"Concentrate," the Hindu god commanded. "Rise above your body."

Utter silence fell as Alan shut all but the single thought from his mind—and it happened! He floated free, while below him lay his physical self. A thought touched his mind. "You have done it! Now think of a place and will yourself there."

A sudden wild idea came to Alan. Elspeth! Could he cross the barrier between the worlds? He pictured the lovely Highland lass, seeking her; instantly he was in the schoolroom in Kilmona, hovering only a few feet away from Elspeth Cameron. She halted in the midst of a sentence, faltering.

Oh, no, Alan thought. He shouldn't have startled her this way. In momentary confusion, he fled—then all was blackness, in a limbo of gibbering shapes that reached out for him. Time stood still. Control—he had no control!

Why had he left his body?

By Lloyd Arthur Eshbach
Published by Ballantine Books:

The Scroll of Lucifer

Lloyd Arthur Eshbach

A Del Rey Book
BALLANTINE BOOKS • NEW YORK

A Del Rey Book
Published by Ballantine Books

Copyright © by Lloyd Arthur Eshbach

Library of Congress Catalog Card Number: 89-92442

ISBN 0-345-32465-X

Manufacutured in the United States of America

First Edition: May 1990

Cover Art by Darrell K. Sweet

For Lester del Rey
with gratitude for help beyond
the normal call of editorial duty,
without whose encouragement this
tetralogy would not have been written.

CONTENTS

The Worlds of Lucifer

Alan MacDougall discovers a long-abandoned tower in the Scottish Highlands while seeking his vanished brother. He finds an ancient scroll, a Druid sword, and a golden armlet shaped like a two-headed serpent. He slips it on—and there's his brother, now become Cinel Loarn, a leader of the Little People—the Sidhe. And now he sees four bronze portals in the walls. He goes through the first.

He's on a road leading to a beautiful city. Attacked by bandits, he is saved by Taliesin, bard of Celtic myths, who says this is Tartarus, created by Lucifer for the ancient Daughters of Lilith, now peopled by men and Celtic gods who died on Earth fourteen hundred years before. Here they are doomed to live on in eternal boredom.

In the city that night, he "hears" Danu, Nuada, and other gods discussing the fact that he must know of the Gate they've long sought. Some suggest forcing that knowledge from him. Danu, Queen of Gods, forbids. But minions of the evil gods attack him. He flees to the Hall of the Dead, a Forbidden Area, where bodies await to replace any slain. And the scroll reveals that any from Tartarus would wither to dust on Earth. But none would believe that.

The hatred of Dalua and Balor of the Evil-Eye increases when they learn that Lord Enki and Queen Inanna, imprisoned in the armlet, are teaching Alan shape-changing, invisibility, and other powers.

In a Golden Tower no other can see, he is welcomed by Ahriman, lieutenant of Lucifer. Ahriman shows him a model with which Ahriman can control everyone and everything on Tartarus.

The gods start a war to determine who will control Alan. He flees, pursued by Balor and Dalua. He dives through the Gate, with Balor behind him. But Balor soon shrivels to dust.

To rest after his efforts, Alan stays with the kindly Camerons and soon begins falling in love with Elspeth Cameron. But the evil will of Ahriman forces Alan back through the second Gate. This time he winds up in Ochren, the gloomy Celtic Underworld. He contacts Taliesin by telepathy, and the Bard soon joins him. None on Tartarus knew of this second world of Lucifer. But they soon win the enmity of Beli, god of the Underworld. They flee and are taken in by the god Manannan, who seems friendly; but he is soon shown to be working with Beli. They steal Manannan's magic boat to cross the sea and reach Tartarus, hotly pursued. Alan reaches the Tower of Ahriman.

There Ahriman tells Alan that he is of royal descent and is destined for a wondrous future in Lucifer's scheme. When Alan again joins Taliesin, the Bard seems to believe Alan may be of royal descent. If so, the Stone of Fal in the Great Temple may prove it.

The gods are convening in the Temple, but Alan and Taliesin slip in. Alan sits on the Stone, which begins screaming loudly to prove royal ancestry. The gods rush in, and one stabs Alan. Near death, he is suddenly transported back through the Gate by Ahriman.

He recovers in the home of the Camerons. But soon Ahriman's spells force him to pass the third Gate. He lands on the island of Scath, where men are forbidden. He avoids the guards by invisibility, but the ruler, the sorceress Scathach, spies him by magic. Mentally calling Taliesin, he hides in a cave, to be confronted by a demon, Amaruduk, who tries to possess his body. The armlet saves Alan, who then surrenders to the guards to be taken to Scathach's castle. There, hidden in invisibility, Taliesin joins him.

Scathach pretends friendship and shows Alan his "past lives," which Ahriman hinted at, trying to gain control of him. He and Taliesin flee through tunnels to the other part of the island, ruled by Amaruduk. Taliesin recognizes the demon as a former god of Sumer and reveals that he, Taliesin, was also once a follower of Lucifer. Amaruduk swears to deal with Scathach and leads them by secret tunnels to the Gate. But Scathach is waiting there, and fighting breaks out between her forces and those of Amaruduk.

Suddenly Alan is transported to the Tower of Ahriman, who puts an end to the fighting. He returns Alan to the Gate. Alan steps through—but Scathach follows right behind, with Taliesin trying to hold her back. She dashes at once through the fourth Gate before she can wither, and Taliesin plunges after her.

Alan knows he must follow them. But for the moment, he lingers with Elspeth, who has come looking for him.

CHAPTER 1

The Perfect Place

Grim-faced, Alan MacDougall stared into the ancient Highland forest, his arm tightening around the shoulders of Elspeth Cameron. The rays of the westering sun filtered through the branches of the great oaks, dappling the rocky floor of the woodland with a constantly changing pattern of light and shade. There was a silence except for the rustling of the leaves high above, swept by a cool breeze rising from a hidden loch to the north, and the faint, high chuckling of a nearby mountain rivulet tumbling down the mountainside.

At last Alan spoke. "I think you had better start for home. Your father will begin to wonder what has become of you, and I'm surprised that your little brother David hasn't already appeared." He glanced with distaste at the massive gray stone tower behind them, the windowless *broch* that had provided access to a fantastic Other World.

"The fourth Gate awaits, and I'd better pass through it before I lose my courage." He forced a short laugh.

Elspeth faced him, her gray eyes looking intently up into his blue ones. "I suppose you have to go; and since

– 1 –

this is the last Gate, there *must* be an end to all this sorcery."
Suddenly, fiercely her hands locked behind his head and she
drew his lips down to hers in a long, fervent kiss. Mac-
Dougall crushed her to him, lifting her from the ground.

At last he released her, whispering huskily, "No matter what happens, my darling, I will return. You will
bring me back. And now you must leave."

Reluctantly the girl drew away, squared her shoulders,
and tried to smile. "It isna fair, my laddie, it isna fair.
But I'll be waiting, and I'll pray a lot." Resolutely she
turned, head held proudly erect, and started down the
mountainside. Alan watched her go. Just before the woods
closed about her she looked back and called, "Be careful, Alan. That sorceress Scathach is very beautiful. And
witches cast strong spells." Then she was gone.

Scowling, MacDougall stared at the spot where she
had vanished. He thought savagely, For one thin dime I'd
chuck the whole damned game and follow her. The ever-
present pressure of the golden, two-headed serpent coiled
about his upper right arm told him he'd do no such thing.
He remembered the enveloping, demonic cloud in his
bedroom at the Cameron farm; the similar attempts by
Amaruduk to possess him; the Sumerian demons for a
time occupying the gods of Tartarus; and Alan knew there
could be no peace until he had seen this experience to
its end, whatever that end might be.

He grimaced as he thought of Elspeth's warning. He
knew all about Scathach's wizardry; and the sorceress
had already entered the land beyond the fourth Gate, so
he knew he had not seen the last of her. In his mind's
eye he again saw Brendah the Warrior, beyond Gate three,
charging into the sorceress to send her sprawling out of
her own world into the *broch*, both women believing that
death would follow instantly. Seconds later, while the
terrified Queen of Scath scrambled to her feet, the Bard
Taliesin had also entered the tower. Both had returned to
the Other World through Gate four, Scathach hastily im-
pelled by fear of death; Taliesin following her after taking a brief glimpse of the Highland landscape, but with
ample time to avoid dissolution.

As MacDougall cast a final, lingering glance down the mountainside, a half-smile momentarily appeared. Womanlike, Elspeth had been aware of Scathach's unusual beauty. She need have no fear of him falling victim to the witch's spell.

Resolutely he entered the ancient tower. He halted just inside the doorway for his sight to adjust to the dimness; the light coming through the entrance and the cold auroral glow from the first and fourth portals—Tartarus and the land Scathach called *Caer Sidi*, visible only through the magic of the armlet—provided inadequate illumination. The second Gate, that to dark Ochren, though standing open, emitted only an occasional uncertain flash; and the third, to Scath, was closed.

He saw his jacket and cape lying in a heap on the oak table and slipped them on. He had dropped them there when exposing the armlet and touching Elspeth with it so she, too, could see the Gates and their world. His sword belt still encircled his waist, supporting the skillfully chased silver scabbard and the longsword that had been his constant companion in the Other World. He drew his flashlight from one of the pockets and swept the round chamber with the powerful beam. There was nothing to indicate there had been visitors.

Visitors. What of his brother Malcolm who had become Cinel Loarn of the Sidhe, and his band? He called out, "Malcolm!"

Instantly there appeared before him the leader of the *Shee*, sturdy, less than four feet tall, brown-haired, clad in forest-green leather, armed with a leaf-shaped bronze sword and a round bronze shield whose striking gave forth the enchanted bell tones of the singing blades.

"Always on guard, Alan. Always at your call."

"Thank you, brother. In moments I will be passing through the fourth portal. This alone will remain open. I will enter there and return by the same way. What is fated to happen will happen in what the Sorceress called 'The Perfect Place.' Did you perchance see my visitors?"

"Indeed." Cinel Loarn smiled. "The dark woman was

very frightened." He paused. "So you return to the Other World for the final adventure." In quick strides he crossed the space between them, and their hands clasped in a strong grip as the Chief of the Sidhe said fervently, "May the one true God be with you!"

As their hands separated Cinel Loarn vanished, and moments later the clangor of bell-notes filled the tower room. Alan heard the swish of scurrying sandals as he crossed to the first Gate and closed it. The second followed; and without pausing he moved to Gate four, crouched, and stepped through.

As he slipped his flashlight into one of his many pockets, his eyes took in the scene, striking in its formal beauty. Observed through the Gate, it had been impressive, but seeing it within the landscape itself made it an experience. In every direction the slightly irregular pastel lawn formed the perfect background for carefully tailored flowering bushes, symmetrical trees, artistically curving white walks, and as far as eye could see, arranged in pleasing random fashion, numerous rounded structures wrought of slender, fluted marble pillars topped by domed roofs of glistening silver. Follies or gazebos they were called in England.

One white-pebbled path, broader than the rest, led to the crest of a distant slope where a great alabaster castle rose, a majestic creation of towers and turrets silhouetted against the aurora. And that aurora, constantly changing, subdued, unobtrusive, formed a backdrop of pastel perfection.

Alan thought of illustrations he had seen in favorite adventure books read during his boyhood, the artist, Maxfield Parrish. An unusual name that had remained with him. This was something Parrish might have painted, lacking only the intense blue of his skies or the billowing white clouds.

"Alan! Welcome to Avilion."

Taliesin's voice; and suddenly, in the act of getting to his feet, the Bard appeared under the nearest tree about thirty feet away. "Beautiful, is it not?" He began walking briskly toward MacDougall, who had not moved. "I have been waiting for you. I knew you would not tarry."

"I'm here," MacDougall acknowledged, "but not because I want to be. And—Avilion? Scathach called it *Caer Sidi*, the Perfect Place—"

Taliesin interrupted impatiently. "*Caer Sidi* or *Tir-nan-og*, the Land of the Ever Young—or Avilion, the Land of Promise—the name matters not. What matters is, this is the final step. All that has happened before has been leading up to this. I have been thinking about the Scroll and its message." He drew the ancient parchment on its ivory spool from a compartment in his cape. "And about Ahriman and what he must be planning. Your coming here was inevitable. Mine was not, and that may be significant." He halted at Alan's side, then added, "No matter what happens, always remember I am your ally; and I am not without power."

Alan's hand closed on the Bard's arm. "You mean at last you're going to tell me what you know?"

Taliesin shook his head regretfully. "No. Better for you to follow your own inclinations, your instincts, at least up to a point—"

He stopped short as a hoarse groan came through the tranquil air. MacDougall heard it, too, and both men listened. They heard a faint cry.

"Help!"

They waited, looking on every side, but they saw nothing and the cry was not repeated. Alan thought of the two Sumerian gods imprisoned in his armlet; directed a thought to them:

"Lord Enki and Lady Inanna, did you hear? And can you tell me its source?"

Mentally the answer came. "We did, and its source is the folly on your right."

"The folly," MacDougall exclaimed, and darted across the lawn, Taliesin following. As Alan approached the structure, subconsciously he noted the artistry that had shaped the slender pillars, the curving tops fanning out into graceful arches; the silver dome of the roof covered by a tracery of engraved designs worthy of the finest jewelry. Beautiful! But the thought vanished in horror as his gaze fell on the floor of the folly with its dreadful occupant.

"Damn!" he whispered.

The white marble floor, sunk a foot below the level of the turf, held a single ghastly figure—a naked man who was mere skin stretched over a skeleton, spread-eagled, his wrists and ankles stretched tightly by coils of gold wire fastened to gold hooks set in the floor. His gaping mouth, staring eyes, and barely moving ribs alone revealed that life remained. He was mired in his own filth.

The eyes rolled and the tongue moved as the sufferer tried to speak; and at that instant a single drop of water fell from the ceiling to splash in his mouth. MacDougall stared upward to see a silver receptacle, another drop of water forming at the tip of a tiny nozzle.

"Hellish!" Alan rasped. "The Perfect Place indeed."

"Only enough water to prolong the agony," Taliesin added angrily.

Again the man tried to speak, and as Alan leaned over, harshly whispered words became clear.

"Hagith . . . your sword . . ."

His meaning in part at least was obvious. Probably Hagith was responsible for him being there, and he wanted his misery ended. As Alan began drawing his sword, there came a single fluttering gasp, the skeletal jaw sagged, and breathing stopped. That final effort had been his last.

Both men turned away from the revolting spectacle, cold anger on their faces.

"Deliberately starving a man to death—and that dripping water . . ." MacDougall groped for words.

"And I called this place Avilion, the Land of Promise," the Bard exclaimed. "Promise of what?"

Alan looked across the parklike expanse at other follies. "I wonder—do those beautiful things hold other horrors?" He strode grimly toward a neighboring creation of marble and silver, the Bard with him. Even before they reached it they saw it was occupied.

It held the nude body of a young woman on her knees

on the floor, calves beneath her, her torso doubled over, all of it compressed under a massive silver grid, weighted down by a huge marble block. A ghastly touch, her long blond hair had been carefully arranged, fanned out like a great halo around her head.

"What a *hell* of a place this is!" Alan rasped as he leaned over to be certain life had ended. No emaciation here. Death must have come quickly, breathing well-nigh impossible. Straightening up and turning, he began, "If this is typical—" He halted, then stared around incredulously.

He was alone!

"Taliesin—where are you?" There was no response. Could the Bard for some reason have become invisible? But he'd still be visible to Alan. Again he called, "Taliesin," but there was no response.

MacDougall's face darkened with anger. There was one likely answer. Ahriman. Lucifer's lieutenant with his fantastic forceps that could pluck anyone from anywhere in this world and place him instantly where the Persian wished. The device that he himself had once used to drop three of his enemies into embarrassing positions. That Ahriman had twice used to rescue him from impossible situations.

He'd soon know. Telepathic communication with Taliesin had become as natural as ordinary speech. He pictured the Bard as he had done so often before, not merely the physical man, but the personality, the entity that was Taliesin. Mentally he reached out.

Nothing happened. He had no awareness of the Bard. His thought was blocked. That had never happened before—but it had, he suddenly recalled. Not his thought but Taliesin's. During his first visit to Murias the Bard was in the midst of communicating when three of the dark gods, Balor, Morrigu and Dalua, had combined their mental powers to block Taliesin's thoughts.

Now Ahriman had not only removed the Bard but was making telepathic exchange impossible.

As a vivid image of the Persian, the greatest power in this Other World, formed in MacDougall's mind, his fury mounted. He could see the supercilious smile on his darkly handsome face, the intensely blue, gem-hard eyes watching. Alan gazed unseeingly toward a swaying curtain of auroral light and spoke aloud.

"So, Ahriman, Taliesin's assessment of the situation was correct. It was not intended that he be here, so you have removed him. Lucifer's lieutenant you may be, and perhaps the master of the fate of all the dwellers on the four islands—though I'm not at all certain that this is so—but I tell you now, there is no chance of me cooperating with whatever you have in mind. I am fed up with your high-handed methods."

MacDougall lowered his gaze and looked toward another folly. There was no response to his speech, nor had he expected one, but he was certain it had been heard, and he felt better after his defiance. He scowled. Making it stick might be another matter.

What should he do now? Investigate more of the follies? He had little stomach for the idea; and it seemed certain that others of the structures had been put to similar use. It was unreasonable to think that only the two they had investigated should be utilized for torture.

The King—or Hagith if they were not the same—should be his objective. That meant the white castle on the northern horizon. He strode to the broader white path and moved briskly toward the striking building. He was still seething inside at the brutal torture he had seen and the removal of Taliesin.

With long, sure strides he followed the road, his gaze fixed on the white marble structure. Visible were three square towers, the central one broad and no more than the height of a normal four-storey building, topped by crenelated walls. The other two, at opposite ends and also square, were far taller, tapering, and no more than eight feet across at the base, apparently observation towers. They also had crenelated walls at their tops and, in addition, near the roof had graceful turrets at each corner. Randomly spaced, tall, narrow windows broke the smooth expanse of the walls.

On each side of the central tower stretched what appeared to be twenty-foot-high marble buildings with regularly spaced windows, probably single-storey structures connecting the three towers.

As MacDougall approached the castle he saw movement, white-robed figures strolling idly about the grounds. There were at least two score, and some were acting very strangely. One had halted and stood rigidly, head cocked to one side. Another continued walking slowly, staring skyward, curved arms outstretched, palms turned upward as if he were expecting something from the heavens. Others sat stiffly on backless marble benches, bodies strangely askew.

As Alan drew closer he was struck by the rapt expressions on every face, euphoric, enraptured. None seemed aware of his approach despite the contrast between his garments—black from head to foot—and their spotless white. He halted a few feet away from the strollers and stared in wonder. All wore identical clothes, white silken robes, gathered at the waist by a heavy white cord, and white, leather-thonged sandals. Some were fair-skinned, others swarthy, their hair—blond, brunette, and even one redhead—cut squarely just above the shoulders.

Suddenly Alan realized that at least one-fourth of them were women. None of the men wore beards, emphasizing his own full yellow whiskers.

MacDougall approached the man who still stood with head cocked and tapped him on the shoulder. Slowly he straightened, as slowly faced Alan; and MacDougall's eyes grew wide. Never had he seen pupils contracted to mere dark points, barely visible against pale-blue corneas, the whites reddened by a tracery of veins. He seemed hardly aware of Alan's presence.

"I want to speak to your King," Alan said loudly.

Comprehension came slowly, the reply uncertain. "But—but no one ever asks to see King Cuchulainn."

"So this is a first," Alan responded curtly, adding "I'm not asking, I'm demanding. Tell me, where will I find the King?"

The other smiled with relief. "In the castle." He

turned away and shuffled across the flagging, smiling happily.

For moments MacDougall watched the white-robed zombies in their aimless walking, his expression grim. Drug-induced euphoria in Avilion, the Land of Promise. A narcotic paradise. If he were sensible he'd head back to the Gate and return to his own world. But there'd still be the armlet—

The Gate! He had failed to mark or even note its position. The distraction of meeting Taliesin and the groan from the folly had been responsible. He looked down the slope, realizing immediately that finding the Gate would be well-nigh impossible, unless the serpent-gods could help. He sent a thought into his armlet. Lord Enki responded.

"You have grown careless, Alan MacDougall. I suppose, given enough time, we can find the Gate."

He faced the tower entrance, a huge silver double door covered by an intricate decorative design in bas-relief, flanked by two round marble pillars. Two massive rings hanging side by side where the doors met provided the means to enter.

Uncertainly MacDougall stood before the imposing doors. Thus far nothing seemed normal—though why he expected normalcy in this unnatural realm he could not have told. For one thing there should be guards. Guards against what? Mentally he contrasted his entering into Tartarus and Ochren and Scath. Impatiently he shook his head. He was here and he was going to see the King. King Cuchulainn, the man had said, a name he remembered vaguely from his reading in *Mythology in the British Islands*.

Still he hesitated. Should he become invisible until he determined what he faced? Or shape-change, perhaps into someone the King would recognize, perhaps Nuada, King of the *Tuatha de Danann*, or Manannan, god of the sea? He had used both forms in the past. To what purpose? Sooner or later he'd have to deal with Cuchulainn as himself, so why not now?

As he reached for one of the silver rings, the doors

swung suddenly outward; and only his reflex leap backward prevented their striking him. In the opening stood
two men as tall as himself, with drawn swords. Evidently
guards. They were dressed alike—light-blue tunics, gaping to reveal hairy chests; dark-green kilts, green leg-
gings fastened with broad cords, leather-thonged sandals.
They stared at him with grim-faced intensity. Here was
no sign of drug use.

There was momentary silence, then Alan exclaimed,
"Thanks for opening the door. I appreciate it."

"You are Alan MacDougall," one of the guards
growled. "We were told of your coming. You are to be
taken to the King."

For a surprised instant MacDougall met the other's
gaze, then his puzzlement vanished. Of course. Scathach
had spoken about him. He responded, "I was about to
ask to be taken to your King, so we have no problem."
He bowed deeply. "Lead on, MacDuff." Confidently he
stepped toward the doorway.

The spokesman automatically drew back, then turned
to lead the way. The other guard fell in behind them.

Alan had given no thought to what the interior might
be like, but what appeared was quite logical: white marble walls and floor. Only the high ceiling was unusual,
glowing with a soft white light like the dome over Murias, the buried City of the West on Tartarus. They were
in a wide corridor, moving past several broad, silver
doors uniformly spaced in facing walls, covered like the
entrance by designs in bas-relief. The hallway ended in
another double door, standing stiffly before it a third
guard.

As the three approached him, the leader uttered the
single word, "MacDougall," and as the guard stepped
aside the doors swung open, propelled from within by
two additional guards.

No element of surprise here, Alan thought ruefully. A
regular reception committee awaited his coming, thanks
to Scathach.

"Enter," his escort growled in his ear; and with a
guard on either side and two behind him they stepped

into a great square marble chamber, the high-domed ceiling glowing with soft white light like that of the hallway. Surprisingly, the floor was covered by a thick rug of utter black. Centered along the far wall, rising high above the floor, stood a round dais of polished black stone, upon it an ornate, massive throne of glistening gold. Except for the five men the chamber was empty.

As the doors closed behind them, others on opposite sides of the dais opened; and two by two a corps of guards marched through the portal, dividing instantly and circling along opposite walls. About a yard away from MacDougall's guards, now facing the throne, the first of the marchers halted, as did those behind him, until all were in position, completely circling the chamber. As one they whipped out their swords and held them rigidly against their breasts, tips pointing ceilingward. All this with smoothness and dispatch born of endless practice.

Silence fell and prevailed for dragging minutes. MacDougall sent his gaze slowly around the circle. A colorful spectacle, approximately one hundred men of uniform height in their yellow tunics and green kilts, beardless, with hair cut to shoulder length, faces immobile. Waiting. Alan thought, What next? The Royal Entrance, of course.

That entrance, when it came, was quite unusual. First a faint golden cloud formed slowly on the dais before the throne. Gradually it thickened; solidified; became the figure of the King. A giant of a man, he must have been close to seven feet tall, the rest of him proportionate in size. And amazingly, he suggested a man of gold. Fully bearded, his whiskers were very like Alan's, and his hair, a great mass, was golden blond. His tunic and kilt were of glistening golden fabric, his sandals likewise golden thonged. His sword belt, of heavy linked chain, the hilt, and the scabbard were of gold. And all visible skin, incredibly in this auroral world, was deeply tanned.

With the appearance of the vaporous cloud the waiting guards as one man bowed from the waist, holding this position until the Monarch's deep voice echoed through the chamber.

"Attention!"

As they snapped erect King Cuchulainn seated himself; and as if on cue a beam of golden light sprang from the ceiling and bathed him in its glow. He sat motionless, his eyes fixed on MacDougall whose black-clad figure stood out against the white marble wall. The King seemed to be studying his visitor, giving him time to be impressed.

His move, Alan thought. So this was Cuchulainn. He *was* impressive. Theatrically so. He tried to remember what he had read about this mythical god of Erin. He recalled that he was reputedly the sun god, bright of countenance, who when angry sent showers and sparks of ruddy fire around him. Heat from his body melted snow within a thirty-foot radius. When he bathed in the sea the water boiled. So it was said. Alan suppressed a grin. Hot stuff!

From the depths of memory came another picture, that of a beardless young man, dark-haired, dead at twenty-seven. Not a large man despite his giant's prowess in battle and his magic. Not at all like the Cuchulainn on the throne.

Shape-changing! Of course.

Alan recalled his seeing through Balor's spurious form after the slain god of the Fomorians was given a second body like that of his twisted subjects. He could do the same with Cuchulainn if shape-changing was the answer. He extended his vision; saw a dark-haired man shorter than himself. And any awe he might have felt vanished. Let him stare.

At last the deep voice rumbled, "Approach, Alan MacDougall!"

Smiling faintly, Alan started across the black rug; after a few strides the smile vanished and his face grew grim as he saw again the tortured bodies in the follies. Casually he sauntered toward the dais, halting a dozen feet away and staring boldly into the King's eyes. Since it required effort to see through the shape-change, he viewed Cuchulainn in the form he had assumed.

"I have been told much about you, Alan son of Dougall, and that you might visit this realm. Is it true that you come from the Other World, the land where once I lived?"

"It is true," Alan answered curtly.

"And is it true that many centuries have passed since I—left Erin?"

"At least fourteen hundred years."

King Cuchulainn stared in shocked unbelief. "And—and you have not died? And can return there?"

"I have not died and can return."

"Then why have you come here?"

Impatiently MacDougall responded, "Frankly, I do not know. Ask Ahriman. I'm sure he has the answer."

At the mention of Lucifer's lieutenant, the King's eyes grew wide with surprise and he stared in silence. It seemed as if he needed time to think over what he had heard.

As Alan waited he thought about his intention to berate the King for the torturing. Would this be wise? Prudent perhaps to learn more about what he faced here. On the other hand, Taliesin had said something about him following his own inclination, his instincts. He gave a mental shrug, then exclaimed, "I've answered your questions. Now you answer mine. What sick mind is responsible for the beastly torturing being carried out in the follies?"

Dimly MacDougall heard a collective gasp from the ranks of the guards; and King Cuchulainn seemed to swell with sudden fury. The golden glow surrounding him intensified, became tinged with red as he cried harshly, "I was warned that you were a meddler, delving into matters that do not concern you. A taste of one of the follies might discourage that tendency. Guards," he addressed the four at the doorway, "deliver him to Hagith the Tormentor. He is to suffer no permanent harm and is to be returned after one sleep. Perhaps then he will have learned respect for the King."

As startled Alan MacDougall grasped the significance of the sudden harsh sentence, and as the King started to rise, another voice, overwhelming in its power, swept through the hall.

"Hold! Cuchulainn, I am not pleased. Your decision was made in haste, out of anger, without sufficient knowledge."

The voice of Ahriman! Alan could not be mistaken. Never had he heard that stentorian voice speaking with the strength and authority his words now bore. He continued: "Alan MacDougall is the Chosen One and is to be welcomed as an honored guest. He is to receive the best you have to offer. Disobedience will not be tolerated."

Without warning the golden beam winked out, to be replaced instantly by one of pallid blue. Fascinated, MacDougall watched as the figure of Cuchulainn became cloudy, hazy; and in its place slowly solidified the raven-black hair, the gem-hard blue eyes, the too-red lips of Ahriman. White vesture, light-blue full-cut oriental trousers, deep-blue cape, all ornamented with intricately patterned threads of gold—all were typical of the Persian. His gaze bored into MacDougall's eyes with hypnotic intensity.

"Alan MacDougall, you are a chosen vessel, prepared for the Master's use. Great events await your word. Consider well your every action. The One who has chosen you generously rewards those who serve him well. Conversely, he does not deal lightly with those who fail him."

In spite of himself Alan felt a sudden chill; yet paradoxically, mingled with the dread was a trace of exaltation. Where was all this leading? An adventure without parallel, unsought, in a world beyond reason where dwelt the dead of millennia, ensorcelled, a land where magic worked and where he was the featured player entirely against his will. Was all this actually happening?

As he blinked to break the spell, the yellow beam returned, and Cuchulainn was again on his throne. He stood up and gestured toward the four guards who had formed Alan's escort. His expression was grim; obviously he was shaken by the appearing of Ahriman.

"You have heard. Join our—guest. Guide him to proper

quarters." He waited while the four marched to Alan's side, then exclaimed, "Guards dismissed."

As he had appeared, so Cuchulainn left, growing ghostlike, nebulous, then vanishing; and in silence MacDougall was conducted from the Great Hall.

CHAPTER 2

In Cuchulainn's Castle

The room to which Alan MacDougall had been ushered was on ground level at the end of a long corridor that began beyond the door through which the corps of guards had come and gone. There were two intersecting hallways; they had turned left into the second one and had gone to the last room on the right, a spacious corner chamber. Walls and floor were of white marble, the ceiling glowing like that in the great hall. A single tall narrow window in each exterior wall verified its being a corner room. A long marble barrier, shoulder high, hid the comfort facilities. Furnishings were simple but sumptuous—a thick black rug, a large bed about a foot above the floor, and a padded contour chair.

After a brief glance at the room, MacDougall went to a window and looked out at what had to be called a small city. From his slight elevation it appeared to be fan-shaped, the point of the fan, the castle; and the oblong cubicles that made up most of the city were formed of marble slabs with glittering silver roofs. He saw white-robed people wandering aimlessly through the streets, with here and there a solitary horseman, the animal, not surprisingly, pure white. Through one of the streets he caught a glimpse of a high marble wall. On his right, just barely visible, he saw the edge of what suggested a clump of woods.

Slowly shaking his head, Alan dropped into one of the chairs. What an incredible place! In the short time he had been here he had seen an unbelievable mixture of physical beauty and gross brutality; euphoric bliss and behind it a drug-induced stupor. The magic of Cuchulainn and his power, overcome by the greater magic and power of Ahriman.

Scowling, MacDougall thought of what the Persian had said. He had referred to him, Alan MacDougall, American engineer of Scottish descent, as the Chosen One, had used the phrase "a chosen vessel, prepared for the Master's use"! The Master? That had to be Lucifer. Lucifer? Why not admit he was the one he had always thought of—if he had thought of a god of evil at all—as the Devil. A wave of dread, instantly denied, swept through him. What had he to do with the Dark One?

If only Taliesin were here. He missed the counsel of the Bard of Bards. It was frustrating, this failure to reach him mentally. Telepathic communication between them had become second nature. He tried again, using the technique that experience had taught him. To no avail. He crossed his arms, his left hand coming to rest on the golden armlet with its twin serpent heads. Could the imprisoned gods help?

"Lord Enki," he sent the thought, "where is Taliesin? Can you find him?"

After a pause the mental reply came. "He is in his home in Falias, pacing the floor in the room where he spends so much of his time. Obviously he is troubled."

"Can you help me reach him with my thought? I seem to be blocked." MacDougall centered his faculties on the Bard.

"We can try."

During a seemingly endless interval that followed, Alan sensed the powerful intellects of Lord Enki and Lady Inanna in rapport with his own. Powers that had countered potent magic spells, that had permitted his accomplishing feats far beyond his own strength; but this time they failed. Finally they desisted, and the Lady Inanna's disgruntled thought came to MacDougall.

"There are powerful entities, not human, blocking our efforts. Entities, many of them, erecting an impenetrable wall about Taliesin. While they continue, we can do nothing to reach him." The Sumerian gods broke contact.

Ahriman, obviously, was behind this, Alan thought. He remembered, during his visits in the Golden Tower on Tartarus, sensing the presence of unseen personalities, especially during his first entry when, impossibly, he had walked through the wall. Demons, without question. And there was significance here. For some reason not yet evident, it was important to Lucifer's lieutenant that he and Taliesin be kept apart.

A grim expression settled on MacDougall's face, his Scots stubbornness rising. He was just as determined— no, even more so—to have the Bard join him. He didn't have the powers Ahriman had; he was merely a mortal man; but they wanted his cooperation in some sort of plan, and they would get it only if they saw things his way in this matter. *If* they got it even then! Inevitably there would be a session with Ahriman during which he'd make his point.

Meanwhile, it might be well if he knew more about his present surroundings.

"Lord Enki and Lady Inanna," he addressed the serpent-gods, "while I'm waiting for King Cuchulainn to make his next move, can I be given any sort of tour of his castle? On occasion in the past you have provided visual access to happenings behind closed doors and across great distances with truly amazing clarity. I recall the grim sights within King Arawn's tower, and the sorceries of the Daughters of Calatin during that mad war on Scath. Not to mention that sham Roman village of Emperor Titus Vespasianus. So, if you will—"

"Flattery is unnecessary," Inanna interrupted somewhat testily, apparently still annoyed by their failure to reach Taliesin. "By this time you should have mastered this ability yourself. However . . . where shall we begin?"

"In the King's quarters. Somehow I don't believe I'll get there in person. I can't picture myself becoming friendly with his Arrogant Highness." In anticipation he closed his eyes.

Instantly a picture formed in MacDougall's mind, a scene as sharp as if he were in the room itself. A single glance took in the setting: marble floors and walls, the glow from the ceiling more golden than that of his own room, a golden-yellow rug on the floor, and massive chairs and tables of metallic gold. If they were the actual metal, they represented a king's ransom anywhere but here. The motif of the sun god with a vengeance.

There were five people in the room: Cuchulainn, two other men, and two women, all seated, the four ranged in a half circle before the King. Cuchulainn appeared as he had in the Great Hall, a blond giant in golden tunic and kilts and gold-thonged sandals. The two men were dark-haired, about Alan's size, one dressed in royal blue, the other in deep maroon. Like the King they wore tunics and kilts, their sword belts of linked silver rather than Cuchulainn's gold.

The woman at the King's right was a beautiful redhead, her skin the very fair tint so often associated with red-gold hair. That hair, high piled, massively coiled, was held in place by great, sapphire-studded silver combs. Her full-bosomed form was clad in a sheath of cloth-of-silver, a great necklace of oval sapphire beads circling her throat, and a silver belt studded with even larger sapphires about her waist.

The second woman was Queen Scathach, still in the garments she had worn during her last appearance in Scath. With the gold circlet around her raven-black hair, the golden breastplates, her lapis lazuli pendant, her purple cape and skirt, and her high cloth-of-gold boots, Alan would have been hard put to decide which of the two was the more suitable consort for the King.

Cuchulainn was speaking.

"I *know* you had warned me, Scathach; but who could foresee the entry of the Mouthpiece into the matter? I should have avoided the visitor altogether. Now I have to welcome him as my guest."

Scathach was apologetic. "MacDougall observes no laws save his own, as I learned to my sorrow; and he has powers beyond those of any man I have ever known. I found him most infuriating. I am convinced he has help outside himself."

"Perhaps," said the man in blue, "the One-Who-Speaks-for-the-Master is his secret aid."

Said the redhead, smiling slyly at the King, "I am eager to meet him. He sounds interesting."

The King frowned at her. "Your jesting is not appreciated."

Grinning, Alan blocked the vision and addressed Lord Enki. "Show me the rest of the castle, continuing with the King's suite."

There followed a rapid tour of Cuchulainn's domain. MacDougall had become accustomed to the fantastic experience, but he never ceased to marvel at the scope and clarity of the mental viewing. Room followed room: the King's dining area, bedchamber, bath, a room that suggested a laboratory but containing the equipment associated with magic. There were other quarters that must be the Queen's, based on their feminine touches.

They moved to the floor above to a great kitchen where a staff of white-clad cooks were abustle with pots and pans, silver and gold, of course; next to it a banquet hall with long tables, and to one side two smaller dining rooms, one with a table set for twelve. Probably the scene of a dinner where he would meet the people who mattered, Alan thought.

The third and apparently top level was divided into four apartments, all similar, evidently living quarters for important members of the King's staff.

Back at ground level they made a rapid survey of scores of single rooms in two wings, each containing a bed and chair, many occupied by guards; and in each wing a single large bath, evidently for general use. Behind the Great

Hall lay the section that held his room, each chamber larger than those in the wings, and each with its own comfort facilities.

Finally he examined one of the end towers. It was what it appeared to be, an observation tower, a spiral stairway winding upward with exits and at the turrets and ending at a trapdoor in the roof. Is there a basement? he wondered—and at that moment a sharp rap on the door cut short his exploration, and a guard's voice called,

"Sir, his Majesty invites you to dinner."

"In a moment," Alan answered, removing his cape, looking for a place to hang it. He found a row of silver pegs in the wall at the end of the bath section; considered his sword and decided to wear it. Just inside the door he paused. He had to make a decision. Should he vent anger against this world by defying Cuchulainn, or should he cooperate to a point, and perhaps learn things to his own advantage? He decided on the latter course. He left the room.

Two guards were waiting, and led him into an intersecting corridor to a stairway that they climbed, and on the next level swung open the door into the small dining room with the table set.

Inside the room, MacDougall halted, his quick glance taking in those already at the table. There were places for five on each side plus one at head and foot. Standing at all but three of the chairs were eight men and one woman, the latter Scathach. At his entrance all eyes turned toward him; and as Alan's gaze met that of the Queen of Scath she smiled and he bowed deeply.

One of the guards led him to what was evidently the foot of the table, where he too stood, obviously waiting the arrival of Cuchulainn and his consort. The guards withdrew. No one spoke.

Following an awkward interval another door opened and the King was ushered in, behind him the redhead of Alan's snooping. Guards followed to seat them, the King at the head of the table and the woman at his right hand. Only the monarch appeared in dress different from that which MacDougall had seen, his tunic now of vivid crimson, its overlapping edges held together by an enormous silver pin, polished to gemlike brilliance; his kilt russet-colored, only his sword belt and scabbard unchanged. A massive gold-link necklace encircled his throat.

After a pause Cuchulainn motioned with palms held downward, and the others sat. Then he raised a hand above his head, and on signal vessels of food were brought from the kitchen, and servers placed generous portions in golden bowls before each diner, beginning with the King and following with MacDougall. Goblets were filled with an amber wine, and when all had been served, the King finally spoke.

"You have come together to meet the Chosen One, or so the One-Who-Speaks-for-the-Master has called him; his guest and mine, Alan MacDougall. He has come from the Other World, and as I have been told by Queen Scathach, herself a visitor, he has visited three other islands in our realm, returning after each sojourn to the land from whence we once came. I trust we will learn more about this later from his own lips. For now, Alan MacDougall, meet the others at table.

"At my right is Queen Eimher, fairest of all the maids of Erin, and fairest now in all this Land of Promise, one worthy to be mate to the god of the sun. At my left is Scathach of Scath, in the olden time Scathach the Amazon who was my teacher in the arts of war and magic.

"Next to her is Laegaire the Battle Winner; and next to Eimher sits Conall the Victorious. These two were my comrades-in-arms in days long gone. Beside Conall is Cathbad the Druid, and across from Cathbad sits Broichan, another Druid of surpassing skill. Beside Broichan is Myrddin the Bard, and across from Myrddin is Artur, Captain of my Guard. Beside Myrddin sits Abred the Vate, and across from Abred, at your left, Alan MacDougall, sits Hagith the Tormentor.

"We will learn to know each other better after we have eaten. But first—" Cuchulainn raised his wine goblet high, fixing Alan with an enigmatic stare. "—to the Chosen One. May his stay among us be all he hoped it would be." All drank deeply except Alan MacDougall who

barely touched the wine to his lips, a sudden vision of
the vacuous smile of an aimless stroller appearing before
him. Caution, Mac, he thought.

When Cuchulainn started eating, the others following
his example, MacDougall flashed a thought to the gods
of the armlet. "Lord and Lady, how safe is this food and
drink?"

The reply came instantly. "Quite safe. Cuchulainn is
genuinely in awe of Ahriman, and he would not dare to
harm you."

Relieved, Alan picked up the large golden spoon and
the twin-pointed dagger and, following the examples of
his neighbors, began eating. The roast beef was deli-
cious, and the porridge of mixed grains and the crisp
barley cakes quite good. Portions were generous, and
surprisingly, he found he was hungry.

While he ate, Alan took advantage of the opportunity
to observe those he had just met, excluding the ones he
had observed earlier. The two Druids caught his eye:
Cathbad, sandy-haired, of medium height, and dressed
in a gray robe; and Broichan with his long, thin face and
deepset eyes, also in gray. He was intrigued by Artur,
Captain of the Guard, like all the guards dressed in a
light tunic and deep-green kilt, differing from the others
only in the gold fringe ornamenting his garments. And
across from him, Myrddin the Bard, a name Alan was
certain he had read was an alternate form of Merlin. He
looked as Merlin should, he thought, keen-eyed, high-
cheeked, dark hair reaching well below his shoulders.
Artur and Myrddin in Avilion! If only Taliesin were here
to give his opinion. The time would come . . . He looked
at Abred the Vate. The Vate? What was a Vate? He had
never encountered the term. Finally there was Hagith the
Tormentor. After a single glance at him, MacDougall kept
his eyes averted from the cruelest face he had ever seen.
Even in repose there was something utterly vicious, utterly cold, about the cadaverous nose, dilated nostrils,
lipless mouth, and close-set eyes buried in shadows.

There was no conversation until all of the food was gone
and the dishes removed; then King Cuchulainn began.

"Alan MacDougall, Scathach tells me she came to our fair land through a portal in the Other World, and that she had entered your land from her island, Scath, through another gateway. She also said—and believed—that anyone from this world entering yours would die. Yet she still lives. What have you to say?"

"She speaks truth," Alan replied, aware of every gaze fixed upon him. "She erred only in expecting death to come instantly. It follows quickly, but how quickly I cannot say. Certainly in far less than half the time of a normal sleep. Probably a fourth of that time. The body from this world, the one supplied by Lucifer, begins to age instantly and in the time I have indicated the decay of fourteen centuries takes place, and even the dust disappears."

"How can you be certain?" the King persisted. "Has anyone died?"

"No, though one shed her blood through the portal into Tartarus." He described the death of Morrigu under the swords of the Sidhe when the crone as a "hoodie crow" tried to force her way through the Gate, her blood staining the wall of the tower and gathering in a pool on the flagstone floor. "In a very short time that blood vanished leaving no trace. But more convincing than that is the prophecy of the Scroll. The Scroll of Lucifer."

MacDougall continued with a description of the ancient vellum scroll on its ivory spool, of Taliesin's deciphering its prophecy that told of Lucifer's jest, of the inborn knowledge of the Gate into the Other World that all leaders possessed, but that, if found and entered, led to the death of the finder with no replacement body, of spirits wandering forever as ghosts of ghosts in a half-world from which there was no escape, unseen, unknown and utterly alone.

Shocked silence followed this revelation, broken finally by Myrddin the Bard. "Taliesin I knew," he ventured, "and I knew of his skills in decipherment. But how may we know if the word of the Scroll is true?"

"Well," Alan answered, "the one you call the Mouthpiece, or He-Who-Speaks-for-the-Master, whom I know as Ahriman the lieutenant of Lucifer, believes in its truth. Since I appear to be involved in the prophecy, he has tried, on the several occasions when I visited him, to convince me of its complete truth.''

King Cuchulainn's eyes widened. ''You have spoken with him—in person?''

''Indeed. Twice he saved my life. Have you not met him?''

There was sudden marked respect in the King's manner. ''Only as you saw him in the Great Hall. But we have seen his powers at work and have felt the weight of his wisdom. So when he tells me you are the Chosen One, I believe.'' Cuchulainn paused, frowning. ''Tell me, Alan MacDougall, for what purpose, what task have you been chosen?''

MacDougall chuckled mirthlessly. ''I wish I knew.'' His expression became grim. ''Whatever the answer, I think I must quickly learn. I've run out of islands and there are no more portals.''

Again silence followed, Scathach finally speaking. ''Where is Taliesin? He followed me out of Scath into the Other World. I saw him. Where did he go—or did he stay in your land?''

''He followed you into this place after we watched you racing toward the castle. Then, invisible, he waited for my arrival. Together we saw—some very disturbing things.'' Alan paused and scowled at Hagith the Tormentor. ''Then the Bard disappeared. Not, you may be sure, his own doing. As for him staying in my world, he who had translated the Scroll, of all people, would be aware of the limited time he could spend there.''

For the first time Eimher spoke, a quizzical look in her violet eyes. ''Why do you return to what for you must be the land of the dead, you who have not died? I am certain I should find the emerald hills of Erin lovelier than this.''

Alan grimaced. ''They are indeed, as are the Highlands of Scotland. Or England and Wales, for that matter. I return only because of a spell that has been cast upon me, and I am drawn against my will.''

Again silence, then Abred the Vate asked hesitantly,

"The other islands—are there Vates performing their duties as we do here?"

"Not only are there no Vates to my knowledge," Alan answered, "but I never heard the term until you were introduced. What does a Vate do?"

The King explained. "A Vate is in a class with Druids and Bards, one commissioned to perform ritual sacrifices. He with the Bards and Druids attend to matters of worship, to the observances of feast days, and other ceremonial matters. But tell us more about the Other World that we left, so you say, fourteen hundred years ago."

Endlessly it seemed to Alan MacDougall he answered questions about the twentieth century. The curiosity of his audience seemed insatiable. As he described scenes in the British Isles, especially those of great antiquity, he could sense their nostalgia, a longing for their former life. This Land of Promise, he thought, somehow fails to satisfy. Of course, those who lived in perpetual narcotic euphoria might believe it fulfilled their every desire. Happiness not of his choosing.

During all the discussion only Hagith the Tormentor had remained silent. At last he spoke, his voice hoarse and grating, in keeping with the rest of him.

"Tell me—in your time how are offending lawbreakers dealt with?"

MacDougall made no attempt to hide his loathing. "As humanely as possible."

Hagith's thin lips curled with disdain. "And does this prevent recurring crime? Here we have none who offend a second time."

With difficulty Alan controlled his anger as he ground out, "I suppose you are the beast who tortures people to death—"

The commanding voice of King Cuchulainn interrupted loudly as he stood up. "Our guest must be tired after his journey from world to world, and sleep-time is at hand." To Alan he added stiffly, "If there is anything else we can do for your comfort, we are at your service."

An idea, half malicious but thoroughly practical, occurred to MacDougall. "My suit needs cleaning. It has gone through a lot during my stay in Scath, and if this could be done I would appreciate it greatly.''

Cuchulainn scowled, then answered, ''Speak to the guard and leave your garments outside your door and it shall be done.''

As his waiting guards led Alan back to his room, he was pleased with what the King probably viewed as an insulting request, but inwardly he was still seething. From somewhere came an irreverent thought. Monsters like Hagith could give Hell a bad name. But somehow the idea didn't seem funny.

In his room he dropped into the chair, mentally reviewing the dinner, considering particularly the people he had met. He tried to shut out all thought of Hagith, the most revolting creature he had ever encountered. There flashed into his mind images of King Arawn of Ochren and his jailers, Pryderi and Pwyll, of Malor and Morrigu, of the Druids Semias and Arias, but none raised his hackles like Hagith.

He thought of Myrddin and Artur. Interesting if they turned out to be the foundation on which the Arthurian myth had been built. He must remember to ask Taliesin. Inevitably he pictured Cuchulainn's consort, the lovely red-gold–haired Eimher with her mischievous violet eyes. A troublemaker, if there ever was one. As if demanding attention the darkly seductive Scathach appeared; and as out of nowhere appeared a vision of the blond beauty of Darthula, Princess of Gorias, who in large part had been responsible for his entering this world in the first place. He hadn't thought of her in a long time. Three women of outstanding loveliness, any of them enough to turn a man's head.

A fourth face appeared on the screen of his mind, not perfect, not exotic, but delightful, one that warmed his heart, the genuine, human Highland lass, Elspeth Cameron. Alan, he told himself with fervor, if you ever forget her and fall for any of these Daughters of Lucifer, you deserve whatever the Old One has planned.

He stood up and strode toward the bath. Sleep-time, the King had said, though how he knew in this land of perpetual day, where time was a variant, he'd never be able to explain.

He halted in midstride as a hoarse scream slashed through the silence. With it came sounds of scuffling, the thud of a blow, and another scream suddenly muffled, as if a hand had been clapped over a mouth.

MacDougall sprang to the door, coming to a jarring halt against the cold metal. Locked! By a magic spell, like all locks in this realm. If only he could see what was happening! And abruptly he could—the same clear image in his mind as provided by Inanna and Enki.

He saw three men in the other extension of the intersecting hallway, two of them castle guards, and the third, one of the white-robed strollers, struggling frantically to escape from their grasp. No euphoria here; he writhed and twisted with maniacal strength, kicking out aimlessly, his head rolling hideously, eyes wildly glaring.

Suddenly the hand over the prisoner's mouth tore away, the guard cursing as blood oozed from bitten fingers, and another wolfish howl burst from lips now freed. It ended in a choking gasp as the other guard lashed his stiffened hand across the man's throat just below his chin, and he went limp. Between them the guards dragged the unresisting form to the end of the corridor; as roughly propelled him down a wide stairway into a room empty except for a long table suggesting the marble slab in a morgue. On this the guards placed their burden.

With their entry a door opened and through the doorway came a powerful man with shaven head, bare to the waist, in black kilt and sandals. Sounds came with him, faint and unidentifiable, a sort of chorus of suppressed cries, choked-off moans, muffled screams, but all merely suggested.

The newcomer scowled with displeasure. "Another one ahead of schedule, I see. The King should be told. It upsets routine. A misjudged application, I suppose." He gestured resignedly. "I'll take it from here."

Dismissed, the guards vanished up the stairway. Alan kept his perception fixed on the broad man who immediately removed the robe from the flaccid body, tossing it through an opening in the wall behind him, a loose white undergarment following; and like a sack of wheat, under one arm he carried the nude body into the next chamber.

Alan MacDougall, in his wildest nightmare imaginings, could not have visualized what met his eyes; nor did he quickly forget the sickening spectacle. A long, dimly lighted room, so long that its farther end vanished in shadow, and about twenty feet wide, it contained three rows of sturdy metal chairs, extending the length of the room. All were bolted to the floor.

Except for a score or so of empty seats at the nearer end, each chair contained a nearly naked man or woman. Arms were rigidly manacled to the chairs at wrists and biceps; broad metal bands held chests and heads. Ankles similarly were anchored to chair legs. And all were efficiently gagged with broad leather bands.

About each middle was a white, rigid, diaperlike contraption that was part of the chairs; and extending into the floor from each seat, a metal pipe whose purpose was obvious. The faint sound of running water came from below the floor. Along the ceiling ran three metal pipes, extending from them flexible tubes ending beneath a white bandage at the manacled left wrist of the writhing, whimpering but helpless sufferers.

As the stocky man entered the room, eyes turned in his direction in hopeless pleading, and lips moved ineffectually in attempted speech. With the new victim being placed in position in one of the empty chairs, Alan cut off his viewing, standing aghast just inside the door of his room. Moments later, without being aware that he had moved, he found himself slumped in the chair, staring at the marble wall.

What had he seen? What mad caprice, what unholy purpose was behind such wholesale torture? The serpent-gods, maybe they could find the answers.

"Lord Enki and Lady Inanna, I have just seen an incredible torture chamber in the basement of this castle. Were you with me—did you perchance aid me in my viewing?"

"Congratulations, Alan MacDougall, on your accomplishment. We did *not* help you; you have finally mastered another power of the mind. In time you should be able to dispense with our assistance altogether."

Impatiently MacDougall responded, "Fine! So I saw without your help. But did you also see it? And if you did, what does it mean?"

"Yes, we saw, but we have not yet fathomed its purpose. We will investigate. Hagith or the King should have the answers. We will report."

In a surprisingly short time Lord Enki's reply came. "The solution is quite simple. Those walking in dreams or who are experiencing inward ecstasy are under the control of drugs. These blended drugs are derived from the fruit of several cacti and certain fungi, all of which are found only on this island. The body can tolerate the narcotics for a certain limited period and in certain quantities or death from rapture will occur. So, periodically, it becomes necessary for all traces of the drug to be purged from the body.

"The process is quite painful and the craving overwhelming. Unfortunately there is no way to counter the— shall we say, discomfort and the frenzy that besets the addict, so logically they are restrained for their own protection. Were this not done, they would destroy themselves. As for the gags, without these their cries and incessant pleading would make it impossible for others to remain in the castle.

"The moral is quite clear. Nothing is free. There is a price to be paid for everything, even for periods of Paradise in the Land of Promise."

MacDougall felt sick. What a price to pay. Those poor devils must be suffering the tortures of the damned. He felt a sudden chill as the phrase formed in his mind. It was entirely too appropriate.

He had a further question for his constant companions. "Lord Enki, what of the guards? They appear to be free of narcotics. And do those in the basement return to the stuff after they are freed?"

"To answer the second question first—of course they

return—again and again. Forever. As for the guards, for them it is prohibited. The same is true for all who have tasks to perform. Theft of the drugs is one of the ways, the chief one, in fact, in which Hagith gains new subjects for experimentation.''

MacDougall grimaced. No mercy extended in Avilion. What a penalty to receive for weakness. He tried to direct his thoughts elsewhere.

The appearance of Ahriman with his startling statement—the Chosen One. What did it mean? It had an ominous sound under the circumstances. Chosen by whom and for what? The ''whom'' had to be quite apparent. Only Ahriman could supply the second answer. Ahriman, the One-Who-Speaks-for-the-Master. He pictured him in his Golden Tower on Tartarus, probably hovering over a gemlike miniature of this island, wearing that fantastic helmet and those magic spectacles that revealed whatever he wanted to see.

He stood up and shrugged. Sooner or later the Persian would supply the answer. Sleep-time—

There came a cautious rapping on his door. What next? MacDougall asked himself.

"Who's there?" he demanded.

The reply, like the rapping, was restrained. "It's Scathach. May I come in?''

"In a moment," he answered; then silently addressed Lord Enki: "A visitor, and the door is locked. Will you counter the spell? Some day you must show me the trick.''

The god's answer revealed amusement. "Interesting guest. It is open.''

"Enter, your Highness," Alan said softly in mock-conspiratorial tones.

The Sorceress pushed open the door and stepped in quickly, glancing over her shoulder as if to be sure she was not seen. "I am sorry if I have disturbed you," she said, "but I heard screaming and I was afraid.''

MacDougall bowed deeply, motioning toward the chair. "I am at your service. Your wish is my command." He repressed a smile, though he doubted that he could hide the twinkle in his eye. The thought of Scathach frightened by a scream or two was quite amusing.

Seated, the Sorceress looked narrowly at Alan, then burst into subdued laughter.

"You mock me, Alan MacDougall." She kept her voice low. "And of course you knew I was not frightened, merely curious. It seemed as good an excuse as any other, and I *do* want to speak with you."

Alan grinned, sinking to a seat on the bed. "I appreciate your diverting my thoughts from a most unpleasant discovery I just made."

Scathach raised her brows. "Tell me."

MacDougall shook his head. "Later perhaps. It has to do with the scream. But what have you in mind?"

The Sorceress looked down at her hands, folded on her lap, her expression almost demure. "This is difficult for me, Alan, but I want to apologize for the way I treated you during those last times in Scath. You must realize that I have had my own way for so long a time that to encounter a will as strong as my own was most upsetting. There is no way I can call back the things I said, but I am truly sorry, and I hope you can forgive me."

What an actress, Alan MacDougall thought, averting his gaze, trying to keep all expression from his face. She sounded *so* sincere. He appreciated the effort her statement must have cost her, despite her insincerity. It would be folly to humiliate her by scorning her request.

"Of course I forgive you. And I owe you an apology. I was hardly a gentleman when I appeared above the assembly in the Circle of Justice and—" He halted when he saw the storm clouds rising in her expressive eyes and added hastily, "But let us forget all that. It is past and done with. This is a new chapter and we appear to be in it together."

Scathach beamed. "Wonderful. Had I known more about you, of what was planned for you—but your Ahriman had said so little—" She stopped short, realizing her slip.

Smoothly Alan covered. "I understand. When Ahriman told you of my coming he said little else. So like him. Even now I have no idea what he has planned for me." So that was the cause of her change of heart. He'd make it easy for her. "When he appeared in the Great Hall and called me the Chosen One, I was the most surprised person there. And I still have no idea what he meant, though I admit it sounded most impressive."

Scathach smiled warmly. "I knew from the first moment I saw you that you were destined for greatness. And you must remember that we—we were together in past lives."

"I am not convinced," MacDougall said, "that what I saw and seemed to experience in Lamashtu's shrine were earlier lives. There was too much coincidence." He paused, then continued, "I have a question for you. Don't you wish to return to your tower in Scath? After all, here you are merely a friend of the King with no authority or power."

She hesitated. "I am enjoying this experience, a change, something new. And how could I return?"

"The way you came, of course."

"Never!" Decisively she shook her head. "There must be another way."

"There is a way," Alan said thoughtfully. "If Ahriman wants to he can place you in your own apartment in an instant."

She smiled. "For the present I prefer to remain right here. I confess I am interested—"

Another rap on the door interrupted her. Startled, she came to her feet, as did MacDougall. It might be embarrassing for Scathach if she were found here. Had the caller heard them talking? They had been speaking quietly. He held a finger to his lips, then pointed to the bath. She understood and quickly hid behind the barrier. At the same instant Alan darted to its end, grabbed his cape, and magically disappeared.

There came a second rap, then the door opened slowly and Eimher the Queen looked in. Incredible, Alan thought—and at that moment he became aware of the sensation of motion at infinite speed; and in less than a breath he was standing in a round chamber flooded with golden light.

An instant later, invisibility gone, he was joined by Ahriman the Persian who said quietly, "I decided it was time to rescue you from two predatory females."

CHAPTER 3

He-Who-Speaks-for-
the-Master

Deliberately Alan MacDougall turned his back on the be-ing who must be the greatest power on Avilion, and prob-ably in all this realm. He did it to gain time while he recovered from the shock of sudden transfer, and because it was the most outrageous act he could think of on the spur of the moment.

"I see you have moved," he observed casually. "This is not the room in which we met on other occasions. It is larger and the furnishings are different, though just as luxurious and pleasing to the eye. I suppose you have residence in both towers." He paused, expecting re-sponse. When none came he glanced around the room, now actually examining the gold-colored rug, matching massive chairs, and a great carved table formed appar-ently of teak and inlaid with gold designs.

He glanced toward the rounded wall, to see again the awesome sight of the aurora surrounding them—and sud-denly startled, he strode to the transparent golden wall and peered out in unbelief.

There was no aurora, only a wall of blackness like that

of starless space! He caught a glimpse of color below eye
level, and glancing down, he saw what appeared to be
an undulating sea of restless radiance, suggesting an expanse of clouds seen from the window of a high-flying
jet, but clouds colored by a surrealistic artist with a pastel palette.

He faced Ahriman in startled question. "We are *above*
the aurora!"

The Persian's gem-blue eyes showed no emotion, but
his red, red lips were curved in a cynical smile. "If you
have finished playing your little game," he said chill-
ingly, "perhaps we can sit and talk."

MacDougall could feel his cheeks flush. He felt like a
child caught with his hand in a cookie jar. His annoyance
was just what he needed to regain mastery of himself.

"Okay," he said in English, adding in the universal
tongue of this realm, knowledge of which had come with
the armlet, "you win. But we are *not* in your Tower in
Tartarus, and we *are* above the aurora. And I don't really
think I needed rescuing from Scathach and Eimher."

"Right on all three counts," Ahriman agreed, per-
mitting his features to relax. He gestured toward a chair.
"Sit, and let us begin at the beginning."

With both comfortably seated, facing each other, the
Persian said, "Once before we began your visit with a
bit of refreshment. You seemed to enjoy my wine." With
his words a round teak table appeared between them, and
in moments a crystal wine goblet and decanter followed,
the red-purple of the wine gleaming through the gemlike
facets of the container. As Ahriman poured, he spoke
casually.

"There is nothing magical about the service, only in
the method of its arrival; that is, by instant transfer, with
which you are familiar, and which in due course you will
master. The wine, by the way, is the same vintage we
enjoyed on that other occasion, though hardly the exotic
creations you shared with Scathach—especially the one
you called 'liquid dynamite.' "

The wine was delightful, Alan had to admit; and when
his host got down to business, Alan was aware that his

truculence had lost its edge. He had noticed the statement "which in due course you will master," but had ignored it as another of the super-abilities he had been promised.

"First," Ahriman began, "the matter of the Tower. Obviously we are in another, on the island you think of as Avilion—a very apt name, by the way. This tower, twice the size of that on Tartarus, is situated on a high mount, and it does project above the aurora. The mount is in a circle that may not be approached by anyone on the island; nor can the tower or hill be seen by anyone but Alan MacDougall. That will change at the proper time, and I feel free to say that time is almost at hand.

"And now," he continued, "I believe you have a quarrel with the system of justice on Avilion. May I hear your complaint?"

MacDougall frowned. Diabolically clever, this lieutenant of Lucifer, taking the initiative. "I do indeed. How can there be any justification for the torturing that Taliesin and I saw in those follies? And I'm sure you know whereof I speak."

"Of course I do. But think dispassionately, if that is possible. Death in itself holds no real terrors in a world where a new body is supplied, as good or better than the old one, and with no loss of memory or change in personality from the previous one. Oh, I concede, all cling to life as long as possible, and there is anxiety that precedes the actual interruption of life, but it passes instantly. So punishment—"

"What you have said is not always true," Alan interrupted. "What about Balor who was given a second body like that of a twisted Fomorian? Or Morrigu, who it seems never reappeared?"

"There are exceptions to all rules, but the cases you cite hardly apply, for both were Earth-created gods with powers beyond those of ordinary mortals. As for Morrigu, her return has been delayed for sufficient reasons that cannot be discussed.

"But as I was about to say when you interrupted me, for genuine punishment, for an effective deterrent, torture alone will suffice. And consider the offense. Those who are punished have with few exceptions been caught in the unauthorized use of drugs. This indulgence, once started, cannot be stopped. The narcotics here utterly enslave the users, who cease to be of use in a carefully balanced society. In the scheme of things on Avilion there must be a certain number of workers in every kind of activity for efficient operation. And this applies to all five cities, as well as farming, fruit growing, fishing, and the rest. Laws must be obeyed, and swift punishment must follow disobedience. Does this satisfy your objections?"

"Satisfy them?" MacDougall exclaimed with growing indignation. "Just the opposite! Why permit the drug addiction to exist? Why continue producing the plants that supply the narcotics? In short, it is a diabolic, arbitrary form of punishment meted out at the will of your Master.

"That spectacle in the basement of Cuchulainn's castle is appalling. With the addicts' plight so desperate, why not let them die in their ecstasy and keep their new bodies free of drugs? No, it's another manifestation of Lucifer's nature."

"Hold!" Ahriman drew himself up stiffly and his eyes bored into Alan's. "You are repeating the error that has prevailed for millennia.

"Who created the place of eternal punishment? Not Lucifer. Who sent all of us here, mortals and angels? Not Lucifer. And now that the Master has tried to make existence more tolerable by creating beauty and purpose and order among men and angels alike, who sends disruption and confusion? Not Lucifer! Alan MacDougall, you place blame on the wrong individual.

"Consider. As the story is told—and I merely repeat what has become widely accepted—the Great Power created all things. That, logically, would have to include Lucifer. He, supposedly the masterpiece of Creation, the highest of the archangels, was given freedom of choice, as later were men. He was given great powers, supernal beauty, intelligence unequaled among created beings—and he exercised his abilities. If not for use, why were they given? And for using what he had been given, he was cast out of the Power's presence.

"Thus began a conflict that has never ceased. It is not confined to your small world, as you may suppose, but it extends through all this vast universe. Of course, these four islands are Earth-centered, as are other and far larger areas of Lucifer's domain; but there are distant worlds where other intelligent life forms have been established, and where the same difference of opinion prevails between the Power and the Master. There, also, are worlds of Lucifer's reforming, with beings confined to what seem endless times of waiting for change, carrying out their little intrigues, fighting their futile little wars, dying to be reborn.

"And change must come! A stalemate cannot last forever. However, you and I are concerned only with Earth and the realm associated with it, the four islands in particular. Have you followed me thus far?"

MacDougall answered slowly, "I suppose so, though I question a lot of it; and I sense a contradiction. If the Power—to use your term for God—created all this, how do you explain the Halls of the Dead where the thousands of bodies await animation? Bodies, I have been told, formed by Lucifer. And how explain all the construction on the islands, the cities on Tartarus, the castles of Ochren and its underground area, or Scath, your own Golden Tower, the cities you mention here on Avilion?"

"The answer should be obvious. Though the Power created—and originally these islands were bleak and barren, those sent here mere spirits—Lucifer re-created, reformed, and adjusted, carrying out his own plans, displaying his own creative and artistic powers. He sought to increase the comfort, the enjoyment of his subjects, to replace the misery that was theirs when first they came here, sent by the Vengeful One whose creation had gone awry, but despite Lucifer's best efforts, constant interference came."

Indignation appeared on Ahriman's face, and he spoke with unusual fervor. "It is evident that you, like most people of your time and world, are guilty of participating in the unjust condemnation of the Lord of Light. Never has a being been more maligned. He has been blamed for every calamity, every catastrophe ever to strike the human race. Every weakness, every moral failure of mankind is attributed to the Master. No one is ever responsible for his own actions. Wars, crimes of violence, especially the more atrocious ones, all are *his* doings. Only man himself could stoop to genocide, making martyrs of an entire people, as was done in one of your recent wars.

"Is it logical to think that Lucifer would lead man to devise the means of his own destruction, possessing the knowledge, as Lucifer does, of man's basic instability? Of course it isn't. At last affairs on Earth have reached the point where he feels compelled to interfere.

"And you, Alan MacDougall, are an important part of his larger plan for your own world, a plan to save it from its own folly. For this you have been chosen."

MacDougall had been on the verge of voicing objections to Ahriman's arguments, but this startling announcement drove them from his mind.

"What did you say?" he demanded.

"I said you have been chosen to play an important part in the fate of your own world. Hence my calling you the Chosen One."

MacDougall slumped back into his chair, shaking his head in mock pity. "You are out of your mind. You must be if you think you can control me on the other side of the Gate. And that despite this cursed armlet."

"I said nothing about control," the Persian responded quietly. "It is an honor that you will accept of your own free will. And little as you think so now, when you do accept, you will be fully qualified for the position you will assume. So it has been foretold." The quiet assurance in Ahriman's voice and manner sent a tremor through MacDougall. He forced a derisive laugh.

"What utter nonsense. And what am I supposed to be doing in my own world of the living?"

"You will right the wrongs of ages. You will establish social justice. You will bring peace among nations. You will give the world what it has never had, the reign of a wise, beneficent, all-powerful ruler.''

If this fantastic statement had come from a wild-eyed zealot, it would have been less surprising; but Ahriman's speaking in his usual, calm, matter-of-fact manner made it all the more incredible. Momentarily words failed Alan MacDougall. Finally he gasped. ''You cannot be serious—or—or if you are, you're stark, raving mad! No mortal man could do what you speak of, and the thought of my doing it is just plain laughable. To think that all this hocus-pocus, this supposed prophecy of the Scroll, leads to this. This *is* the secret of the Scroll, is it not?''

Ahriman ignored the question. ''You will have help, of course, the help of many expert assistants. You will have the counsel of advisors wise with the wisdom of the ages. You will have power such as no man has ever had, under certain restraints, of course. Whatever you desire will be yours, limited, naturally, by the demands of your responsibilities.''

While the Persian was speaking, MacDougall caught the reference to advisors and in the same breath ages-old wisdom. There arose in his mind the image of a dark cloud closing about his head, demons attempting to possess him. Demonic helpers! After all, this whole unbelievable plan was Lucifer's.

There *were* demons on Earth, fallen angels. He knew little about such things, though he vaguely recalled records of demon possession in the Bible. And everyone had heard of exorcism, of multiple personalities that some said were many demons possessing a single individual. That demonic helper of Amaruduk in Marduk, Ashack had been his name, had told of a game once played among demons, who tried to see how many of them could crowd into one body. He wanted no part of any of this.

''You have been tested.'' Ahriman's words came through his racing thoughts. ''Time and again we have tested you during your visits to Tartarus and Ochren and Scath, and I am pleased to tell you that you passed every test. This necessitated some degree of control on our part, but—''

"If I recall," Alan interrupted in annoyance, "you once told me you did not want to control me, that my interest for you lay in my independent action. Do you remember your statement? It was during our first interview."

Ahriman smiled depreciatingly. "I recall—and it was true, then. Strangely enough at that time I had no idea of your ultimate destiny. I should like to project the image of my being all-knowing," he added smoothly, "but the Master imparts knowledge progressively. However, all that is past. The present is all that matters."

MacDougall was unconvinced. "Then why did you make the offers you did during that same conversation—powers and abilities beyond any possessed by the gods of Tartarus if I but cooperated with you?"

Looking annoyed, the Persian gestured with his right hand, as if brushing all this aside. "You have a retentive memory. But what is important now is the fact that you are not yet ready for the Great Adventure. There is still some intensive training that you must undergo here on Avilion.

"At the end of the training period you will have mastered all of the powers you will need to perform the supernatural feats, the—miracles, shall we say—necessary for you to establish yourself as the Great Leader you will have to become to accomplish your destiny. You will be as a god in the sight of the world.

"Think! You will be able to appear inside closed rooms. You will know what people are thinking before they speak, and you will know whether they are lying or telling the truth. No mental secret can be concealed from you. By reading signs and portents you will be able to foresee the future. I need not mention invisibility and shape-changing or thought transference, abilities already yours. You will not only be able to transfer yourself from place to place, but others as well, even sending another wherever you wish without yourself going there."

As Ahriman paused briefly, a vague memory from childhood Sunday School teaching came to Alan's mind, and he said with an attempt at sarcasm, "I suppose you'll soon say I will be able to heal the sick and raise the dead. And, I suppose, cast out devils.''

"Not actual infections or true sickness or crippling infirmities; but much illness is imaginary, or is the result of outside possession, and such you will be able to heal. As for raising the dead, if it becomes desirable, as a demonstration, shall we say, it would be possible for a newly vacated body to be reanimated by one of your agents, prepared for the task. And obviously you will be able to cast out demons, since Lucifer's angels will be subject to your command. But this will not be your province. You will be dealing with larger matters.''

"But I want no part of any of this," Alan objected vehemently. "This is not for me, understand? I want nothing to do with it. What must I do to make this clear?"

The Persian ignored his protests, adding "All this power will be second nature to you, a part of your mental control!"

As this thought registered to MacDougall's mind, he began with sudden hope, "You mean—" then halted. He had been about to ask, You mean I can shed the armlet? Better not ask, came an inner warning. If that happened he would reach his goal. He would be free!

Instead, he continued with simulated interest, "You mean I will be master of all the magic of the *Tuatha de Danann*, of Manannan and the Daughters of Calatin, and—"

"All that and more. And all because the Master made a promise to a sixteen-year-old Saxon boy named Vollmar, bastard son of King Vortigern, fourteen centuries ago!"

"So we're back to my visions in the shrine of Lamashtu," Alan scoffed. "I suppose next you'll tell me that Lucifer placed the Sumerian gods, Enki and Inanna, in their twin-headed serpent form six thousand years ago for my benefit. As punishment for their offenses, of course, but secondarily so that millennia later I'd be able to wear the armlet and thus find my way into Tartarus."

Ignoring the sarcasm, Ahriman said, "Obviously that would be absurd. But the Master was able, after the visitation with Vollmar, to arrange for the armlet's making its way into the possession of Caermarthen the last Druid, so that when he died under the sword of your brother Malcolm, you would find the jewel. He was able to bring the unnatural line of the Sidhe into your ancestry so that Malcolm would choose that particular time to visit the Scottish Highlands.

"I could carry the picture further by suggesting that he arranged for the *Shee* to be in the *broch* so that Malcolm, as Cinel Loarn, would be waiting at the portal when you fled from Tartarus, to drive back Balor and Morrigu; or that he arranged for him to be waiting when I placed your grievously wounded body through that same Gate so that he could bear you to the Cameron farm—but I will not do so." Ahriman looked quizzically at MacDougall.

"Why does this involvement of the All-Wise with matters spanning many centuries seem strange to you? Do you not see that a thousand years are as one day and a day as a thousand years to the Lord of Light?"

His face became suddenly stern, his eyes burning into Alan's. "Never," he admonished, then repeated the word for emphasis, "*never* underestimate the abilities of the Master. Such misjudgment could be costly, very costly." There was a chilling quality in his words; and Alan fully expected to heed the admonition.

Abruptly Ahriman stood up. "I believe we have discussed all that requires our attention at this point. There will be other sessions after you have seen more of what lies before you. We leave for another level."

Still seated, MacDougall looked up at the Persian who obviously expected him to rise, then drained his wine goblet.

"There are questions still unanswered," he said as he got to his feet. "But then, there always are when I leave you."

"You are not leaving at the moment. I have far more to show you." The Persian grasped his hand firmly; and in that instant the setting changed. MacDougall caught his breath and grasped the railing before him.

They were standing on a round platform at the apex of a great golden arch, a narrow band about two feet wide with a slender but sturdy railing on both sides. And they were high above what appeared to be a landscape as viewed from an airplane. Directly overhead arched a domed golden ceiling, glowing with internal light. Immediately Alan realized they were perched above a miniature of Avilion, as on other occasions he had viewed Tartarus and Ochren. Despite this awareness, he clung to the railing, fighting a queasy feeling in his stomach.

This was not the same vantage point as that in the Tower on Tartarus, despite similar opaque golden walls. This chamber was far larger, indeed, twice the size of the other. A single glance sufficed to reveal the great ten-foot-wide lens suspended below them, the small golden table and chair, and the now-familiar domelike cap with its attached lenses, and the great twin-handled padded forceps that made up the working tools of this device.

After that single glance MacDougall fixed his gaze on the miniature landscape below, the fantastically reduced replica of Avilion. It shone with gemlike brilliance under the radiance emanating from beneath the catwalk circling the round chamber.

Without warning that light vanished, and from the ceiling sprang a spotlight, spreading over the outer portion of the island. Slowly it followed the shoreline, revealing a broad expanse of cultivated fields.

"That spotlight," Ahriman commented, "is a great help when I use the forceps. You will observe that Avilion has some characteristics which are unique to this island. Obviously it was greatly changed by the Master and now bears no resemblance to its original shape."

Unlike the other islands, which had the natural contours one would expect, Avilion was totally and obviously the result of planning and design, symmetrical in every way. It was round, its shoreline smooth, its beach of uniform width around its entire circumference. There were minute fishing villages along its shores with tiny toy boats evident in the sapphire waters, but each was balanced by a comparable village on the opposite shore.

There were farms with tiny dwellings nestled among the fields of grain, some green, some tawny and ready for harvest, and picture-perfect orchards. There were fields where white cattle grazed. Other farms filled areas in corresponding positions on opposite sides of the island. Through all this ran a tracery of threadlike white roads.

It looked, MacDougall thought, as if a master lapidary with artistic taste to match his skills had designed and created the largest and most perfect gem ever imagined. A sudden wild idea—had the gem preceded the actual island, this Lucifer's model? Hmm—not logically, since the Tower had to exist to hold the model. No matter.

The beam moved inward, sweeping over the complex of towns—cities?—at the island's heart. There were five, all surrounded by high walls, each completely different from the others, and each equidistant, forming a great circle at the center of which towered an immense hill, its slopes a carpet of pallid green. And from its peak, like a golden beacon, rose the Tower of Ahriman. There the light lingered.

The base of the mount of the Tower was girdled by a circle of giant trees; and descending the slope were five white lines, barely identifiable as stairways, each pointing to one of the cities. From them, beyond the trees, projected white roads, arrow-straight, crossing the pale-green meadow, ending at city gates.

Again Ahriman spoke. "Quite impressive, is it not? And different." As an afterthought: "You will understand that the area inside the circle of trees and for a mile outside them is forbidden to all the dwellers on Avilion. In fact, they can see nothing beyond the trees. Hill and Tower are invisible to them."

Forbidden! A strange characteristic of all the bodies supplied by Lucifer, an instinctive recognition and an inborn dread of "forbidden" areas, making it actually impossible for them to trespass. Fleetingly he thought of the Druid Semias whom he had placed in the heart of one such area with dire results. For Semias and himself.

"I call your attention to the cities," the Persian continued. "They are important to you, hence this view of the island. You will recognize the white city of Cuchulainn. Now you have an overview.'' The beam highlighted the marble city.

Dominating it was the massive, square central tower of the castle, with the two slender, tapering observation towers at opposite ends of its face, and marble walls extending diagonally away to form two sides of a triangle. The third side, sweeping in a great, graceful curve, completed the fan shape he had observed through the window of his room. The numerous dwellings with their glittering silver roofs completed the jewellike city of Cuchulainn. A striking picture set against the pallid green meadow. Tiny white-clad figures in arrested motion were barely visible.

MacDougall looked for the follies that had provided unpleasant greeting on his entry into Avilion, found them scattered about on the approach to the castle, minute silver-topped gems set on a landscaped slope. To their right was a great rounded clump of trees, a clear area at its center. Off to one side lay what appeared to be a white marble disk. Oddly, a mistiness hung over the clearing, obscuring details.

''Where did all the marble and silver come from—'' Alan began, then checked himself, remembering the unnatural deposits of metal mined by the Trolls of Tartarus. ''I know. Any mineral Lucifer wants can be claimed from the infinite supply in the universe.''

Ahriman smiled faintly. ''You learn, young man.'' The beam moved on to the city next in line, clockwise around the circle.

''The dwellers call this Magadha, which was the name of the area in the Other World where the Gupta kings came to power. You will meet King Kumaragupta, as well as Varuna the Seer, in whom resides the knowledge and power of the ages, and Kalidasa the Poet. These three reign in Magadha, the city of the Hindus. There is another man you had better avoid, Mihiragula his name.''

MacDougall's attention was fixed on the gemlike city, so, though he heard the Persian's words, he gave little thought to their import.

Magadha, as large or larger than the city of Cuchulainn, was square, its surrounding wall built of black stone blocks. At regular intervals from the top of the wall rose pyramidal domes ending in needle spires, also formed of black stone. An ornate double bronze door was centered in each of the four sides. The buildings, set in a crisscross grid of narrow streets, were multicolored, some red, others yellow, still others white and deep green. Most of them were flat-roofed and of identical size. Only what appeared to be a temple suggested the Indian architecture that Alan knew, with its stepped-up, four-sided spire, multistoreyed, tapering as it climbed upward to its peak. And even from where MacDougall stood, he could see that every inch of surface of the temple was covered with intricately carved ornamentation. To the right and left of the main temple rose two smaller ones, far less imposing, three storeys high. They were wrought of dark-gray stone.

"Tell me," MacDougall asked curiously, "how far apart are these cities? And why are there no roads connecting them?"

"The distance, about twenty of your miles. As for the lack of roads, there is no commerce of any sort, no interchange whatever between them. Indeed, were it not for my control there would be constant warfare between every city. Each has its own food suppliers; and each considers itself the reason the island was created."

"Each its own private Paradise," Alan commented, "or Hell."

"One might say that." Ahriman waved toward the third city, the spotlight moving with his gesture. "Now consider Shenzhu, the City of Jade."

As MacDougall bent his gaze on the next city, he marveled. If any deserved comparison with gems, it was this one. Indeed, it *was* a jewel, a model city wrought of jade. Its walls formed a hexagon, its six uniform sides built up of spinach-green blocks, topped by tapered turrets of black nephrite. The curved gable roofs of the houses with their upswept corners were formed of long convex tiles of varicolored jade, polished to mirror

brightness. The asymmetrical arrangement of the individual houses created a beauty that could not have been
matched by any formal layout.

Three tall, six-sided pagodas, all of equal height, rose
above the rest of the city, one of apple green, another of
white, and the third of a delicate mauve. Beautiful but
impossible, Alan thought as he marveled at the model.
There couldn't be that much jade in existence—not if the
actual city duplicated the miniature. Not to mention artisans to polish a mountain of jade. And all those colors!
He gave voice to his thoughts.

Ahriman shook his head sadly. "You are not logical,
Alan MacDougall. As with marble and silver, jade is also
available in infinite quantity. The colors? Even in the
Other World, jade in its two varieties, nephrite and jade-
ite, has been found in every color of the aurora—or the
rainbow, if you prefer. With an infinite source of supply,
and in a world where time is what you want it to be, why
should this be impossible? You will find your visit to
Shenzhu most fascinating."

After a pause he continued, "Now observe Atu, whose
dwellers call this world Khert-Neter, the home of the *Ka*.
Atu was the chief city in Khert-Neter in their beliefs. Its
rule is divided between Osiris, god of the dead, and the
moon-god Thoth, though they exist for them only as images of stone."

Obediently the beam fell on the fourth city; and again
it was totally unlike the others. It was surrounded by a
broad border of palm trees, which softened its lines and
added greatly to its beauty. The palms, incredibly, were
a deep, natural green. The city itself, obviously Egyptian
as the Persian's references to Osiris and Thoth had indicated, was built primarily of oversized bricks. Yellow
bricks formed the thick walls that made up its four sides,
and brick walls formed its oblong, tapering, flat-roofed
houses. Only the imposing entrance to the city, rising
twice the height of the wall, was stone, topped by a cor-
nice, intricately carved, either of wood or painted stone.

Also built of tan blocks of stone was what must be a
temple, four times the height of the other buildings and

proportionately broad, erected on a great stone platform with four majestic square pillars marking its entrance. It was built in three sections, the central one most imposing. Leading up to it was a long, wide stone ramp.

But most unusual about this city were the graceful palm trees scattered freely through its streets, rising high above every building except the temple.

"One more city for your inspection," Ahriman said quietly; and the light moved to the fifth and last lifelike model. "They call it Axume, the African city from whence the dwellers came."

This was a study in gray and brown—gray rock and the brown of rusted iron. It was round, about the same size as the others; and the houses within its rough granite walls were likewise round. The roofs topping the hutlike dwellings of granite blocks appeared to be cones of weathered sheet iron. As they probably were. Scattered among them were small, squat, round-topped cylinders suggesting to MacDougall granaries or storage bins. There were no streets, turf growing between the buildings. The circling wall, built of rough-hewn granite blocks, was without ornamentation except for evenly spaced, skyward-pointing iron spearheads of great size, obviously wrought for their present purpose and not to be the heads of weapons.

As with the other cities, a single group of buildings dominated. These stood inside the massive granite gateway with its brown iron double gates. The central structure was a round stone tower that suggested to Alan a larger version of the Highland *broch*. It was flanked by two tall gray obelisks bearing intricately chiseled designs, too small to be seen clearly in miniature.

In Axume also were barely visible human figures.

The spotlight vanished and the full radiance of floodlights and ceiling returned. Ahriman faced MacDougall.

"Now you have gained something of an idea of the makeup of Avilion. No doubt you noticed that each city represents a different civilization or culture. Cuchulainn, the British Isles; Magadha, India; Shenzhu, China; Atu, Egypt; and Axume, Africa. These—"

"You mean to tell me," Alan interrupted, "that these groups and their cities were established here at the time the promise was made to Vollmar and the prophecy of the Scroll was written? And all for my benefit fourteen hundred years later?"

Ahriman nodded soberly. "It is difficult to believe, is it not? Yet that is the fact. And all of the dwellers in the cities are from the same time span, though of course you could not know this."

"But why? Why? What possible reason can there be for this diversity of peoples?" More than ever before, MacDougall felt like a puppet dangling from Lucifer's strings, and his frustration increased with each passing moment.

"This will become clear—all in good time. But now, before you visit Magadha and the others, we have one more task before us, a journey, or better, a tour. And this is not the place from which we start."

Again the Persian grasped Alan's hand, and instantly they were back in the room at the top of the Tower. They seated themselves on opposite sides of the teakwood table, and the Persian fixed unwinking eyes on Mac-Dougall's, frowning thoughtfully. At length he spoke.

"I want to show you some scenes in the Other World. There is no trickery in this, no deceit. I want to reveal to you some phases of life in the world you call home. When you see what I plan, you will recognize the settings either by personal knowledge or through hearsay.

"In order for me to do this it will be necessary for you to place yourself under my mental control. You can do this willingly or resisting every step of the way. The end result will be the same." As MacDougall began to protest Ahriman interrupted, "Ask the gods in the armlet. You have no reason to doubt them. They will verify what I've said."

Scowling, Alan asked mentally, "Lord Enki and Lady Inanna, can he do as he says? Can he force me to yield to his control?"

The serpent-gods gave silent assent. "He speaks truth. It might be an interesting battle if you resisted, but in-

evitably you would lose, so you would gain nothing
through resistance. So why resist? You had less reason
to yield to Scathach and Ereshkigal back on Scath, and
there, if nothing else, you had an interesting experience.''

True, Alan thought; and though it went against every
instinct, he said aloud, ''Very well. Do what you must.''

Ahriman responded, ''To be fully truthful, my powers
end at the line that separates the worlds. I can communicate with others yonder, nothing more. You will be
conducted by one named Ophiel. It will be a mental journey, but you will sense fully whatever you are shown.''

He stood up and walked behind MacDougall, placing
his hands over Alan's forehead, the fingertips meeting.
His touch was cool and though he exerted no pressure,
there was strength and energy flowing from him. As the
moments passed Alan became drowsy; and out of his
lassitude rose a sudden feeling of panic and the impulse
to fight. But he no longer had strength, and from his
weakness came the thought, Why bother?

Through the corridors of his brain echoed, ''Why
indeed?'' And he became aware of another presence, another personality in his mind.

''I am Ophiel, and I obey the instructions of the 'One-
Who-Speaks-for-the-Master.' We journey about the
Earth.''

Fleetingly MacDougall was aware of travel at infinite
speed; and the thought came ''Observe.''

Suddenly sight and sounds and smells smote his senses.
He heard a subway train roar by to grind to a halt several
hundred yards down the track. The commotion of rush-
ing riders blended into a blur of noise; but his attention
was caught by a group of people doing little or nothing,
a dozen feet away, some sprawled or sitting on the con-
crete floor along a tiled wall, others partly hidden amid
cartons under a closed stairway. All of them, men and
women alike, were unkempt, roughly but heavily dressed,
the men bearded or unshaven. Every face, black or white,
bore an expression of stoic resignation. Over the scene
hovered the effluvium of stale sweat and urine.

His guide sent the thought, "Obviously we cannot be seen, though all your senses are functioning. This is the first of many scenes you will see. These people live here, and there are thousands like them in the City, homeless, many less fortunate than these because they haven't even the shelter of a subway station."

Abruptly the scene changed; and they were in a spacious apartment furnished in luxurious good taste. Visible between heavy draperies framing wide windows, countless lights like stars glittered against a night sky. One man, faultlessly dressed, sat alone at a dining-room table, being served in silence by a man obviously a servant. Soft music and the blended aroma of savory food soothed the senses.

"Contrast." The thought came from Ophiel. "And there are thousands like him in the City."

Again the scene changed. Alan was in what appeared to be the waiting room of a doctor's office, a white-clad nurse in attendance; evidently the office of a gynecologist since all those waiting were women.

MacDougall sent a protesting thought. "Ophiel, why have you brought me here? I can see no reason for my seeing a physician specializing in women's problems."

"It is that in a way; but we thought you should know about a situation that the Master finds most disturbing. This is one of many thousands of abortion clinics in your country, where countless lives are destroyed before they are born. The cries of the innocent never cease . . . But we shall forgo the details."

Again the scene changed. Hot, dry, dust-laden air rose from parched ground. Huddled in the uncertain shade of a few sparsely leaved trees were thirty or forty scantily clad black men, women, and children, the children especially pathetic with their pipe-thin legs and arms, their bony faces, ribs clearly visible above distended stomachs. In the background before a few frame buildings a man and three women in wrinkled whites were ministering to a column of the starving, dispensing a heavy gruel in tin pans.

"Contrast," came the thought. The desert was replaced by mountains of grain in enormous overflowing bins, extending to the horizon. The picture blended into a view of the interior of a warehouse where uncounted tons of cheese and butter and containers of powdered milk gave mute testimony to a tragic and ironic imbalance. Finally this blended into a vast landfill where scores of trucks were emptying their cargoes, disturbing great flocks of seagulls, and almost as many children and some adults scavanging for hidden treasure.

"Why am I being shown this?" MacDougall mentally demanded. "I know things are out of balance. But it has always been that way. And there's certainly nothing I can do about it."

"So you *are* aware?" came the response. "Is this also familiar?" Alan seemed to be looking down at a riot. Hundreds, perhaps thousands of men and women, black, brown, and a few scattered whites, were advancing toward him. Some bore signs nailed to sticks, others simply waved and shouted, while still others continued their steady forward march.

Then shots were fired and marchers fell; and uniformed soldiers and policemen waded into the crowd, truncheons swinging—and abruptly the scene vanished. And MacDougall suddenly realized that he had seen this very happening on television, a protest march against apartheid in South Africa.

"This is not happening at this moment," Ophiel commented, "but iron-fisted oppression continues. And unless something or someone brings about change, South Africa will experience one of the bloodiest revolutions ever to strike Earth." And even as the thought formed, Alan saw, in rapid succession, views of blacks sweating in the depths of mines; the hovels on unpaved streets in which they lived; the luxury of Afrikaners; and a meeting of an all-white Parliament in which a great majority shouted down the voices of a few favoring compromise.

How long this world tour continued, Alan MacDougall had no idea. It seemed endless. It included visits to Afghani refugee camps in Pakistan, with close-up views of children without hands, the victims of booby-trapped toys

thoughtfully distributed by Soviets. There was a visit to
North Ireland to observe civilian bombings perpetrated,
as Ophiel pointed out, in the name of Christianity. On
and on it went, with a visit to a mountaintop in Jamaica
with mansions of the opulent covering one slope and the
hovels of the wretchedly poor on the other. He saw a
dawn in the streets of Calcutta where the homeless un-
touchables yielded up to collectors the bodies of those
who had died during the night. He saw muggings and
murders, rapes and adolescent suicides.

Finally Alan sent an explosive thought. "Enough,
Ophiel! Whatever I am supposed to have learned should
be clear after all this. The world is a mess, I freely concede it. And I can even fill in areas you have missed. No
more!"

With the last exclamation Alan opened his eyes to meet
the steady gaze of Ahriman. After a brief silence the
Persian said, "I regret that I could not journey with you;
but I am certain you found Ophiel an efficient guide. He
knew my reason for the guided tour; and I am certain
you now see the need for something to be done. And
need I add, there was no deceit in what you saw. These
conditions exist."

"Of course they do; any thinking adult is aware of the
problems. But there's certainly nothing I can do about
it."

"You shall see. In due time you shall see." Ahriman
stood up. "Now you will return to Cuchulainn's castle,
and there you will mount a horse and ride to Magadha
to begin your final training."

Also on his feet, MacDougall shook his head decisively. "I will do no such thing. You can return me to
Cuchulainn, or you can transfer me to the Indian city,
but you can't make me do anything else."

MacDougall saw the darkly handsome face of Lucifer's
lieutenant express shock, then grow darker with fury, but
he kept his own face immobile. "I have not mentioned
your high-handed return of Taliesin to Tartarus—at least,
I assume that is what you did. And you've blocked all

mental communication. I will not take one step until he joins me. And you can't compel me to do so."

Inwardly Alan quailed at the mounting wrath evident on Ahriman's face, but he managed to keep his own face expressionless. He meant what he said; he needed the Bard's company and support. As he watched the Persian's struggle for control, and the satanic play of emotions, he knew why he was called "He-Who-Speaks-for-the-Master." In the end MacDougall won.

"Very well," the deep voice announced. "Taliesin will join you in your room. And Cuchulainn will provide two horses for your use."

He drew a deep breath and added frigidly, "Don't try my patience too far."

He lifted a hand and waved as if giving a signal—probably, Alan thought, to an assistant in the room of the model. An instant later he felt sudden indescribable motion; and he stood alone in his marble-walled bedroom.

CHAPTER 4

Magadha

Slowly Alan MacDougall felt his tense muscles relax, his iron control give way; and only then did he realize how rigidly he had been holding himself. He inhaled deeply and dropped to a seat on the bed. Alan, he told himself, you've been swimming in deep waters.

As he had done after each visit with Ahriman, he mentally reviewed all that had happened, all he had been told, and as he thought of the Persian's outrageous declarations, he felt a rising tide of panic, panic mingled with resentment. How had he gotten into this mess? It was like a game of cards with the deck stacked against him; he knew there was no chance of his winning, but he couldn't stop playing.

The claims Ahriman had made, that all the crime and misery on Earth were God's fault, not Lucifer's—God's and Man's. Equally absurd the idea that he, Alan MacDougall, was to become a world dictator; that he would right the wrongs of the world, bring about peace between nations, end crime. Those visions, the street people contrasted with the very wealthy. Dividing the wealth had never worked and never would. Communism was an appalling failure. Of course there were problems, but he didn't have the solutions.

The four cities he was to visit, to complete his education, Ahriman had said. This at least could be interesting, and he would be free of the attentions of Scathach and Eimher. If ever he had actually had the attention of the redhead. What had led her to visit while the sorceress was already in his room? Which, of course, she may not have known. He wanted no part of even a suggestion of a liaison with the wife of King Cuchulainn. That was a complication he did not need.

He heard a sound behind him and swung about. There, between the bed and the window, stood Taliesin, his brows arched in surprise. As Alan stood up, beside the Bard in mid-air appeared his cape, dropping to the floor as it materialized.

"Welcome!" MacDougall exclaimed. "So Ahriman kept his word."

Mechanically Taliesin picked up the garment and draped it over his shoulders, smiling broadly. "I left quite suddenly and returned the same way. Ahriman's work, of course. Not the first time he has done this to me, as you know. I tried to reach you but the way was blocked. I knew you would not be idle, so I just waited."

Alan indicated the chair. "Sit and I'll bring you up to date." Half reclining on the bed, MacDougall switched to mental communication. "*You sense my thought?*" he asked, and at Taliesin's affirmation he went on. "*I'm certain Ahriman is watching. He can't read my mind, and I hope you also can block out his prying.*"

"*I believe I can. Despite his position in Lucifer's hierarchy, he is no more powerful in certain respects than others of the dark angels. Once having been one of them, I have knowledge of such things. If he were to combine with others, he might penetrate the barrier I erect, but his excessive pride prevents that. He delegated to others the blocking of our mental exchange as a task beneath him, but this would be another matter. So we may safely exchange thoughts.*"

"Good. Then this is what happened after Ahriman re-

moved you.'' In flashing images, far more rapid than words, he told of all that had taken place. At its conclusion the Bard had shared in MacDougall's experiences almost as fully as if he had been present.

"As I see it,'' Alan commented finally, *"the next move will be Cuchulainn's. He will receive or has already received instructions from 'He-Who-Speaks-for-the-Master,' which is what they call Ahriman, and will act upon them. No one on Avilion, I am certain, questions his authority.''*

Frowning, Taliesin stared at the floor, evidently considering what he had learned. Finally he sent a somber thought to MacDougall. *"I believe Lucifer has the power to do all that Ahriman has said he would. But that is not to say it is certain to happen. There is a Power greater than the Lord of Darkness, one who confounded his plans on other occasions. Do not lose courage, my friend.*

"You may have forgotten, but shortly after I had deciphered the Scroll I said I did not believe you were part of Lucifer's plan. I honestly thought so, believing the obstacles to this ever happening were too great. Obviously I was wrong. But I am certain of this—nothing in the prophecy is inevitable. By the way, I no longer have the Scroll. Ahriman took it. But I remember it well.''

MacDougall yawned and said aloud, "Until the King makes his next move, I could stand some sleep. Despite the crazy time in this world, I feel as if it has been a long day. Now if the serpent-gods could transfer you into the next room—"

From Enki came the thought, "It should be quite easy to enter by way of the corridor. Or is that too simple?"

Both men grinned ruefully, and moments later Alan was alone. As he prepared for bed he remembered his brash request for cleaning service. In his pajamas he opened the door and summoned the guard, giving him not only his suit but all of his soiled garments.

"They must be back," he said brusquely, "by the time the King calls me after the sleep."

The guard bowed. "It shall be done."

* * *

How long he slept, Alan could not tell, but it seemed to be a short night when a rap on the door awakened him and a deep voice announced, "You are summoned by the King, and your garments are here."

After he had dressed he was joined in the corridor by Taliesin. With two guards guiding, one before and one behind, they were led to the small dining room where Alan had met the "people who mattered." They were ushered to seats at the table where places were set for two.

As the silent guards withdrew, two food servers entered through another door, each bearing a heavily laden tray. As they placed their dishes before MacDougall and Taliesin, one said, "The King has instructed us to tell you to prepare for your journey." Bowing, they left.

Alan grinned at the Bard. "Notice, your presence is acknowledged though Cuchulainn has not seen you. Ahriman's word carries a lot of weight around here. Eat heartily. We don't know where our next meal's coming from."

In apparent silence they consumed a light meal of barley loaves, slices of cold roast beef, cheese, and stewed mixed fruit; their beverage was an herbal tea they could not identify. As they ate, MacDougall tried to recall and mentally relate details of his visit with Ahriman that he might have overlooked during his initial summary to the Bard.

"Tell me," he concluded, *"is what Ahriman predicts for me the Secret of the Scroll that you've been keeping from me? After all, you deciphered it."*

After a long pause Taliesin answered, *"In part. There is more."*

"More! Tell me."

"I'm sorry," the Bard responded, *"but it would not be wise for me to say. Your not knowing may increase your chances of escaping it. Lucifer is not God."* And there the exchange ended.

When they had finished eating, the guards reentered and again without speaking led them through corridors to a small audience chamber where the four of them waited. Alan and the Bard were seated on a narrow marble bench facing a golden throne on a marble dais, the guards standing stiffly at their backs.

At last yellow draperies behind the throne were spread apart and a double column of guards entered to take their places to right and left of the dais. Then as before King Cuchulainn materialized, standing before his throne. At his appearance the Bard automatically stood up, and a second later, reluctantly, Alan also rose.

As the King seated himself he motioned for his visitors to do the same. He spoke.

"He-Who-Speaks-for-the-Master told of your return, Alan MacDougall, and of the one with you, the Bard Taliesin." He looked keenly at Taliesin. "I knew you in a day long gone. You were more slender then."

Taliesin nodded, smiling broadly. "Far more slender. Part of the added girth came with the new body and part is my doing. But I am nonetheless the Bard you knew."

"Whence come you? Not from the Other World, surely, like MacDougall."

"I came from there, but I was only passing through. I have spent the centuries since our time in Britain on another island under the aurora."

"Passing though?" Cuchulainn asked with sharply quickened interest. "You must tell me—but not now." He frowned with barely concealed annoyance at MacDougall. "I may not delay your departure to Magadha. I am sure they will greet you . . . warmly. Two horses await you outside the rear of the castle with a guard ready to guide you to the west gate." Addressing himself directly to Taliesin: "We shall speak more fully of this matter when next we meet."

Without warning King Cuchulainn became wraithlike, then disappeared. Too late Alan thought he should have exerted his acquired power to see things as they actually were, to determine the true manner of the vanishing. Moments later the guards who had brought Alan and Taliesin there led them through the curtain behind the dais, down another hallway, and out of the castle.

Awaiting them were two pure white stallions, ready for

mounting. They were handsome animals, well groomed and high-spirited. With them was a third horse already bearing a rider, another guard. At a word from him, they swung into the saddles and were led through the streets of the city to a gate that was opened at their approach and closed behind them after they rode through, their guard remaining behind. On the way they had passed white-robed pedestrians who wandered aimlessly about and ignored them completely. It was all very efficient, impersonal, and unnatural.

"Very strange," Taliesin remarked.

"I believe we'll find Avilion the strangest of the four islands," MacDougall agreed, "though each of the others had its share of oddities. I think of that strange pillar of light projecting from the mouth of the brazen serpent in Findias on Tartarus; or the ghostly cloud of intertwining, whispering souls in the abyss of Annwn on Ochren; or the Grove of the Spirits of the Daughters of Lilith on Scath. But these cities promise to be strange indeed."

They rode away from Cuchulainn across green turf for roughly a mile, their mounts, though hardly docile, responding well to the reins. Alan called a halt.

"We don't really know where we're going," he said. "We'd better get on track. With no road to follow, we need points of reference. We've been riding directly away from the Cuchulainn gate. To my right should lie the Mount and Tower of Ahriman."

He turned and stared across the plain. "In this clear air and on a flat world I should be able to see it even fifteen miles away." And there it was, made small by distance, the circle of trees like a pale-green girdle about the base of the conelike hill with the Golden Tower at its apex, vanishing into the sky. It was barely visible, but unmistakably the Tower of Ahriman.

"I see nothing," Taliesin said ruefully. "Nothing but a gray mist where land and sky seem to blend into one. But your seeing it is enough to guide us. If we keep it to our right we should reach our destination."

"Another possible help," MacDougall added. "The

armlet.'' He addressed a thought to the serpent-gods. ''Will you keep us on track?''

''If you were to use your own sense of direction—but of course we will.''

They set out at an easy canter, side by side, Alan on the right. As they rode along they engaged in mental conversation. The Bard began with a comment on Ahriman's repeated defense of Lucifer during Alan's visit. *''Never forget who he is and from whence he fell. He was and is the Great Deceiver. I should know, having been one of his from the beginning. And he chose to become what he is. Nothing, nothing I say, is permitted to stand in the way of his ambitions and plans. And his hatred for the Most High, whom Ahriman calls the Power, is all-consuming.''*

Bitterly MacDougall responded, *''And somehow I have been drawn into the center of his plans.''*

The mental dialogue ended for a time, each man occupied with his own thoughts. A low outcry from the Bard ended MacDougall's reflections.

''Alan, I see Ahriman's Tower! It is just as you described it, on the crest of a conical hill. What has happened?''

They drew rein, halting their mounts and staring toward the distant tapering pillar of glistening gold. Recollection came to MacDougall.

''Ahriman said this would happen, and soon; that all could see the Tower. I gained the impression that this would somehow mark an approaching climax.'' Grimly he added, ''If it's the end of this fantastic affair, it can't come too quickly for me.'' He prodded his horse into motion. ''On to Magadha.''

With mounting excitement Alan led the way across the grassy plain, spurring his stallion to a brisk gallop; and at last the walls of the Hindu city appeared on the horizon, a black box with the ornately carved, many-storeyed spires of its temples thrusting upward into the aurora. As they drew closer, they headed their mounts toward the great bronze double gate, set in the center of the black wall. Massive stone pillars, ornately carved, held up a great arched capstone, the doors themselves an intricate montage of figures of erotic nymphs, serpents, monsters, and dancing girls, all intertwined.

Alan could detect no sign of life, no activity; but when they were within thirty feet of the gate, the bronze masses began moving inward, slowly, then with increasing speed. And standing abreast in the gateway appeared six bowmen, steel-headed arrows nocked, bowstrings drawn back.

Startled, both men drew sharply on their reins, horses rearing; even as Alan cried, "Vanish," the six arrows were released!

There came a loud, metallic *bang*, and as if the missiles had crashed into an invisible wall they ricocheted or slithered aside or simply fell to the turf. It had happened in seconds, the horses dropping to all fours as the arrows landed, then vanishing with their riders. The bowmen stood frozen in consternation.

There had been no time for fright. Alan's thought to the Bard, *"Did you—?"* was answered immediately, *"Not I! Perhaps Lord Enki—"* And the serpent-god responded in the same moment, *"Not our doing."*

Ahriman! came the simultaneous thought. And Alan added grimly, *"He sent me here; he should have prepared the way."* On its heels another thought: *"Inside the gate, Taliesin, then reappear while the guards are still in shock."*

Seconds later, as the archers began moving, MacDougall and Taliesin, only a yard away from their assailants, seemed to materialize out of the air.

"Who are you?" one of the guards gasped.

"Who are you to ask?" Alan demanded sternly. "He-Who-Speaks-for-the-Master sent us. We would see—" As he hesitated momentarily, only one name came to mind: "We would see Varuna the Seer."

"The god Varuna!" The response was little more than a whisper. "But he sees no one."

"He will see us," MacDougall said with complete conviction. "Do not keep us waiting. Send to someone in authority and say we have come."

The spokesman hesitated, then said uncertainly, "Better we take you to the Despot. He, I am sure, can arrange what you wish—if he wills." He halted and became even more hesitant. "Your horses—it would be well if they were left here. We have no horses in Magadha, since only the King and his attendants ever travel outside the city. The cattle pens are nearby. Better I have them taken there, then they will be ready whenever you need them. And as you can see, our streets are not intended for horses."

MacDougall repressed a grin. The blocked arrows and their disappearance had certainly made a deep impression on this bowman. Frowning as if considering the suggestion, Alan inspected the guards. Heads smoothly shaven, feet bare, upper bodies clad in loosely fitting sleeveless and collarless blouses of tan fabric, buttoned down the front and ending at the waist. Their lower bodies were covered by an odd arrangement of voluminous red cloth, fastened about the midriff, gathered to create a trouserlike effect, ending at midcalf, with the excess cloth drawn up between the legs and fastened in the rear above the hips. In addition to their bows, each had a quiver of arrows strapped to his back, the feathers projecting above the right shoulder, and a long dagger in a sheath strapped about the waist.

"Very well," he said, dismounting; and as Taliesin followed his example the Bard sent the thought,

"Have them lead the way. I don't like the looks of those knives. Not in the hands of men who tried to kill us on sight."

As two of the guards led the horses away, and as the four divided, two in front and two behind the visitors, Alan shook his head decisively. "We follow."

The spokesman shrugged, scowling. "As you wish." And with Alan and the Bard bringing up the rear, they started into the city.

Gray flagstones were underfoot; they walked at a brisk pace, the guards apparently anxious to be rid of them. MacDougall remembered the varicolored houses he had seen in the model in Ahriman's Tower; he saw now that

the boxlike structures were built of red and yellow sandstone blocks, with here and there one of dark green. The
roofs were slate gray. Yet strangely, despite the bright
colors, an air of somber gloom hung over Magadha.
There was an oppressive silence; a mental question from
Taliesin suggested the reason.

"Where are the people?"

There were none! Not quite true; after crossing two
intersecting streets and approaching a third, they saw
three men coming toward them, naked except for dark-
red loincloths. They shuffled slowly along with shaven
heads bowed, seeming barely able to take the next step.
They turned into the cross street. As they passed, Alan
stared in disbelief. All were dreadfully thin, little flesh
on their bones.

A bit later they saw another man, equally emaciated
and slow-moving. As they approached him, he reeled
and fell to his knees. The archers passed him without a
glance. Indignantly Alan reached down and set him on
his feet, a figure amazingly light, and the man mumbled
something faint and unintelligible. He leaned against a
wall, panting with weakness.

After passing four others in like condition, one a
woman partially wrapped in a sari, an end dragging on
the street, MacDougall called out, "Guard, what is
wrong with these people? They look starved. Where are
they going?"

"They are Tantrics who have been meditating. They
sit for very long times. They are going to one of the halls
where food is served."

MacDougall grimaced with frustration. Did he mean
they literally starved themselves? What of the houses?
"Taliesin," he flashed the thought. *"Join me."* With
minds linked Alan mentally scanned the interior of the
house they were passing. The front wall held a single
window and a closed door, the window set too high to
permit peering in. But for the newly acquired sense of
MacDougall, this presented no problem.

The room was dimly lighted and sparsely furnished,
the stone floor covered by a thin, plain rug. There were

three men in the room, clad only in loincloths, each
seated cross-legged on a pallet, head bowed as if contem-
plating his navel. And from each of them came a low
repetitious chant, rhythmically uttered, but with no re-
lationship to the chants of the others. They were chanting
different sounds, with a humming "mmm" dominating.
But what struck Alan most forcefully was their near-
skeletal emaciation. He sent his perception from house
to house, to see essentially the same scene, varying in
details and some including women.

"*This is mad.*" Mentally he addressed the Bard. "*I
suppose this is somewhat like the Transcendental Meditation craze that invaded my country during the last de-
cade, only carried to the ultimate.*"

"*This is probably its source,*" Taliesin said, "*since
this is far older than what you speak of.*"

"*The mumbling we sensed must be the mantra, the use
of a combination of sounds, supposedly sacred and magical, without apparent meaning but of great significance
to the initiate. But these meditators are going to insane
lengths. Perhaps the serpent-gods can shed some light on
all of this.*"

"We can indeed," the Lady Inanna responded without
being asked. "We have explored the thinking of some of
these. They are following the Tantric path, the way of
knowledge gained by integrated reflection. They have
transcended the path of action and hope to obtain the full
realization of self. These are not our words but theirs. In
time, if they do not give up and seek food and drink,
they will become too weak to remain seated and will
collapse on their mats, still meditating with minds open
to ever-wilder visions. Unconsciousness will follow with
death not far behind. This is what they seek, believing it
will lead them to a higher plane of existence. They seek
liberation, what they call *mukti*."

MacDougall was aghast. "*You mean they deliberately
starve themselves to death?*"

"*And I suppose new bodies follow,*" the Bard observed dryly, "*only to go through the same futile circle.
Over and over and over.*"

"Literal Hell," MacDougall muttered under his breath.

During this telepathic exchange, MacDougall and Taliesin had continued their brisk walk behind the bowmen; and now they followed them into a side street, wider than any they had seen. At its end towered Magadha's Temple complex.

Four-sided, the three structures rose in uniform steps from a massive base fully fifty feet in diameter, each of the storeys substantially narrower than the one beneath it. Long stone stairways led to the first Temple level. From the corners on each level projected a rounded dome topped by a tapering, four-sided spear of stone. Larger domes of the same shape crowned the triple Temple.

Dominating all of this, obscuring the basic structure, was an incredible profusion of ornamental carving. Not a single visible surface had been left untouched by the sculptor's chisel. Cavorting dancing girls mingled with stone serpents, demons, and dwarfs. Sculptured panels were crowded with Hindu gods and their attendant spirits, with figures of elephants, crocodilian monsters, with pot-bellied princes on palanquins—a potpourri of the sculptor's nightmare skills.

A stone wall surrounded the Temple grounds, with a single pillared gateway, ornately carved, providing entrance. The four bowmen halted before two challenging guards armed with double-edged swords, blocking their way. They stared incredulously as they caught sight of MacDougall and Taliesin.

"Who are these and whence have they come?"

"From—from the Other World. He-Who-Speaks-for-the-Master has sent them. Before I learned of this, they stopped six arrows in flight. And—and vanished. Like gods."

"As we could again," Alan interjected impatiently. "We grow weary of this delay. Take us to someone in authority."

The bowman began hesitantly, "I suggested Despot Mihiragula—"

"Excellent idea!" The guard seemed amused at the thought. "He will make them welcome." His expression changed. "But he might blame us for bringing them. You know the rule—"

The four bowmen who were facing the Temple suddenly stiffened. "Here he comes!" one exclaimed in a hushed voice. All snapped to attention. The two Temple guards turned sharply and froze.

"A vicious-looking brute." MacDougall flashed the thought to Taliesin. *"I believe Ahriman warned me to avoid him."*

He was a giant of a man, about Alan's height, but at least twice his breadth and girth. He made the Bard look slender. He was—surprisingly, Alan thought—a blonde with a tremendous mane of hair a shade darker than MacDougall's and a massive, unshorn beard. Dark eyes glared through puffy pouches, overshadowed by eyebrows of tremendous size.

He wore a sleeveless maroon vesture of silken fabric, open in the front, exposing a hairy chest, and one of the typical voluminous wraparound garments like those of the bowmen and guards, his of black, differing in its having the excess cloth suspended from the waist in front. He differed also in that he wore thonged sandals, profusely jeweled. And both arms were circled with broad gold armlets and bracelets, heavily set with colorful gems. A wide, white sash girdled his waist, about it a belt of gold chain from each side of which were suspended curved scabbards topped by black, gem-encrusted hilts.

The Despot had approached in silence, his glare expressing mounting fury. Suddenly he bellowed, "Visitors in Magadha! You know it is forbidden. Why have you not slain them? Your swords—now!"

"They would not dare!" MacDougall responded coldly with a confidence he did not feel. "He-Who-Speaks-for-the-Master protects us. We come at his command." To Taliesin he thought: *"Be ready to disappear. And run."*

"He speaks truth." A new voice came with quiet assurance from Alan's right; and, unnoticed during the

Despot's approach, a second figure of power entered the picture, coming, apparently, from a secondary Temple. All eyes turned in his direction as he continued speaking.

"The Great One appeared to me only moments ago and told me to hasten to greet them. I was also told that both King Kumaragupta and the Lord Varuna were informed of their coming." His lean face broke into a smug smile. "So I fear, Mihiragula, for the present you must restrain your savagery." As he continued his approach, a low growl came from the Despot's throat, his only response; he remained motionless.

With great interest Alan observed the newcomer. Of average height, slight of build, he was dressed much like Mihiragula except that his garments were of pale blue and he wore no weapons. His hair, cut to shoulder length, and his eyes were black, the latter close-set and shifty. He wore a domelike helmet of silver, heavily set with blue gems. His face, somewhat swarthy, beardless, and youthful, was that of a schemer.

As he reached the group he said to Alan and the Bard, "I am Kalidasa, and I am a poet. With Kumaragupta and Varuna, I am one of the rulers of Magadha. And—" He bowed toward the glowering Despot, visibly gloating. "—though he likes it not, he must obey my commands. Is it not so, Mihiragula?"

The scowling giant barely nodded; growled to guards and bowmen, "Dismissed"; and, after a single baleful glance at MacDougall, he turned and stalked back toward the main Temple. An ugly, vicious man, Alan thought.

As Kalidasa led the visitors toward the lesser Temple, he stepped smoothly between them and spoke directly to MacDougall.

"You are Alan MacDougall who has come by some strange means from the Other World, where once all of us dwelt. And you have been Chosen, so I was told, to be greatly honored by the Lord of Light, the Fairest of the Fair. Indeed, you are called the Chosen One. You have come seeking audience with the Lord Varuna. This is not easily gained, so until he calls you we will provide rooms and food for both of you in my quarters." He smiled ingratiatingly. "I am happy to do this for you. The Lord Varuna is very old and sufficient unto himself. Even the Chosen One must await his pleasure; but I will do my utmost to have you meet him." He turned his attention to Taliesin.

"You, I understand, are Taliesin, also a poet, from another island in this land, and a Bard of renown in the other life. They call you the Bard of Bards." He smiled with simulated warmth. "If there is opportunity, we must talk. It will be stimulating to speak with a kindred mind after—forever. Here there are none who think as I do, save perhaps the Lord Varuna. And his thoughts are his own."

A note of genuine awe crept into Kalidasa's voice. "From my window I saw the hill and the Tower of the Great One, which until now has been hidden from all. Its appearing must presage change, the coming of great events, perhaps the passing of our imprisonment."

They had reached the foot of the stone stairway leading into the lesser Temple. There had been no opportunity for response, and none seemed expected. Inside the wide, sculptured doorway they were met by guards, one of whom was directed to take them to rooms that Kalidasa designated.

Before they followed their guide, MacDougall said, "We appreciate your hospitality and your coming when you did. This Mihiragula had become somewhat difficult."

Taliesin added politely, "It will be interesting to speak with a fellow poet."

Kalidasa bowed. "May Surya again shine upon you."

They were led through a maze of corridors to adjoining rooms on the first level, each with a single window and the same sort of facilities Alan had found in his room in the city of Cuchulainn. There was, similarly, a low bed, a single chair, and a small table. Same architect and interior decorator, Alan thought. He sent a mental comment to Taliesin: *"Kalidasa is not a man I would trust."* After a pause: *"A change of subject. Which is worse— torturing people to the point of madness to keep them alive, as in Cuchulainn, or encouraging them to fast themselves to death for their religion, as in Magadha?''*

"You don't really expect an answer, do you?'' the Bard responded. *"Four islands—and Tartarus continues to grow more satisfactory with each visit to the others.''*

They continued their telepathic conversation while preparing for bed, mainly discussing the mysterious Varuna whom the bowman had called a god. Alan, minus shoes, cape, jacket, and shirt, stretched out on his bed. As his eyelids grew heavy he asked belatedly, *"Is there any chance that food will be brought at this time? I cannot fathom how periods for eating are determined. I'm not hungry, but I am sleepy.''*

"No chance,'' the Bard replied. *"We know instinctively, and this is not the time. It is time for sleep. Rest well.''*

With a sleepy thought to the serpent-gods to keep alert for possible intruders, MacDougall rolled on his side; and as drowsiness became overpowering and his thoughts became a disconnected hodgepodge, familiar thought patterns, as voices, touched his mind.

The *Tuatha de Danann!* A discussion already under way, and he an unwitting eavesdropper as had happened several times before, just before sleep. Voices in his mind as speakers in a dream. The first was that of Danu the Mother.

"Will you repeat what you just told me, Nuada, for the benefit of those newly joining us?''

Came the familiar voice of Nuada, King of the Celtic gods. *"I have just returned from Manannan's copper ship, Wave Sweeper. It lies motionless in the midst of a shoreless sea. As you know, it has neither sails nor rudder, not even oars, for it obeys the voice of its master, Manannan, god of the sea. But now it will not respond to his magic. Food is gone and those still on board are in a sorry state.''*

"And you forsook them?'' the deep voice of Gobniu the Smith demanded.

"You know better than that,'' Nuada snapped indignantly. *"I've come back for food. With my transfer power*

I could have brought them all, two at a time, but Manannan will not abandon his coracle, and the others are staying with him. He asks all of you to exert your powers to counter the magic that holds Wave Sweeper in thrall.''

Diancecht the Physician asked, "How did you get into this fix?"

"As most of you know, we learned through Taliesin, who found out from MacDougall of the charmed life, that there is a third island in this world. Manannan decided to visit it and took nine others with him. Beside me these included Balor; Beli; Pryderi; Mathony, Manannan's master magician; and four of his Druids.

"We reached the third island and met its Queen, Scathach the Sorceress. Of course we also met MacDougall and Taliesin. Some of us had known Scathach in the olden days—but I will tell of our experiences at another time. Now it is imperative that I secure food and return to the others. When we left Scath we started toward a fourth island. We believe powers on that island have blocked Manannan's control of his ship.''

Nuada's last remarks reached MacDougall faintly and waveringly, finally merging with the confusion of dreams. He slept.

A sharp rap on his door awakened him, and as he sat up a deep voice announced, "The Lord Kalidasa invites you to join him in breaking fast."

"Very well," Alan responded, getting out of bed and stripping off his clothes. He needed a bath. He heard a rap on Taliesin's door, and a similar dialogue followed. As he prepared for the day—he was more comfortable thinking of it as such—he greeted the Bard.

"You slept well?"

"Indeed. And you?"

"Very well—after I listened to part of a conference of *the* Tuatha de Danann." He repeated the conversation that had come to him unsought.

Taliesin commented in amusement, *"Can you picture that group packed tightly in* Wave Sweeper, *sitting or standing idly, waiting for something to happen? They can't even lie down except perhaps for one or two at a time. What frustration!''* He added thoughtfully, *''The work of Ahriman, of course. He will restore Manannan's power when it suits his purpose, perhaps to bring them to Avilion.''* Solemnly he concluded, *''Strong magic.''*

In due time both were ready, each wearing his cape at Alan's suggestion. There was no assurance that they would return to their rooms. On signal they went out into the hallway. Two waiting guards bowed obsequiously, then led them through several corridors, finally leaving the building.

Towering before them rose the central Temple with its bewildering display of sculptured walls. They crossed an arched bridge, likewise intricately ornamented, and passed through a wide doorway into the graystone edifice. Inside, the walls and much of the ceiling were a continuous mosaic in which the unlikely blending of gods and monsters, of dancing girls and demons, of serpents and spirits, was repeated, but in vivid and unfading colors. A luminous band in the center of the ceiling and extending its length provided light.

The guards halted at an open doorway and motioned for MacDougall and Taliesin to enter.

''The Lord Kalidasa awaits within.'' Turning, they marched back the way they had come; and Alan and the Bard entered the room.

''Greeting, my friends!'' Kalidasa, who had been sitting at a teakwood table inlaid with silver and set for four, rose and came toward them, a smile of exaggerated warmth on his lean face. ''I trust you had a refreshing sleep and are ready for whatever the gods have in store.'' He paused briefly, glancing toward a second doorway behind him, then his speech rushed on.

''We are awaiting the arrival of King Kumaragupta, who is anxious to meet you, which frankly I find rather surprising. We would have invited the Lord Varuna to join us but he never leaves his quarters. We have sent him word of your coming and have asked for audience.''

Up to this point the flow of words from the poet had made response unnecessary and difficult; now he halted at a faint musical sound. It was the tinkling of tiny distant bells, coming from beyond the doorway across the room. The three turned and waited in silence, Alan and Taliesin in growing wonder as the bell-tones drew closer. Then came the dancing girls.

Two by two they entered, posturing, jeweled arms waving, begemmed fingers gesticulating, bare feet moving in intricate steps, jeweled and bell-spangled ankles flashing. A colorful spectacle from their high-piled floral headdresses, wide gem-beaded necklaces covering shoulders and the upper curve of their bare breasts. Nude to the waist, they wore voluminous wraparound skirts of lacy fabric, a bright red. There were at least a score of them; and behind them came the King.

Like Kalidasa he was black-haired and dark-eyed, and he wore the usual wraparound lower garment, a vivid purple, drawn up into quasi-trousers with the excess cloth drawn up between the legs, but there the resemblance ended. Not quite Alan's height, but broad of shoulder, King Kumaragupta had a prominent mustache, curled upward at the ends, and a close-cropped beard trimmed to a point. He wore an open-fronted lavender tunic, beneath it a pale-yellow undershirt. Like the dancers, he was heavily jeweled, starting with a dome-shaped golden crown, armlets, and bracelets; and there were gem-studded sandals on his feet. He was unarmed.

As he approached the table he waved in dismissal to the dancers; and still moving to the rhythm of their tinkling bells, they retreated from the room.

"I welcome the Chosen One and his companion," the King announced sententiously. "We are honored by your presence." He gestured with both hands. "Be seated, my friends. We should be standing in your presence."

Alan caught a look of surprise on Kalidasa's face, quickly erased; and he thought, What a selling job Ahriman has done to bring about this phony reaction. He'd take it as his due. Bowing deeply, he responded, "The honor is mine, O King; and your graciousness will not be forgotten." To Taliesin he flashed the thought, *"Sickening, is it not?"*

When all were seated, Kumaragupta raised a hand; and

immediately two servants came through a third door, each with a wide golden tray held high above one shoulder. They served a hot wheat porridge sweetened with honey and cooled with fresh milk, plus generous portions of fresh and stewed fruit. The food was good and Alan ate heartily.

During the breakfast, Kalidasa, surprisingly, had little to say, apparently in awe of the King. The latter, on the other hand, kept up a running conversation in an obvious attempt to make a good impression on Alan. He asked questions about the Other World; and after he had learned of Taliesin's origin, about the other islands. When all had eaten their fill, leading up to the subject gradually, the King asked casually, "And what do you expect to learn from the Lord Varuna?"

"As for that," MacDougall answered, "you know as much as I do. I am here only because Ahriman, the one you call the One-Who-Speaks-for-the-Master, suggested that I do so. I was with him in his Tower at the time. I trust Varuna will know the answer."

The King's brows arched with surprise. "You have been in the Tower? Only since you arrived has it been seen. This is an area unseen and forbidden—" He stopped short.

Sharply in Alan's mind—and he saw immediately in the others' as well—formed words of power, an almost audible command.

"Bring them to me—now!"

Kumaragupta looked at Alan solemnly, then stood up, as did the others. "You heard? The Lord Varuna will see you now." He spoke to Kalidasa. "Guide them."

The poet bowed to Alan and said, "Follow, if you will." He turned and strode toward the doorway through which the King had come.

A final word came from the latter, a positive note in his voice. "We will meet again. And you will have gained that which you seek."

Their way led through a long corridor and up four stone stairways to the top level of the Temple. As they hastened along, the Bard commented mentally, *"No question about the real ruler of Magadha, and it is not the King.''* He was puffing from the unwonted exertion. *''Why the haste? I would have preferred a bit of time for that fine meal to digest.''*

They were on the third level when MacDougall called out, ''Lord Kalidasa, slow down. I am certain the Lord Varuna will still be there when we arrive.''

Reluctantly Kalidasa halted; and they waited until the Bard caught up with them. After a brief rest, and more slowly, they climbed to the fourth level. A single corridor led to the left, ending at the far wall; there were four doors, evenly spaced, in the right wall. A faint, indefinable aroma permeated the atmosphere.

''This level is entirely Varuna's,'' the poet said in a low voice, ''his and those who serve him. He never descends the steps—though if he wished to go elsewhere he has other ways.'' Direct transfer, Alan thought. ''We await his permission to enter.''

With his engineer's eye, MacDougall estimated the size of the area. Due to the upward tapering of the Temple tower, this was substantially smaller than the lower floors, but it was nonetheless a very large apartment.

Startlingly a shrill and quavering voice burst from beyond the nearest door. ''Enter, Alan MacDougall and Bard Taliesin. And you, Kalidasa, begone! You are no longer needed.''

Kalidasa pointed to the proper door, then turned hastily and scurried down the stairs. With a dubious look at Taliesin, MacDougall thrust open the door to face a heavy drapery of deep blue. He separated its folds and entered Varuna's quarters, Taliesin at his heels. A wave of strange incense swept over them, exotic yet subtle; and dimly, little more than a whisper, a high-pitched humming note rose and fell, barely audible yet persistently there. These impressions were momentary as their eyes were drawn and held by the lone occupant of the room.

Varuna—it could be no other—was *old*, small, and thin, with a beardless, pallid face contrasting with his intensely black hair and eyes and with the swathings of gold-colored cloth that enveloped him. He was seated cross-legged—in yoga, Alan thought, they called it the lotus position—on a square, padded stool, like an over-sized ottoman. At the moment he shook with silent laughter, his incredibly wrinkled face contorted with a mirth somehow suggesting the demonic. Gaining control of himself, he wheezed.

"They fear me greatly, Kalidasa and Kumaragupta, and I find it so very amusing. They have no powers; and I fear I have not spared them with the demonstrations of my own."

Abruptly his demeanor changed, all traces of mirth vanishing. Cocking his head to one side, he carefully surveyed MacDougall, then as carefully examined Taliesin. Neither man displayed any emotion during the appraisal.

Varuna nodded approvingly. "I am impressed. Both of you conceal your thoughts well. I doubt that anyone can read your minds. You, MacDougall, have been well chosen, I think, for the task and honor that lies before you. As for you, Taliesin, your part in all this is unclear. In what follows here, you will merely observe." His eyes narrowed. "Make no comment, no suggestion at any time." He clapped his hands twice. "There is no reason for you to be standing."

Instantly the heavy blue draperies, which covered all four walls, were spread apart and two female servants in red saris entered, each carrying a stool like Lord Varuna's. As if under orders, they placed them before their master, one directly in front of him, the other off to one side.

As Alan seated himself facing the Seer and the Bard occupied the other stool—neither sitting cross-legged—Varuna fixed his eyes on MacDougall.

"Do you know why you have come to me?"

"I have not the faintest idea, except that I am to be taught a skill that will be useful to me in the future."

"So I thought. The one you call Ahriman told me what that skill is to be." He pursed his thin lips. "What do you know about the land called Bharate-Varsha and its gods?"

"Nothing," Alan began; then as a swift thought came from Taliesin: *"India; and Varuna was one of the chief and early gods,"* he corrected himself. "Rather it is a land we call India; and you were its greatest god. I know little beyond that."

"At least that is a beginning"—the Seer nodded—"but the task will be difficult. And there will be danger. You are to be taught in one lesson what adepts spend half a lifetime mastering." He closed his eyes and bowed as if in deep thought.

"What powers have you gained?" he asked at last.

"Nothing of great consequence," MacDougall said deprecatingly. "I can shape-change, become invisible, receive and send thoughts, distance seeming no factor. Oh yes—and I can observe happenings in closed rooms. All this, of course, in this world." He thought of mentioning the serpent-gods but decided not to.

Varuna nodded approvingly. "Better than I hoped. You have mastered some of the *Riddhi*. The others should not be too difficult for you to master. You do well for a mortal . . . We will prepare for your lesson."

"Mithila," he called, his voice only slightly louder than his normal tones. Instantly one of his female attendants came through the curtains and knelt before him, her forehead touching the heavy black rug that covered the floor.

"Rise, Mithila," Lord Varuna said, "and summon the *apsaras*, all of them, to engage in the *sankirtana-yajni*. Go."

Keenly interested, MacDougall watched, thinking of all the god had said. Mention of him being a mortal had raised a question. Silently he asked of the serpent-gods, "Enki and Inanna, his referring to me as a mortal—does this mean—"

The Lady Inanna interrupted; and there was impatience and annoyance in her thought. "About time you called on us. One would almost assume you had forgotten us. Of course he is one of the ancient gods, one of Lucifer's host. He does not know of us, nor should he be told. He is one possessing great knowledge and power, who in the pantheon of his land was second only to Brahma the Creator. He was the guardian of that creation, the judge between the true and the false, a god greatly feared. In your world today he is forgotten, a decline that began when the warrior god Indra gained the worship of men—Indra and Agin and Prajapati. And now an upstart they call Krishna has become their idol.''

Alan's respect for the wizened Varuna grew at Inanna's comment. ''Then he is able to teach me this mysterious power?''

''He can do whatever he wishes to do.''

Meanwhile the curtains parted and fully three score girls—*apsaras*, the Seer had called them—glided into the chamber. All were dressed alike in full-cut, ankle-length skirts of pale green and short-sleeved flesh-colored bodices, their black hair uncut and held in place by a band of pearls. As they entered, from each came a musical humming, wordless, but by varying volume establishing a tempo, with their bare feet moving in rhythm, their outstretched arms and hands describing figures in the air. They danced along the walls, the movement of each a perfect duplication of the one before her.

MacDougall watched intently as the circle grew until finally all had entered. Now the humming changed. It appeared that each knew her part and that groups automatically formed, to create a rhythmic and harmonious chant. The first group began with what sounded like ''Ommm,'' repeated in perfect tempo. The second in a different but harmonizing note repeated ''Kraum,'' the third ''Vam,'' and the fourth ''Hum.'' Beyond that MacDougall could not follow, though each new word ended with ''mmm''; the blends of sounds so similar made differentiation impossible. The effect of the music, coupled with the endless rhythmic motions, voices, arms, hands, and feet never missing a beat, was incredible and hypnotic.

Alan tore his eyes away from the dancers and fixed them on Varuna. Even this did not shut out the sights and sounds of the *apsaras*, for the unbroken line kept moving by. He was barely aware of a thought from Taliesin.

"Fantastic."

The god had begun speaking, his voice barely rising above the endless chanting, and Alan tried to concentrate on his words.

"Have you encountered the thinking of the Tantrics on time? I find it interesting. It is their belief that everything that happens has happened before and will happen again. Anything that has not happened will not happen. Time is a circle without beginning or end. Yet, strangely, time has no constancy. It is determined solely by the duration of events. In short, time is a variable. You agree?"

MacDougall checked an impulse to shake his head to clear it. What had this to do with anything? The last idea he had heard from Taliesin a long time ago. Or so it seemed. His sight of the Seer had grown dim; and Alan realized that his eyes, without direction, were following the dancers, snapping back only to move again, like a spectator at a tennis match. He realized that Varuna had continued talking. What had he said? He lowered his eyelids, trying to concentrate on his words, trying to shut out the endless humming.

"The mantra," he was saying, "is a sequence of sound units with single pronunciation and intonation, a combination of *bijas*—seeds you would say—without apparent meaning yet with great significance. 'Om,' for example, addresses the Master, the Lord of Light. Listen and you will hear it."

Mentally MacDougall protested. How could he pick out the single sound among the others so very like it? And all of it had grown faint, barely audible. Only the words of Varuna remained clear, though even they were soft and distant.

"Your mind is now in control of your body. It will obey your every command. It is weary, and the floor is soft. You will command your body to lie down and sleep, though you will remain alert and fully awake."

Of course. It was so logical. His body needed rest, and it *would* lie down. It was strange, almost as if there were two of him—himself and his body. He felt the cushioning rug against his back. So soft. He heard Varuna's voice.

"And now you will leave your body. You will rise above it. It will remain below you, resting. So easy—so little effort. You see it now, lying so comfortably."

The voice of the Seer had become faint; he could barely hear it. There was a stillness, breathless and tense; then he felt an airy buoyancy, and he was floating upward. He was swaying from side to side as if moved by a gentle breeze. Below him, sharp and clear in his perception, lay the form he knew as Alan MacDougall, eyes closed in sound sleep, lips slightly parted. He could see the chest rise and fall with normal regularity.

For an instant he felt a stab of fear; then the lightness, the inexpressible freedom brought euphoria, a sensation almost ecstatic. And suddenly his senses possessed a new sharpness; there was a new awareness. He not only heard the unending harmony of the singers, he felt it with every atom of his being. And he saw not only his sleeping body, he was looking down at Varuna, who sat with bowed head, and at Taliesin at one side, staring at the sleeping MacDougall, his brow furrowed, his lips drawn, tight with concern. He was leaning forward. And the incense, its aroma was almost a tangible thing.

As all this registered on his consciousness, Lord Varuna raised his head and said softly, "Return, Alan MacDougall, to your body, and awaken. Now!"

It was an instantaneous thing. Alan felt the solidity of his flesh as he leaned on one elbow, looking up at the Seer, then getting to his feet. Uncertainly he sank to a seat on the ottoman. What, really, had happened? He could see Varuna eyeing him speculatively, giving him time to think. He recalled all that had transpired, or that had *seemed* to transpire. Obviously he had been hypnotized, a combination of what must have been the mantra the Seer had referred to, chanted by the *apsaras*, possibly aided by the rhythmic arm movements, the dancing, the incense. Plus the droning voice of the hypnotist. Had he imagined the exit of his spirit—soul?—from his body?

Came a startling thought: Was this the new ability he was to learn for his future use?

As if sensing the tenor of his thinking, Varuna said quietly, "The sleep was induced, but the separation of your spirit self from your body actually happened. And, yes, this is the power you are to gain."

About to protest, MacDougall crossed his arms, his left hand closing on the armlet. "Lord and Lady, did it really happen?"

"It did," came the instant reply. "The essence that is really you left your body and returned."

"But why?" Alan exclaimed aloud to the Seer. "Of what possible use can this ever be to me?"

"That," Varuna answered, "you will learn during the second part of your lesson." He called out,

"Mithila, dismiss your *apsaras*. They have done well."

One of the dancers stepped out of line, raising both hands high. Instantly the melodic organ tones fell to a faint humming and the swaying arms were lowered as one. The dancer at the opening in the draperies stepped through and the others followed in rhythmic stride. With the last one gone, Varuna rose, sweeping his garment around him and flinging the excess cloth over one shoulder.

"Follow," he said, leading the way through another opening in the curtain. They entered a chamber even larger than the one they left, this one furnished with a thickly quilted pallet and another ottoman. Again at a clap of his hands the Seer, on orders that must have been given telepathically, had a second pallet placed on the floor beside the first. He addressed the Bard.

"Taliesin, MacDougall and I will be going on a journey, with our bodies remaining behind. You will remain here on watch. I could summon guards, but nothing can happen. It is prudent, however, under the circumstances for a watcher to be here." To Alan: "The journey will be yours; I will be with you as your guide."

Momentary indecision assailed MacDougall. This idea didn't appeal to him at all. This leaving the body was too much like dying. And in this world there were demons who might want to take possession, to fill the vacancy with the resident gone. He brightened. The serpent-gods could reach him instantly. He thought of the feeling of incredible freedom, of lightness, and curiosity awakened. He recalled reading about people who practiced what they called OOBE, out-of-body experience, though he had always considered it nonsense, something the Hindu adepts did. A sudden recklessness swept through him. He had returned safely from the first separation; and there was the zest of a new adventure. He would see it through.

"And what are your instructions, Master Varuna?" he inquired.

"We will be lying on the beds on our backs," the Seer replied. "You have mastered concentration to be able to assume other forms and to become invisible. Now to gain the freedom you seek, the freedom from your material body, you will center your mind, all your faculties, on your goal to the exclusion of all else. You will command the separation. And since you have done it once, though with my assistance, you can do it again."

Crouching, MacDougall stretched out on the pad, Varuna sinking to his knees with surprising agility and in moments lying on his back. Alan flashed a thought to the Bard. *"You'll be with the body, so if there's need, you'll call me."*

"We will be with the body and the spirit," the serpent-god corrected. "And remember, we are yours to-command."

MacDougall heard the Seer's soft voice. "Concentrate. Think only of your purpose. Rise above your body."

Utter silence fell as Alan MacDougall shut all but the single thought from his mind—to rise above himself, to see his motionless form lying below him.

And it happened! He was again aware of the sensation of floating free, of the lightness of thistledown. And below him lay his physical self, beside the still form of Varuna.

A thought touched his mind. "You have done it." Alan's perception—not exactly sight—sensed a wraithlike figure floating beside him. "And now we travel. Think of a place you have seen on this island; will yourself there. I will stay with you."

MacDougall pictured the entrance to Cuchulainn's castle; with the thought the white marble pillars towered before him, while several white-clad figures wandered aimlessly about.

"Now," Varuna directed, "select a more distant place. Perhaps another island, and inside a building."

Scath, Alan thought, and with Scathach the Sorceress here on Avilion, who if anyone occupied her apartment? He pictured the luxurious dining room where he had sampled her special wines, willing himself there. And he was! The room was occupied, and incredibly, by Brendah the Warrior who had thrust the Sorceress through the Gate into his own world! Fascinating, he thought. How had she managed it, and how did she control the three Daughters of Calatin? Now was not the time to find out.

He sensed the presence of the Seer. "An even greater distance." Tartarus. Trollheim, the underground city of Einurr Gurulfin. Wherever the King of the Trolls might be. He pictured the white-haired little man, willed himself beside him—and he was there, floating at his elbow through one of Trollheim's streets. He wondered momentarily if he could gain his attention, perhaps communicate with him; the words of Varuna reached him.

"It would not be wise, would only confuse him. This, too, is a power, but not for a novice. Later perhaps . . . And now whither?"

A sudden wild idea came to MacDougall. Elspeth! Could he cross the barrier between the worlds? He pictured the lovely Highland lass, seeking her; at the same instant was conscious of strong negation from the Seer.

He was in the schoolroom in Kilmona, hovering a few feet away from Elspeth Cameron, the teacher, who was speaking to a group of children. He was keenly conscious of her nearness; longed for the ability to speak to her.

She halted in the midst of a sentence, faltering, glancing about in wonder and uncertainty.

Oh no, Alan thought. He shouldn't have done this, disturbing her. Varuna was right. Varuna! The awareness of his presence was gone. He was alone. Of course. An angel of Lucifer, condemned to that Other World, he could not leave it. In momentary confusion MacDougall fled—anywhere to gain time to think.

Then all was blackness, and he floated in limbo. Time stood still. And the tangible blackness seemed swarming with other shapes. They reached out to grasp him; they gibbered soundlessly in the midst of wild and formless gyrations. Terror grew in Alan MacDougall. Control— he had no control! Why had he meddled with this thing? Why had he left his body?

"Alan! Alan MacDougall!" Out of the void came a thought, strong and sure, the familiar and so-welcome call of Lord Enki, the serpent-god. With it he sensed the words of Lady Inanna. "Return at once. An emergency. Seek your body. Now!"

With relief welling up within him he pictured his supine body, with all of his being willed himself inside it— and recovering instantly, he sat up, then sprang to his feet.

"What happened?"

First he saw the Bard sitting on his ottoman, leaning forward, his head held between his hands. There was an ugly bruise and a great swelling in the middle of his bald pate. The Seer stood on his pallet, facing MacDougall; and to one side, frozen in statuesque rigidity, stood the hulking form of Despot Mihiragula, the leader of the guards.

"What happened?" Alan demanded again.

"What happened to you?" Varuna countered with annoyance. "When you conceived the brilliant idea of returning to the Other World, you left me behind. You should have known I could not follow. So I returned here." The Seer glanced malevolently toward the motionless Despot. "A fortunate thing, as it turned out. I awakened to see *that* poised above your form with drawn sword.'' His high-pitched voice grew shrill with wrath.

"He will pay—how he will pay! Somehow he must have learned of our absence. He entered my rooms, struck Taliesin, and probably would have killed both of you had I not appeared.

"But you—did you encounter trouble?''

"Oh, a bit,'' MacDougall replied, forcing a smile. "Nothing I couldn't handle. I admit I lost my way, but I made it back safely. I realized I shouldn't have gone to the other side. I want no more lessons now. With practice I believe I can master this skill.'' Reluctantly he added, "I suppose on occasion it could be useful.''

He turned to the Bard, now standing. "How do you feel?''

"Except for a tender spot and a thumping headache I am quite all right.''

"I am anxious to leave,'' MacDougall said. "The City of Jade awaits.''

Varuna bowed. "I have done what I was told to do. You are free to leave when you wish.''

CHAPTER 5

The City of Jade

The great bronze double gates of Magadha clanged shut behind MacDougall and Taliesin as they sent their white mounts galloping across the grassy plain.

"Seems they're happy to be rid of us," Alan said aloud.

"No happier than I am to leave," the Bard replied, holding his forehead. "There are violent people among them."

"Miserable people, too," Alan added. "Tortured drug addicts in Cuchulainn; and fasting fanatics starving themselves to death in Magadha. I wonder what we'll find in Shenzhu. And I wonder what I am supposed to learn."

"The ability to transport yourself—and others—instantly from place to place would be most convenient," the Bard suggested.

"We shall know in due time." They fell silent, concentrating on their riding, keeping the distant hill and Golden Tower to their right. Odd, Alan thought, that Varuna had not mentioned its appearing; though if the other rooms in his quarters were as heavily draped as the two he had seen, existing windows might well be covered. And perhaps he had known of Ahriman's Tower before it became visible, since he was one of the ancient gods.

They rode on in silence for a time, Alan's thoughts inevitably reverting to his out-of-body experience. Frightening yet fascinating; too real to be imaginary. But not a toy to be treated lightly, this traveling in what had seemed to be a ghostly realm of almost-sensed spirits.

He thought of the diverse characters they had met—the ancient, wizened Varuna; Kalidasa the politician; overly gracious King Kumaragupta; and the vicious Despot Mihiragula. Better forget them and think about what lay ahead.

"Taliesin," mentally he addressed the Bard, *"I think we'll approach Shenzhu with caution. Invisible, I mean. I don't like bowmen who shoot first and ask questions later. Could be embarrassing. So—will you join me?"*

With the skill acquired through much practice, MacDougall vanished, his horse disappearing with him.

"Excellent idea," Taliesin agreed, exerting the magic he had taught Alan at long range so long ago, to help him escape when trapped in Balor's apartment in Murias. That first time the serpent-gods in the armlet had helped greatly without Alan's knowledge. But now the ability was his own.

They settled into a more leisurely canter; and about midway in their ride they halted to rest the horses. Twenty miles between cities, Ahriman had said; and with the sameness of the landscape the trip seemed endless. During their rest the men drank from their canteens, but they had no water for their mounts. When they removed the animals' bits the stallions began cropping the lush turf. In a land where it never rained and dewfall watered the land, considerable moisture clung to the grass.

"It just occurred to me," Alan said aloud, "when Ahriman showed me the model of Avilion, I saw no sign of streams. There's the fresh-water sea, of course, but the five cities are far inland. I imagine each must have its own well."

"Quite logical," the Bard commented. "There's far

more symmetry here than appeared on the other islands. From your description of the model, Avilion appears to have been designed and constructed by a master architect." After a brief pause he added, "You failed to mention the white buildings you called the Halls of the Dead."

MacDougall raised his brows. "Hmmm. You're right. I saw none. Yet there should be one for each city, since five different peoples are involved. Maybe they're underground. True, there's no warfare, with Ahriman keeping them apart; but people die. Most assuredly people die among the fasting in Magadha and are replaced."

On their way again, MacDougall mentally reviewed what he knew about their destination. The incredible City of Jade, the model a veritable gem. Closing his eyes he could picture it, the deep-green jade walls forming a hexagon, atop a wall at each corner a white jade turret. And the typically curved gable houses, randomly spaced, without sign of streets, the roof corners tilted upward. The roofs formed of polished jade tiles. Colorful! Walls and roofs of every color of the spectrum. And there were three six-sided pagodas forming a triangle in the heart of the city, one white, another apple green, and the third mauve. It was a fantastic toy wrought by a Fabergé for a wealthy princeling.

When the city itself appeared before them, the actuality far outshone the miniature. In part this was due to the auroral backdrop, a shimmering veil of pastel beauty with its restlessly dancing curtains of pink and blue and violet reflected from the mirror-bright fluted jade tiles. Alan caught his breath; and he heard Taliesin exclaim in a hushed voice.

"Fantastic!"

Riding closer, MacDougall caught a glimpse of what must be a guard seated in the nearer turret. He could not see the man clearly in the shadows, but he appeared to be asleep. Alan's attention shifted to a wide arched gateway in the facing wall, behind it a latticed bronze gate. Through the interstices he saw movements as of several people milling about, and he heard voices.

Secure in his invisibility, Alan motioned for Taliesin to join him, and side by side they rode up to the gate. Handing his reins to the Bard, he sent the thought, *"A little eavesdropping could be interesting."*

Close to the gate he peered between the strips. There were three men, Chinese, all dressed essentially alike in long yellow tunics open down the center, with overlapping sides held together by a gray sash, below it baggy, ankle-length trousers of deep blue, and straw sandals. All had long black hair, tied in a tight topknot perched on their heads. One differed from the other two in that he had a sword belt around his waist, a black hilt eight or ten inches long projecting from the scabbard. Probably a two-handed, single-edged blade. The others bore no visible weapons.

"I tell you," the armed man was saying angrily, "no one visits Shenzhu. And why should the Emperor send such as you when real men are about? But if visitors should come they will receive a warm greeting." He laid a hand on his sword.

One of the messengers shook his head sadly. "You but try to provoke us to anger, but you cannot succeed. And in truth the Emperor sent us. There will be two men, not of the Han people, one tall and yellow-haired, dressed in black, and the other short, heavy, balding, and wearing a blue cape. They will be riding white horses, and they should arrive soon. So the Emperor's servant told us."

"Two of the round-eyes coming here? They would not dare." The guard drew his sword, clutched it with both hands, and waved it wildly above his head. "I will cleave them in two!"

MacDougall motioned for the Bard to join him on foot, as he sent a thought to Lord Enki. "Will you freeze the violent one where he stands?"

Even as the guard stiffened with the sword held high, Alan had a fleeting thought. That would be a magic trick worth learning.

"Open!" he commanded loudly, suddenly visible, joined instantly by Taliesin and the horses.

The messengers, glimpsing them through the gate, leaped forward hastily, unlatched the gate and swung it open.

"Welcome, Honored Guests," the spokesman said timidly, bowing low. Belatedly his companion also bowed, tearing his gaze away from the statuesque guard. "We greet you in the name of the Emperor Khau Ch'in Khih."

"It is well," MacDougall said with just a trace of condescension. "We need our horses cared for; then one of you will take us to your—" He almost said "leader." "—Emperor. We come in the name of the One-Who-Speaks-for-the-Master, the Lord Ahriman." Sounded quite impressive, Alan thought.

Eagerly the silent one volunteered. "I will lead the horses to food and water. I will remain with them until you require their services."

"Good." Alan nodded approvingly.

As eagerly the other said, "And I will delight in leading you to his Majesty."

As they were about to start out, Taliesin asked, "What of the statue?"

"Oh, yes." To the messengers Alan said, "Remove his sword and give it to me. He cannot move and will know nothing of what you do."

With difficulty they pried the weapon from the rigid fingers. After taking it, MacDougall stepped outside the gate and hurled it, javelinlike, as far as he could throw it. It landed point down in the turf and stuck there.

"I'll release him when we are out of sight. Let him figure out what happened."

One of the messengers began to smile, the beginning of a chuckle in his throat, instantly suppressed at his companion's disapproving glance. To MacDougall he explained, "It is not allowed that we find amusement in another's misfortune. Not even that of one of the followers of Mo Tzu." Again he bowed. "We start."

The horses were led away in one direction and the visitors in another. As they threaded their way through the narrow paths, about six feet wide, winding and twisting aimlessly between the jade cottages, MacDougall's wonder knew no bounds. The walls of the structures were indeed jade, every shade of green, including the emerald color called Imperial, warm grays, old ivory, clean whites, robin's egg blue, peach, lavender, yellow. Each cottage was its own color with darker, harmonizing jade tile roofs, the walls of polished blocks, fitted together without mortar, with the perfection that reminded Alan of the masonry of Machu Picchu where not even a knife edge could be forced into the joints. No matter what Ahriman said, this was impossible.

MacDougall's imagination began to work. He pictured an alien world where jade was as common as limestone or granite, where the gem material was quarried, and where giant craftsmen labored at the behest of their master, Lucifer. They shaped and polished the blocks and tiles as Terrestrial lapidaries might form cabochons for jewelry. Wild fantasy, but no other explanation made sense.

They passed numerous strollers, all of whom looked at the visitors wonderingly, several smiling and bowing in greeting, one even speaking hesitantly to their guide. "Can I help?" Politely his offer was refused.

They came to two men seated side by side on the sill of an open doorway. They were the picture of dejection, one sighing deeply as the three passed.

"What's wrong with them?" MacDougall asked.

"I know them. One is Chih T'ang. He has lost count. The other, Wang Teh, fought back when the Mohists tried to steal his cloak. Both must start over."

MacDougall stopped short as did Taliesin. "What do you mean, they must start over? Lost count of what, and why shouldn't a man resist a thief?"

"We are followers of *Tao*, the Way, as set down by our revered ancestor Lao Tzu, as is our Emperor. We are here in this waiting place, though we do not know why. But we need not remain. We can earn our release by performing ten thousand good deeds without a failure. If we fail we must begin again, or if we lose count we must go back to the beginning." He sighed. "It is so hard to find good deeds to perform when everyone is trying to be helpful. My guiding you is my six thousand and forty-first.''

Incredible, Alan thought. "You spoke of the followers of Mo Tzu," he said. "What of them?"

"Fortunately they are few. We call them Mohists. Their hearts are filled with hatred. Were they able by lifting their little finger to save a thousand, they would not lift it. The teachings of Mo Tzu have been more fatal than the sting of scorpions. His followers are the only ones among us to bear arms; and if it were not for the control of the Emperor and the power of the Sage, Wu Chuangtse, none of the *Tao* could live.''

Mention of the Mohists reminded Alan of the statue-like guard; with a thought to the serpent-gods, he released him. Without further interruption they made their way through the maze of houses until they reached a clear circle in the center of which stood a mauve pagoda. It was a thing of beauty, the translucent, gemlike lavender jade gleaming in the light of the aurora. Six-sided, it tapered upward through eight steps, curving gently inward, a narrow balcony marking each level.

As they approached the pagoda-Temple, MacDougall for the first time in Shenzhu saw the carving he automatically associated with Chinese jade. It took the form of deeply cut bas-relief figures surrounding the arched doorway. His brief glance as they entered the building gave little time for identification of the figures, but he thought he saw stylized dragons interwoven with what looked like grotesque fans and gourds festooned with gracefully curved ribbons, all in mauve jade.

Within the pagoda, as in the buildings of Magadha and Cuchulainn, a glowing ceiling provided light. They were met in the hallway by four smiling doubles of their companion, except that these men wore yellow and purple. As the guide bowed and turned to leave, MacDougall said, "You have been most helpful," hoping this would bring to a satisfactory close his six thousand and forty-first good deed.

"We go to the Emperor," one of their new escorts said

with the usual bow; and they started through the corridor. They halted before a doorway covered by heavy purple silk draperies embroidered in gold with the same design Alan had noticed in the carvings at the entrance—dragons, fans, and gourds, and a profusion of ribbons. Beside the doorway a gold bell dangled from a gold chain; at its ring a voice came through the curtain.

"Enter, Alan MacDougall and Bard Taliesin. Liu Pei, wait."

Alan pushed the curtain aside and with Taliesin entered a softly lighted chamber. A glance to right and left revealed walls of deep-purple fabric, and facing him the room's lone occupant. The wall behind him was a single great carving in lavender jade, a work of incredible artistry. The dragon-fan-gourd motif was repeated, but in addition there were symbolic representations of other objects, only two of which Alan recognized—swords and lotus blossoms. All of this was obscured by the great seat that was part of the carving, and its occupant, who must be Emperor Khau Ch'in Khih.

He was a broad, impressive figure clad in a yellow silk robe, a pattern of purple dragons embroidered down its entire front and on the outer surface of both voluminous sleeves, a jeweled belt of gold about his waist completing the royal dress. The impassive, oriental face caught and held the attention—narrowed, slightly slanted black eyes under thinly penciled brows, a drooping black mustache extending well below the corners of his thin-lipped mouth, below the lower lip a tiny tuft of hair, and extending from the tip of his chin a long, stringy black beard. His large topknot was almost covered by a gem-encrusted crown of gold. He was the first to speak.

"Welcome, Alan MacDougall and Bard Taliesin. I regret that I have no seats to offer you, but ordinarily none sit in my presence. They kneel. I do not expect this of you. Your audience, really, is with the Sage, Wu Chuangtse. I merely wanted to extend greetings from all who dwell in Shenzhu. At least all who follow *Tao* and the worshipers of Buddha. The Mohists—we will not speak of them. Have you any questions before you visit the Sage?''

''We appreciate your welcome,'' Alan answered. ''Evidently He-Who-Speaks-for-the-Master has told of our coming. I have no question of importance, but I *am* curious. There are three great pagodas. Are they temples, and if so, why three?''

''They are temples. This one is the Temple of Tao. The white one, the Temple of Buddha; and the green one for the score or more of other gods, including Mo Tzu.''

Alan hesitated. ''Again, mere curiosity and an impudent question. Emperor—of a mere city?''

The Ruler's eyebrows rose in surprise, then he smiled. ''I was Emperor in the Olden Time, with many cities and vast numbers of subjects. Here there is only Shenzhu and few people, but to them I am still Emperor.'' He clapped his hands. ''I trust you will receive whatever you seek.'' As the four waiting escorts entered he directed, ''Conduct our visitors to the Sage Wu Chuangtse.''

Both visitors bowed before they left, and Alan said, ''Thank you, your Majesty.''

There followed what seemed to be an endless climb around and around, up the inside of the Temple-pagoda. When they finally reached the top level, both Mac-Dougall and Taliesin were puffing, despite their having stopped about midway for a brief rest.

There was a single room on this level—the eighth, Alan counted—surrounded by a corridor that appeared to have a narrow doorway in each of the six sides, through which they glimpsed the aurora. In the wall of the hexagonal chamber, at the head of the stairway was a curtained doorway. From within came a single word in a commanding voice,

''Come!''

With a half grin at the Bard Alan sent the thought, *''Here we go again, back to school. I'll insist on seats.''* He thrust aside the heavy drapery and they entered.

This room, like that of the Emperor, held a single occupant. The softly glowing ceiling revealed a chamber more spectacular than the other; and the Sage was a more striking figure than Emperor Kha Ch'in Khih. His deep-crimson robe of glistening silk, swathing him in voluminous folds from chin to toe, caught the attention. But his round face immediately drew the gaze—a face strangely familiar, Alan thought, though he felt he could never have seen it before. Then it struck him. An oriental Taliesin, despite the bushy, drooping mustache. It had to be the twinkling eyes and the balding head with the fringe of hair above the ears that created the resemblance.

He was seated on a wide dais of black jade, elevated about five feet above the black, heavy pile of the floor. The room itself, six-sided, had panellike walls of alternating black and mauve jade, each a giant landscape in high relief. But what landscapes! The rugged mountain ranges, lacy waterfalls, islands in placid lakes, gracefully arched bridges, grotesquely branching trees, lone, gabled cottages nestled in unlikely nooks—and all achieving the almost infinite depths typical of Chinese art. Paintings in monotone wrought in imperishable jade.

The voice of the Sage brought MacDougall to the realization that he was standing like one in an art gallery lost in contemplation. "You find my chamber pleasing?"

As one Alan and Taliesin answered, "It is fascinating." MacDougall added, "The jewel of this incredible city."

Sage Wu Chuangtse beamed. "If you were to spend time with me, we might venture into the depths of one or more of the Six Worlds, each a marvel in itself. Most of its wonders are concealed behind the surface." His gaze lingered on one of the vast panels. "Within, I live again in the Olden Time, and in lands I alone have seen . . . But sit. You come with a purpose."

He motioned toward a low, slightly curving backless seat of black jade, until then unnoticed. Upon stepping over, Alan and the Bard seated themselves.

After greeting both, the Sage concentrated on MacDougall. "I have been told by the one you call Ahriman of your need for certain knowledge. I am to teach you one specific gift or power."

He closed his eyes in apparent meditation. His visitors

watched expectantly, tension mounting. Finally they saw Wu Chuangtse slowly floating up from his seat to hang motionless in midair. He had not changed position, even his robe remaining as it had been, defying gravity. Then lightly he floated around the room, hovering near the ceiling, finally settling back to his seat on the dais.

Watching in wonder, MacDougall momentarily thought, Hypnotism; but he knew better. After all, in a world where some could transfer themselves and others instantly over long distances, this was not extraordinary. The Sage smiled faintly, the twinkle in his eyes revealing his enjoyment.

"Very convenient," he said, "when ascending and descending that long stairway, and it has other uses. I believe you call it levitation. This I am to teach you."

Worth knowing, MacDougall thought. Combined with invisibility, it would have been most helpful during his escape from Scathach's Tower. The more he thought of it the better he liked the idea.

"When do we begin?" he asked.

"Now. Were it not for the unusual abilities you already possess—invisibility, shape-changing, thought transference, creation of mass illusions, and others—this would not be possible except through long periods of meditation, but since you have learned true concentration, we should encounter no difficulty. Begin by clearing your mind of all extraneous thought, or as much as is possible, and breathe slowly and deeply."

MacDougall closed his eyes and started deep, regular breathing. But clear his mind of thoughts—not easily done. How, for example, had the Sage learned of his abilities? From Ahriman, probably. And creation of illusions had really been accomplished by Enki and Inanna.

"You did more than you realized," came a thought from the Lady Inanna, "though of course we played a major part. But stop thinking. You accomplish nothing this way."

Wu Chuangtse echoed the thought, a slightly impatient

note in his voice. "Your mind continues actively thinking. Open your eyes."

As Alan did so he continued quietly, "Select a detail in the scene on the black panel behind me. Concentrate on that small portion. Think of nothing else. Probe its depths. Deeper. Deeper."

MacDougall fixed his eyes on the black jade bas-relief, selecting for his attention a misty valley with a narrow, lacy waterfall pouring over a high cliff into a deep chasm. There seemed to be a tiny cottage clinging like a swallow's nest to a precipitous mountainside. The detail was incredible; and as he sought to look more deeply into the very substance of the scene, he heard the droning voice of Wu Chuangtse:

"*Tao* proceeds in stillness, and in stillness all things are produced. The methods of creation proceed gently and gradually, and thus it is that the yin and the yang overcome. The one takes the place of the other. Life is the root of death, and death is the root of life. The crash of thunder and the blustering wind come without design and have power to create nothing. The *Tao* in quietness does nothing, so there is nothing that it does not do."

What was he saying? Like an intrusion the confusing words floated into Alan's awareness. They made no sense, yet somehow they seemed to be trying to create a picture—

"*Alan!*" The single word like a silent cry came from the mind of Taliesin, jarring its way into his own consciousness. Like one rudely awakened, he turned quickly to his right where the Bard had been seated. Had been— he was not there!

MacDougall sprang to his feet, glancing swiftly about. No Bard. "What's going on?" he demanded angrily, meeting the startled gaze of the Sage.

In immediate response the face of Ahriman appeared in midair beside that of Wu Chuangtse.

"Control yourself." The deep voice of Lucifer's lieutenant rebuked him. "There is no reason for a childish tantrum. You have been having your way with him joining you, and nothing has changed. A meeting is under way in the green pagoda that may well be important to you; and since Taliesin was not needed here I decided he should be an unseen observer. You will be reunited when the meeting ends. Communication between you is open so you can verify what I have said.'' The image of Ahriman vanished.

"*Taliesin*—'' MacDougall began; and the Bard interrupted,

"*I heard through your ears, Alan; and what Ahriman said is true. I am in the green jade Temple and outside a room where Emperor Khau Ch'in Khih is meeting with what appears to be a group of Mohists. There are angry words; and I had better concentrate on what is being said.*''

"*Good,*'' Alan silently commented. "*See you later.*'' To the Sage he said apologetically, "Sorry about the interruption. I was concerned about my companion's disappearance.'' He added, "What you said made no sense to me.''

Wu Chuangtse smiled blandly, his voice soothingly calm. "We must begin anew. Have you fathomed all that lies within the scene you selected? If not, look more deeply.''

Again MacDougall fixed his eyes on the carving, seeking the dwelling on the cliffside. Again he heard the droning voice of the Sage.

"All, all is the *Tao*. With it there is no effect that cannot be produced; without it there is no effect that can. Is not the Great *Tao* the Grand Source and the Grand Origin of all things? Well has it been said, 'To remain whole, be twisted. To become full, be hollow. The Sage does not show himself, therefore he is seen everywhere. He does not contend, therefore none can contend with him.' This is the wisdom of *Tao*.''

Again the pretentious words filtered into MacDougall's consciousness as something heard in a dream. What was the Sage saying? It interfered with his concentration on that tiny dwelling. Almost he had seen its true shape emerging from the mist. He tried to shut out the flow of words. Faintly they persisted.

"Through *Tao* one becomes as a piece of uncarved wood, blank; yet receptive as a hollow in the hills. Murky as a storm-swollen stream, yet clear and still as a spring welling up in a rocky gorge. Through rest and quiet both body and spirit will become as a wisp of cloud, ethereal, and in union with *Tao*."

With his eyes fixed on the carving, MacDougall thought dreamily, If he could become as a wisp of cloud he would float into the mist and see clearly that dwelling on its precarious perch.

The droning voice continued. "Great through *Tao* is the mind of man. Now exalted, now depressed; pliable and soft or sharp enough to chisel jade. Now as hot as scorching fire; now as cold as ice. Resting, it is still as a deep abyss; moving, it refuses to be bound. The mind commands and the body obeys."

Faint as a distant echo the phrase lingered: The mind commands and the body obeys. Light—he felt so light— light as thistledown. Buoyant, he floated; and he *was* floating! The waterfall and the cottage—the cliff and the stream—he was almost within the black and gray landscape, the clouds of mist about to part . . . and faint as a whisper he heard the voice of the Sage,

"You *are* floating, Alan MacDougall. You are above me. You have mastered levitation."

Alan glanced down, suddenly coming out of a near trance, to see the face of Wu Chuangtse tilted back and looking up at him. He started to sink; he felt again the airy lightness and commanded his body to circle the room. It obeyed! He hovered, aware of a feeling of freedom beyond any he had ever experienced. Save one—that out-of-body flight. At last, reluctantly, he sank to the jade seat from which he had risen.

He grinned at the Sage. "I suppose it was your mind implanting in mine the confidence that I could transcend the bonds of the material world, escaping normal physical restrictions."

"True," Wu Chuangtse responded, "but the power was yours. Now, with the experience so recent, do it again."

MacDougall closed his eyes, the better to recall his mental state during his floating—and without conscious effort he rose slowly into the air, hovering there.

"A power once gained," the Sage said approvingly, "remains with you, available for use when you need it."

"Combined with invisibility—" Alan began, then halted at the sound of rapid steps on the stairway. Several people racing up to the top level. There came sounds of a scuffle, and a voice pleading between gasps.

"But I must see the visitors! Please! I have run—all the way."

On his feet MacDougall faced the doorway as the Sage commanded, "Bring him in."

The guides who had ushered Alan and Taliesin to Wu Chuangtse thrust through the curtain, clutching the arms of a third, all three with chests heaving. The central figure, dripping perspiration, was on the verge of collapse. Alan recognized him as the man who had led away the horses.

"What is the trouble?" the Sage asked quietly.

"The horses," the man wheezed, "the horses—the Mohists have made off with your horses." Gulping air he added, "The ones who tried to stop you. I—I could not prevent it."

"Well," MacDougall said reassuringly, "any horses will do. The pair we rode were provided by Cuchulainn."

"It is not well." The Sage looked troubled. "We have no horses. Only cattle for fresh milk."

"Where have the thieves gone?" Alan demanded in exasperation. "It will not be possible for us to walk."

"Out of the city—riding west—toward the farms."

"Taliesin! I must join Taliesin. Somehow we'll have to pursue them. Ahriman must—" He broke off as the Lady Inanna's impatient thought interrupted him.

"Alan MacDougall, sometimes I despair of you ever learning to think. Can you not see that by combining what you learned in Magadha, the out-of-body experience, with the power to levitate, you will have instant transfer? Instead of leaving your body behind in instant flight, you take it with you. And after you join Taliesin, you take him with you with no more difficulty than transporting the garments on your back.''

Lord Enki added, ''Picture the Bard and will yourself beside him. We will add our strength to yours.''

Alan felt sudden doubt. It seemed so easy—*too* easy. But, why not? Just more magic—and magic worked here. Others did it—the *Tuatha de Danann*—and he had floated around the room; he had taken his spirit out of his body, sending it about at will . . . He faced Wu Chuangtse.

''I will be leaving in moments,'' he said with confidence. ''I must join the Bard Taliesin, then go in pursuit of the horses. Thank you for your great help. Perhaps we will meet again.''

He closed his eyes the better to visualize Taliesin; centered all his faculties on the thought of joining him—for an instant felt the extraordinary lightness, the indescribable sensation of infinite speed—and he was standing beside the Bard.

Taliesin was a ghostly image, telling Alan instantly that he was invisible to those around him, as he himself was a moment later. But not before he had been seen by several in the bright-green chamber. Sharp outcries followed, and one of the Mohists pointed and shouted,

''There—behind the Emperor—one of them! Spying. Kill the intruders!''

The Bard, instantly comprehending, sent Alan the thought, *''Outside!''*

''A better plan.'' MacDougall grasped Taliesin's arm, visualizing the city gate through which they had entered Shenzhu; and following the formula he had so recently learned, the two in a breath stood just outside the bronze latticework. The change was startling, all commotion gone, silence around them, no one in sight, the dancing aurora overhead, and the two like gray ghosts as they saw each other, back where all of it had started.

Slowly in wonder and disbelief the Bard Taliesin shook his head. Aloud he said, ''Alan MacDougall, you never cease to amaze me. By the one true God, I would never have believed this possible. Not long ago I left you at

Ahriman's persuasive invitation. Except for the power to separate spirit and body, you were as I had known you, with the long-familiar magic powers. The Sage of Shenzhu had started to teach you how to float. And now, all of a sudden, you have mastered what we have called instant transfer! Something that I who have been a dweller in this world for fourteen centuries cannot do. How can it be?''

"Credit the gods in the armlet, Lady Inanna and Lord Enki. It was they who recognized that the power to levitate and the out-of-body experience when combined would result in—'' He gestured with open hands. "—this.'' MacDougall changed the subject. "Is there any reason why we should return to the green pagoda? I barely caught a glimpse of that room and have no idea of what was going on.''

"None,'' Taliesin answered. "There was nothing more to be learned. The Mohists violently objected to us being in Shenzhu, and it was their intention to kill us on sight. No reason except their general hatred for all except their own kind. It was their intention to bar all gates and to then hunt us down. The Emperor, who is Ruler of all in Shenzhu, forbade this; but double-cross and disobedience is part of their makeup, and they were arguing that our presence here was a violation of an ages-old law . . . What is our next step? Getting the horses?''

"Yes,'' MacDougall answered, "but not as you think. Two of the Mohists, apparently on their own—one of them the graceful statue Lord Enki created when we arrived here—have stolen the horses and are headed west toward the farms and, I suppose, the sea. There are no other horses in Shenzhu. Learning this is what sent me to you.''

"Perhaps,'' the Bard suggested, "you could transfer us to our next stop without the need for the ride. I'm getting hungry. No one thought of offering us food in Shenzhu.''

"I'd rather not attempt it,'' Alan replied. "All I have seen of Atu, the Egyptian city, is the miniature; and I'd find it embarrassing to wind up beside the model in Ahriman's Tower. Then too, I'd like to have the horses in reserve.'' Abruptly he scowled. "A further thought. It annoys me to have those two horse thieves think they're getting away with their mischief. It will give me great satisfaction to make them walk home.''

Taliesin opened his canteen. "Though we have no food, we *do* have water.'' He drank heartily.

MacDougall followed his example, then said, "I suppose we need a plan. How do two men on foot stop two men on horseback?''

They discussed several ideas, finally deciding to transfer to the vicinity of the horsemen—invisible, obviously—then jump ahead a quarter of a mile on their course. There the Bard would shape-change into the likeness of a richly dressed and bejeweled Magadhan, lying in seeming unconsciousness. Assuming they would dismount to investigate—and probably rob—Alan would then make off with the horses. If only one dismounted voluntarily—unlikely since neither would trust the other—MacDougall would "assist" the mounted man to dismount. Taliesin, with precise timing, would vanish, as would the horses; and with sufficient space between the Bard and the Mohists, MacDougall would circle back for Taliesin; and they'd be on their way.

The plan worked to perfection; and Alan had the satisfaction of gazing back to see the Mohists plodding across the turf, angrily berating each other.

CHAPTER 6

Atu in Khert-Neter

They were well on their way to the next city, the horses traveling at a leisurely pace, when MacDougall said, "I think we'll go invisible again. Due to our side trip, we don't know just where we are; and invisible we have time to adjust to any situation." In moments horses and riders vanished; and only the faint sounds of hoofbeats on turf showed they were there.

They had already discussed the meeting Taliesin had observed, which had dealt primarily with the Mohists' objections to the visitors' presence. The Emperor had been criticized for his constant siding with the Taoists, a neverending source of contention. A real politician, Alan had commented, to be able to juggle the contrasting lifestyles and philosophies.

After a period of silence MacDougall mentally observed, *"Atu, the city of the Egyptians, is next. According to Ahriman, they call this world Khert-Neter, the home of the Ka, or soul, which I equate with the land of the dead. Atu, in their belief, was its chief city.*

"This is a strange set-up. Five cities, each inhabited

by a different people—Celts, Hindus from India, Chinese, Egyptians, and finally black Africans. All isolated from each other for at least fourteen centuries, the result of Lucifer's planning for my benefit, I'm supposed to think, to fulfill a prophecy on an ancient Scroll. Completely ridiculous."

Solemnly the Bard answered, *"Not as wild as you may think. Remember, time means nothing to the one they call the Lord of Light, and his plans have always been far-reaching."*

Abruptly Alan changed the subject. *"What I learned in Shenzhu is very worthwhile, with thanks largely due to the Lady Inanna. The ability to levitate could be of value; but combining it with soul-flight, as the goddess suggested, to produce instant transfer is terrific. Now I won't have to depend on one of the Tuatha de Danann, or on the whims of Ahriman to go places."* He added a mental chuckle.

"On occasion, I've called on the serpent-gods to stop enemies in their tracks, like the Mohist at the Shenzhu gate. That would be a trick I'd like to master."

Lord Enki interjected his thought with fatherly tolerance, so both could sense what he said, "You've had that ability for a long time, but you haven't known it. It is a simple trick, somewhat akin to your mental control of Scathach's mirrors. You forcefully plant the idea that he cannot move in the mind of the one you wish to stop, that everything about him has halted. Doing it to a group of people simultaneously is difficult, but even that you should be able to master with practice. Try it on Taliesin. He won't mind. However, prepared as he is, it might be difficult."

Somewhat doubtfully the Bard agreed, but before MacDougall could make the attempt, there came an interruption. The horses suddenly reared back on their haunches as if frightened by something in their path. At the same instant a low, vibrant voice exclaimed, "Alan MacDougall, your invisibility spell is no better now than when I first met you. It is no concealment to the penetrating eye."

Momentarily startled, both riders drew rein. Alan stared toward the source of the voice with the extra energy needed to see through invisibility, catching a fleeting glimpse of a tall, swarthy, malformed figure, flanked on both sides by shorter but similar beings. The central one was gone instantly, to be replaced by the familiar regal individual he had met in a tunnel on Scath. The ruler of half the island, this was the demon who had begun by trying to possess his body and who, accepting failure, had ended by helping him leave Scath. He was dressed as he had been at that time in a long silken yellow robe with a gold link belt about his waist, a curved sword in a jeweled scabbard at his side. He became fully visible.

"Amaruduk!" MacDougall exclaimed in astonishment. "You here!"

"Indeed. And why not?" The one-time Sumerian God of gods smiled with obvious self-satisfaction. "The journey posed no problem. I simply used you as a focal point. I knew if you were in the Other World I would remain where I was, and if you were in this one I would join you." His expression grew grim. "You may recall, I once told you that I would no longer be confined to Marduk. Though I cannot return to your realm, I can at least see the rest of this one."

He held out both hands. "I do not come unattended." He snapped his fingers, and at the sound the two shadowy figures solidified, became Annunaki, judges in ancient Sumer, now servants of Amaruduk. Alan and the Bard had met both before. One was Kindazi who had helped them on several occasions; and the other Ashak who had guided them to Amaruduk's realm.

"And now that you're here . . ." Alan left the question incomplete.

"I have no immediate plans," the other responded with a faint smile, "except to learn from you as much as possible about this island. I have one ultimate aim, which I may or may not disclose." He glanced about, then shook his head. "There doesn't appear to be a place where we can sit in comfort while we converse."

"Except for the turf." Swinging out of the saddle, Alan

waved one hand. "It may lack dignity, but it should suffice."

Amaruduk shrugged, watching the Bard dismount. "If Taliesin can do it, so can I."

They formed a sort of circle on the grass, the Annunaki sitting a foot or two behind their master. Casually MacDougall remarked, "Interesting development, your arrival on Avilion. Scathach is also here, as you may already know, and Manannan and his companions are on the way—if Ahriman ever permits them to complete their journey. At the moment they're lost at sea." Alan saw a flash of deepened interest, instantly concealed by the Sumerian god.

"Including those, I suppose, whom my Annunaki possessed," Amaruduk observed quietly, then changed the subject. "Tell me, if you will, how does this island—I assume it is an island—differ from that of Marduk and the others?" Amused, Alan noted his refusal to use Scath as the name for Island Three.

"It *is* an island, circular in shape with five unusual cities evenly spaced around a central Tower." Briefly he described the succession of cities, the three already visited and the two remaining. "Strangely, each city is the home of a different race or nationality, and there is no commerce between them."

A thought came from the Bard. *"I would not be so free with my information, if I were you. Remember who he was in the Olden Time. We know nothing about his reason for coming here."*

Alan gave the faintest nod, then concluded, "The Tower can barely be seen in the distance on the crest of a hill to your right."

Amaruduk gazed in the direction indicated, staring with narrowed eyes at the tapered golden cylinder, its top vanishing into the aurora. Finally he asked, "What is the significance of the Tower? Though I think I can guess."

"That is the headquarters of Ahriman, the lieutenant of Lucifer." Alan watched for a change in the other's expression, but his face remained under rigid control.

After a brief pause the visitor asked, "Do you consider yourself in debt to the one you call Ahriman?"

Surprised by this abrupt question, MacDougall answered noncommittally, "He saved my life on two occasions—but on the other hand, had it not been for him, my life would not have been in jeopardy."

The Sumerian god waited for more, but Alan added nothing. At length Amaruduk responded, "Oh."

During the silence that followed, Taliesin volunteered, "Perhaps we should inform our visitor that Ahriman is most interested in our movements and may well be observing us this very moment."

At the words Amaruduk stood up, his acolytes also rising. An instant later they became invisible, wraithlike to Alan and Taliesin.

"Thank you for your help. We shall meet again, I am sure." They were gone.

With a chuckle Taliesin commented as they mounted their horses, "I assume you agree we did not want them for traveling companions."

"Indeed," Alan responded; then added telepathically, *"I have a hunch he plans some sort of an attack on Ahriman. If so, I want no part of either side."* What did the serpent-gods think of Amaruduk's sudden appearance on Avilion? Mentally he addressed them.

The Lady Inanna responded, "He is in serious trouble. His willful awakening of the Sleepers to attack Scathach, which Ahriman checked and certainly reported to the Lord of Light, will not go unpunished. So, it appears, he feels he has nothing to lose by an attack on Ahriman, or perhaps by trying to strike a bargain. Your guess is as good as mine. But it is certain mere curiosity has not brought him here."

Another complication, Alan thought, then mentally shrugged it away.

After some brisk riding they saw the fourth city appear in the distance; Atu, Ahriman had called it, its people Egyptians. Unlike the others, it was surrounded by a broad border of trees, palms they appeared, honestly green, giving the city the appearance of an oasis in a pale-green prairie. They could see three sections of a single tan building jutting high above the palms, the only visible sign that a city was there. At Alan's suggestion horses and riders again became invisible.

"The palms give me an idea," MacDougall announced aloud. "We'll tether the horses under the trees and then explore the city—rather, the sandstone Temple. In the model, as I picture it, the building is constructed of three square-cornered units, tapering upward to flat roofs, with one great entrance. We'll transfer just outside that entrance and see what we shall see. The city itself also has but one entrance, facing Ahriman's Tower."

At little more than a walk they approached Atu. When close enough to see the wall, they spied a single guard, armed with a bow and a quiver of arrows, listlessly pacing the length of the wall. What a pointless pursuit, Alan thought, endlessly guarding a city with no enemies to attack. Under the palms they dismounted, removing the bits from the horses' mouths to permit grazing and tying the animals to the trees with cords they found behind the saddles.

Taking Taliesin's hand, MacDougall centered his thoughts on his newly acquired ability, cautiously setting his target the far corner of the city wall. Instantly they were there.

"I'm taking it easy," he thought to the Bard, *"until I feel I've mastered things. Frankly, it's exciting, but almost frightening. I am not aware of my using any of my own energy; I seem to be drawing on power outside myself."* In a sudden, fleeting moment he remembered Ahriman's reference during their first meeting to limitless energy everywhere.

Ahead he saw the great portal leading into Atu, towering high above the palms and dwarfing the walls; and seconds later the two men stood before it. It suggested a building in itself, all of ten feet across at the base, its tapering walls fully five feet thick with a flat, slabbed roof, the doorway surprisingly small. A single guard, about ten feet beyond the open doorway, paced slowly back and forth, the picture of boredom. Behind him on a broad expanse of flagstone other Egyptians strolled aimlessly about, or stood talking in little groups, still others visible under the palms, idly wandering hither and yon through narrow streets. The houses lining the streets were single-storey yellow brick oblongs with high slits of windows in tapering walls, flat-roofed like the Temple.

The people were swarthy, black-haired, the men with locks shorn square slightly below the earlobes, that of the women ending about midway between breast and waist. There was little variety in dress, the men bareheaded and bare to the waist, clothed in short, wraparound skirts overlapping in the front; the women clad also in single garments like shifts with straps over the shoulders and ending a few inches above the ankles. All wore single-thonged sandals.

Stealthily MacDougall led the way into Atu, undetected, moving toward the broad ramp leading into the Temple. At the foot of the slope he halted, looking at the Bard with a rueful half-smile. He sent a thought.

"I keep forgetting one of my new powers—that of seeing inside closed rooms, an ability I always credited to Lord Enki and Lady Inanna. I still think they're involved."

He closed his eyes and sent his probing gaze into the section of the Temple to his left, opening his mind for the Bard to see with him. There were high-vaulted corridors with glowing ceilings, and walls and floors of sandstone blocks, large and untenanted rooms lying on both sides of the hallways. Some were living quarters, simply furnished; and there was a large dining room, behind it a kitchen where cooks were busily preparing food.

I'm hungry, MacDougall told himself—then thrust the thought aside as his probing sight came upon a large hall with row after row of backless stone benches set in a half curve, the floor sloping downward to a raised dais of black marble. On the benches were seated a hundred or more men, all dressed in coarsely woven gray skirts, black hair uncut, some with straggly beards, all with bare feet.

A woman, tall, commanding, and lovely of face, stood on the dais addressing this strange audience. She wore a simple black, long-sleeved, ankle-length robe, drawn in at the waist by a heavy, ropelike cord. Lovely of face, but with chestnut hair drawn back tightly and unbecomingly and tied with a black cord at the base of her neck. At one end of the dais, at the woman's left, stood a man of lighter skin, gray-haired, wearing a long robe of blue, about his neck a long string of beads ending in a black *ankh*, a looped cross, and upon his head a tall, bejeweled miter. Strangely, a heavy iron chain came from beneath his robe, extended a few feet along the floor to end at the top of a massive pillar. Chained!

Along each side wall, evenly spaced, stood ten guardsmen, armed with swords and bows and bronze-tipped arrows, grimly alert.

"That looks interesting," MacDougall mentally exclaimed. *"Let's join the party."*

"Excellent idea," Taliesin agreed; and an instant later they were standing at the rear of the room. Still invisible, they slid into vacant seats in the last row. The speaker was using a low-pitched, well-modulated voice that carried clearly throughout the chamber.

"Mind itself and the divine are the ultimate end, marking the true intellectual and reflecting the epitome of love. Reason and prudence have no part in theoretic wisdom; it is by the power of living the life of theory that we differ from lower animals, that we are humankind. Is this clear?"

Not to me, Alan thought wonderingly. Sounded like double talk.

The speaker continued, "From knowledge we rise to wisdom, as knowledge of first principles, and finally as theology. In the part of the soul that has rational discourse is the intellectual principle; for its sake and for the sake of the thoughts that it energizes, all else exists." She turned to the man chained to the stone pillar.

"Do you agree, Most Holy Cyril?"

The priestly figure hesitated. "If I understand your meaning, theoretically I suppose—"

"Vacillation, vacillation!" the woman cried scornfully. "Always temporizing. Never a clear-cut answer from the all-wise Bishop of Alexandria, self-appointed judge, whose theology was not allowed to influence his life." She turned to the audience.

"Class," she called out, "what is the Sixth Commandment of Moses?"

As one a hundred voices shouted, "You shall not commit murder."

Again she addressed the one called Cyril. "You have not forgotten, Most Holy Bishop?"

Hoarsely came the reply. "I have not forgotten."

Again she called out, "Class, what is the Ninth Commandment of Moses?"

"You shall not give false evidence," the chorus responded.

"You remember, Cyril?"

"I remember." Cyril's answer was a groan. "I remember."

"Five lashes," the speaker exclaimed. "And this time you, Khianias, will strike the blows."

This time, MacDougall thought; there must have been other times.

Reluctantly one of the gray-clad men rose and came forward, mounting a short stairway to the dais. He stooped and picked up a metal-tipped whip that Alan had not noticed, crossed to the Bishop, and tore off his robe. A strange figure, pot-bellied, wearing only a loincloth and his Bishop's crown, a heavy chain about his waist. He cringed and moaned as the blows fell.

At their conclusion the woman exclaimed, "And one for you, Khianias, for being the Bishop's tool."

Savagely Cyril grasped the whip; and as the other bared his back, he swung a single vicious blow.

MacDougall stood up, Taliesin rising with him; and while the Bishop put on his robe and Khianias returned to his seat, the speaker continued, "Theological knowledge, unless it manifests itself in the life it professes, is anathema. Hypocrisy is the bane of all philosophy—''

Grasping the Bard's hand, MacDougall returned in less than a breath to the entrance of the Temple. Mentally he exclaimed, *"What was that all about? A strange situation."* At Taliesin's *"I have no idea,"* Alan concluded, *"Maybe the Lord Enki and Lady Inanna can tell us."*

The latter answered, "I read the woman's mind, so I know. She is Hypatia, daughter of Theon, a renowned mathematician and philosopher, as she herself was. She was famous throughout Egypt for her eloquence and beauty, and by her outspoken defense of her theological position she gained the enmity of Cyril, Patriarch of Alexandria. At his instigation a mob of fanatical monks, stirred to frenzy, dragged her from her chariot into one of the churches of the day, stripped her naked, hacking her to death and literally tearing her limb from limb. Then they burned her body piecemeal.

"Now all are here, including the Patriarch and the monks; and their positions are reversed, with Hypatia in control. Now they have to listen to her lectures again and again—and again—with lashings between." An amused note entered Inanna's thought. "It may well be that her lectures are intentionally obscure so that Cyril remains eternally confused."

"Justice," MacDougall commented silently; then unuttered, his alone, came a thought. *All* the participants in the tragedy are here in Lucifer's domain. To the Bard: *"We'll investigate the other wing of the Temple."*

Alan had expected an architectural duplicate of the left building, but this section was totally different. Here was no corridor, but direct entry into a large chamber. In Hypatia's area—at least what he had seen—there had been no carvings in bas-relief; here the walls were covered by column after column of Egyptian hieroglyphics as well as typical two-dimensional representations of men, women, and gods.

Seated in splendor at one end of the room on a gold-encrusted ebony chair was an impressive figure of authority, a man taller than most Egyptians. Penetrating, deep-set eyes dominated a strong face with a large, sharply chiseled nose, thin lips that seemed on the verge of a sardonic smile, high cheekbones, and a resolute chin. His expression was sober, arrogant, and of an unapproachable frostiness. A broad gold band encircled his head, holding a mass of black hair in place; rising from it, centered above his high forehead, was a jeweled head of a cobra, arched to strike. A white tunic was draped over his left shoulder, leaving his muscular right arm and chest bare. He wore the usual Egyptian kiltlike skirt, overlapping in the front. He was speaking to several guards standing uneasily before him.

"Why have they not been seen? He-Who-Speaks-for-the-Master told me of their coming, and they should be here. Two of them, one tall with yellow hair and beard, dressed in black; the other short, heavier, balding, and in blue. Has the guard at the gate been alerted? Or has he been sleeping as usual, and have they already entered Atu?"

One of the group answered apologetically, "We have been watching with all care. We have posted extra guards on the wall and at the gate; and when they arrive messengers will report with speed, and they will be escorted to you immediately."

MacDougall squeezed Taliesin's arm. *"That's our cue to appear. We'll materialize suddenly inside the doorway. But first, Lord Enki, what is his name and position?"*

The serpent-god answered, *"He is Horsaneb, formerly the General of Egypt's armies, and Ruler of Atu. He calls himself Commander."*

"Thank you. Now, Taliesin, on the count of three we appear." Alan grasped the Bard's hand, counting, *"One, two—three!"* And as one they were on the opposite side of the closed door, facing the Ruler.

As Horsaneb's eyes grew wide with surprise, MacDougall said quietly, "Greetings, Honorable Horsaneb. We were delayed, else we would have been here earlier. Because of that delay we chose to appear in this unusual manner. Your guards are not at fault. There was no way they could have known of our arrival.''

After Horsaneb's first surprised reaction, he banished all expression from his face. He nodded approvingly. "I see you are aware of the value of the unexpected, Alan MacDougall. When I learned of your coming and its purpose, and considered the source of that knowledge, I anticipated someone unusual. My first reaction is favorable.'' He looked keenly at the Bard. ''The One-Who-Speaks-for-the-Master had less to say about you, but in my judgment you too are worthy of attention. Welcome to Atu.'' He stood up and bowed.

The visitors returned the bow, waiting for Horsaneb's next move. It followed immediately. Curtly he said to the guards, ''Go about your duties. Tell those at the gate and on the wall that the visitors are here.'' Leaving the dais, he joined Alan and Taliesin. Cordially he said, "You have arrived just in time to be my guests at dinner. And since the one you are to meet will not see you until after sleep-time, you will be shown to rooms where you may rest. I trust you approve.''

"I am delighted with your plans," MacDougall said warmly. ''Frankly, I am hungry, and sleep will be most welcome. I can never become accustomed to a world without night and normal time.''

As the two were escorted by the Ruler himself to a sumptuous dining room where a table was set for three, Alan sought to recover from his surprise at their reception. They were being treated like visiting royalty. The Ruler's attitude remained unchanged during the excellent dinner—meat, fruit, vegetables, and crisp-crusted loaves—and his conversation seemed designed to make his visitors feel welcome. Like all who learned of Alan's coming from the Other World without having died, he asked the usual questions; but on the whole he was a perfect host.

Later in his room when MacDougall prepared for bed, the mystery remained unresolved. Horsaneb's interest and cordiality seemed genuine, though it hardly conformed with his grim visage. What had Ahriman told him?

Still later, stretched out on a low, hard bed, a duplicate of that in Cuchulainn's castle, Alan's mind, still active, relived his experiences since arriving in Avilion. So much had happened with so many new people that events tended to blur and overlap. He closed his eyes to block out the constant light. If only there were periods of old-fashioned darkness in this world, or switches to shut off the ceiling glow. He could sleep better in darkness. A sudden wild thought struck him. The doors locked by mental control; why not the lights?

"Lord and Lady," he addressed the serpent-gods, "can you shut off the ceiling glow?"

Came the response "Can you? Have you tried?"

Feeling foolish, MacDougall centered his thoughts on darkness, picturing the ceiling becoming dim, the light vanishing—and even as he visualized darkness, a heavy blackness filled his room. Only a faint line of light beneath the door prevented total darkness.

Startled, MacDougall lay with eyes wide open. Were there no limits to what his mind could accomplish—in this world, of course? Methodically in thought he recited the list of his extraordinary powers: mental telepathy, invisibility, shape-changing, mental control over animals, vision through solid objects, out-of-body flight, levitation, instant transfer—there was little left to master in magic abilities.

He felt momentary exhilaration, then as he continued staring into the darkness he became aware of sudden revulsion. This was Lucifer's domain! Not the accepted idea of Hell, but a realm of life after death nonetheless. These powers were his through the agency of Lucifer. He was taught by demons or their agents, under the direction of Ahriman, the self-styled lieutenant of the Arch-Demon himself. Why? Why Alan MacDougall? None of this was his seeking. He didn't belong here!

He closed his eyes and with no conscious direction on his part his mind re-created a scene in the Scottish Highlands, his first night as guest in the Cameron home. Clearly he pictured what Duncan Cameron had called "a readin'." Elspeth seated with the great family Bible on her lap, reading the one hundred twenty-first Psalm. The lad David seated quietly, Norah in a far corner, all reverently listening. Again he heard Cameron's prayer, especially its conclusion.

"An', Father, we pray for the stranger who has come into our house. Be wi' him i' his travelin'. Keep a firm hold on him an' on a' of us. Deliver us from evil. An' tak' a' the glory unto Thyself. Amen."

Cameron asking the Almighty to keep a firm hold on him. Fervently he hoped the Scot's prayer was being answered.

MacDougall thought of the Bard in the next room. He needed wise counsel. He sent a solemn thought.

"Taliesin, I am troubled. A short while ago I caught myself beginning to delight in all the powers I am gaining. Then I suddenly realized their source. All of this—the visits to these cities, the way prepared by Ahriman—is at his behest, and behind him is the Lord of Darkness. Why should I be given this instruction? Certainly not for my benefit. Oh, I know—the wild idea that I am to rule the world—but that's just plain silly. I'm troubled."

Gravely the Bard responded, *"I have been wondering at your rather casual acceptance of all that has been happening. I am convinced that your possible escape from all of this depends upon your own resistance and that Scots stubbornness that is part of you. Some of the abilities you have acquired were necessary for your survival. You had to meet magic with magic. But the out-of-body experience, for example, is hardly needed here. I know— it led to your grasping instant transfer; but that could have come by other means, and would have come, since you have the ability to draw from original power.*

"Friend Alan, you have reason to be troubled, though not yet have you reached the point of defeat. But you need to resist as never before."

"Two more lessons," MacDougall commented. *"What magic is left for me to learn?"*

"You will know in due course. I foresee one possibility that you should by all means refuse."

"What could that be?"

"I could be wrong, so let us wait for the fact."

Knowing the Bard, MacDougall did not insist on an answer. He felt better for having shared his troubles. Maybe now he could sleep. About to doze off, he thought of the door. It should be locked. As with the ceiling light, perhaps it too was mentally controlled.

"Lord Enki," he sent the thought, "how do you lock the door as you've done for me in the past?"

"It is time you learned. There are two methods. With the first you mentally freeze the hinges so in effect they become solid metal. Easily done, but just as easily undone by anyone with magic powers. The second method is more complex. There is a bolt embedded in the door itself that fits into a socket in the frame. You move it by tripping a complex combination of pins that you predetermine—"

"Never mind," MacDougall interrupted. "Will you lock the door, please?"

Enki gave vent to a mental snort. "Very well."

Chuckling to himself, Alan thought drowsily that locking doors was an ability he didn't have to master so long as he wore the armlet.

"Alan! Time to awaken." The penetrating thought of Taliesin brought MacDougall sharply awake. Yawning, he stretched and opened his eyes, momentarily confused by the darkness. Remembering, he reactivated the ceiling glow.

"I'm awake," he answered. *"Haven't slept so soundly in a long while. Have I time for a quick shower?"*

"I suppose so," the Bard answered. *"We haven't been called yet, but I caught the thoughts of two guards in the corridor. They are awaiting a signal from the Commander before summoning us to breakfast."*

MacDougall found a primitive sort of spray in the necessary room, and though the water was cold, the quick bath was stimulating, and after an energetic rubdown and brief calisthenics he felt ready to tackle whatever lay before him. He was fully dressed when the summons came and he joined Taliesin in the corridor.

They were led to the same room in which they had dined; but there were three additional dignitaries present for breakfast. Commander Horsaneb introduced the philosopher Hypatia, whom he called the Oracle, and with her, Hor-Amon the Enforcer, a brawny Egyptian who maintained order in the other section of the Temple. The third was the white-robed deputy of the Priest of Thoth. The latter, named Hamti, who said almost nothing during breakfast, was there to conduct the guests into the presence of Shepsut, the Priest of Thoth, after they had eaten.

Breakfast was a hearty meal, hardly less sumptuous than the dinner had been. Broiled fish, crisp rolls, fruit, and hot porridge were placed before the five in lavish abundance. Alan was plied with questions about his own world by Hypatia and Horsaneb; the Oracle's greatest concern was whether or not she or her teachings were remembered.

At this point the Lady Inanna sent a hasty thought. "I have been inquiring, and, yes, Hypatia is remembered by philosophers of your day."

"Are you remembered?" Alan responded. "Though philosophy is not my field of interest, I believe you are remembered as is your father Theon, even after fourteen hundred years." Innocently he added, "Your name is associated with a Bishop of the day, Cyril his name. I seem to remember hearing of a Saint Cyril—but I'm sure he must be another priest with the same name."

Hypatia grimaced in distaste and indignation. "It *must* be another. Even the Roman church could not make so grave an error. Cyril of Alexandria is in this Temple; and he is far from being a saint." She would have said more, but Horsaneb asked an unrelated question, and Alan was spared the necessity of stretching his very limited knowledge.

The breakfast ended; and almost regretfully, it seemed, the Commander bade MacDougall and Taliesin farewell and consigned them to the care of Hamti the deputy. Silently he led them through a wide doorway with carved columns on both sides, into the great central section of the Temple.

Immediately they came face to face with two white-robed priests with shaven heads, barring entrance to a heavily curtained doorway. Recognizing Hamti and apparently aware of whom he was guiding, they bowed deeply and stepped back, sweeping aside the draperies. The guide paused briefly before passing between the priests, murmuring a faint invocation.

As they entered a great and shadowed hall, Mac-Dougall gained a fleeting impression of ancient evil, as if they were in a place not intended for the living. The ceiling, unlike all the others they had seen, was a dead black, studded with winking lights like stars, suggesting a normal moonless night in Alan's world; yet oddly this did nothing to dispel the feeling of evil.

The walls, barely seen, were decorated from floor to ceiling with symbolic designs and scenes. Great, dark pillars towered in each corner, covered with intricate carvings like the walls. Between them on three sides, heroic stone statues stood guard—some human-appearing, men and women, others human bodies bearing heads of various animals and birds. There were eleven in all. Before each stood a low, three-armed golden lamp, providing dim illumination. The lamps were wrought in the shape of three lotus blossoms, the central bloom rising above the others, oil-filled, faintly aromatic vapors rising from broad wicks.

For an instant Alan had the unsettling thought, Were these images possessed by the demons who had empowered them during Egypt's day of glory? Nonsense, he told himself.

Demanding full attention was a single towering figure at the far end of the hall. On a low-backed chair of gold, in regal dignity, sat a god cut from black stone, its garments carved of alabaster; the face strong and grim with its stylized Egyptian beard projecting from the point of the chin. On the god's head rose an enormous domed crown of gold, golden plumes decorating right and left

sides. Six circlets of alternating gold and gems starting
at the base of his neck formed a wide ornament covering
the upper chest. Outthrust forearms, broad bands of gold
about the wrists, held what to MacDougall looked like a
hooked cane, or a shepherd's crook and a flail.

He had little time for observing these fascinating details, the guide hastening through the chamber, stepping
as lightly as possible, heading toward a narrow doorway
in the farther corner. As they passed the huge image,
Lord Enki sent Alan the thought, "Osiris, God of the
Dead."

They left the great hall to enter a short corridor extending along the end wall of the Temple of Osiris. The
glowing ceiling of the hallway was a relief after the shadowed dimness of the hall. There were three curtained
doorways in the facing wall; they halted before the central one. As if their coming was foreknown, a deep voice
came from within.

"Enter!" With the word unseen hands inside the room
drew the curtains, and Hamti drew back and bowed.

Side by side MacDougall and Taliesin entered the room
and stood rigidly, staring in wonder. Alan had not had
any idea what to expect, but certainly not this. Before
them stood a fantastic hybrid figure, its head and shoulders that of an ibis, black and shining with a great,
sicklelike beak. The shoulders emerged into the arms and
body of a muscular man. Tight-fitting garments, vesture
and wraparound skirt, ended at the knees; and like the
statue of Osiris, he wore a pectoral of gold and gems as
well as armlets and bracelets of jeweled gold.

Strange bird eyes stared and the beak opened to emit
the incongruously deep voice. "Welcome, Alan Mac-
Dougall and Bard Taliesin. I have been awaiting your
coming. I am Shepsut, Priest of Thoth."

Before Alan answered, a thought came from the Bard.
"Shape-changing, Alan! Don't believe what you see."

Instantly MacDougall beheld the Priest as he really
was—rather short and stocky, with an angular face and
intense dark eyes. He was dressed in white, differing from
his deputy chiefly in his possession of a full head of dark

hair. Evidently he had taken on the form of the god he served for his visitors' benefit.

Alan chuckled. "The change doesn't improve you at all, nor does it impress me. Shape-changing was one of the first unusual abilities I learned after entering this world." Casually he added, "I could match you, but that would prove nothing."

Instantly Shepsut appeared as himself, his manner completely serious. "I should have believed the One-Who-Speaks-for-the-Master. There will be no more games." He spoke to Hamti.

"Chairs for the visitors and one for yourself. You will participate in our lesson."

The Priest of Thoth turned and seated himself in a broad black chair, apparently carved of jet, inlaid with gold designs featuring the head of an ibis, a single eye, and columns of hieroglyphics. As he did so MacDougall glanced around the room, noting the heavy blue rug and the murals on the walls, all involving the ibis-headed god Thoth in action scenes and painted in the two-dimensional style of Egyptian art, the colors rather subdued.

Most prominent in the room's contents was a huge statue of Thoth, about twice life size, standing on a low platform of black stone directly behind the Priest. Amazingly lifelike, it would not have surprised Alan had it moved.

Hamti's return cut short further observation; and after they were seated in a half circle about six feet from Shepsut, the latter spoke, addressing Taliesin.

"You will learn something of what I have been instructed to impart and, it may be, enough to venture an attempt to put the ability into practice. I strongly advise against this. As I suppose you know, you were not included in my word from the one you know as Ahriman. I felt you should be warned."

"Thank you for your warning," the Bard replied.

To MacDougall, Shepsut began, "I think it would be well for you to understand why I have been chosen to guide you into this knowledge. Thoth, as you may be aware, in the Olden Times was the 'Measurer,' the scribe of the gods of the Underworld. It was he who recorded the weighing of the heart of those who, after leaving the body, entered the judgment hall of Osiris. He it was who constantly dealt with the *Ka*, the double of the soul; and the *Ba*, the life principle of man; and the *Khaibit*, or the soul's shadow. All of these, with the *Khu*, make up the spirit-soul of a man.

"I as Priest of Thoth have mastered the secrets of the god, which accounts for me having been chosen for this task." He frowned in thought as if deciding his next step.

"You, with your ability to free your spirit from your body, as I understand you have been taught, have been well prepared for the next step. As I will reveal, you may accomplish your purpose silently, subtly and without warning, or, for its impression on the one you chose, accompanied by a black cloud, misty and intangible, but very real to the victim. And Hamti will be your subject for demonstration and practice."

As the other talked, MacDougall had begun to suspect where all this was leading. Now he could see why he had been taught to free his spirit from his body. At mention of the black cloud, recalling his own terrifying experience when he was its subject, he sprang to his feet, upsetting his chair and sending it flying.

"Hold everything!" he exclaimed. "Am I to understand that you're leading up to me learning how to possess another's body?"

"Yes," Shepsut answered, his brows arched in surprise. "Either by sharing or by dispossessing—"

"Forget the whole idea!" Alan was genuinely angry. "I want nothing to do with such diabolic acts, now or ever. It has been tried on me, and I want no part of it. If Ahriman thinks I can be induced—or for that matter forced—to learn that trick, he's mad. And you can tell him I said so."

"Sit, MacDougall," the Priest said calmly. "There will be no attempt at forcing. I was warned that you might object, but I hardly expected so violent a reaction. I have been given an alternative, an ability quite in keeping with powers already yours."

"Very well, I'll listen." As he turned to pick up his chair, Hamti was already there; and as he set it upright, MacDougall thought he saw a look of relief on his face, a reaction he could well appreciate. Possession, even when unsuccessful, was a frightening experience.

"Because Ahriman felt you might object to the power of possession—though it would be very useful in your future task—he directed that I teach you to read minds. I am surprised, in view of your other abilities, that you have not yet gained this power. In passing, I find it interesting to note that both of you have closed your minds against my best efforts. This indicates a power that should make your own development of mind reading quite simple."

Why not? Alan thought. It could be a help when dealing with enemies, an ability possessed by many in this world, even though his own thoughts were beyond their invading.

"I see no reason—" he began, then paused at an urgent interruption by Lord Enki.

"Alan, sorry to intrude, but it has become important that this session be terminated and that you be on your way to the next city as quickly as possible. As closely as you can, repeat what I am about to say."

Alan gave instant assent to the serpent-god's unprecedented action; and as the words formed in his mind he echoed them aloud.

"It hardly seems necessary. You, Honorable Shepsut, are about to say 'The creation of thought requires the expenditure of energy, and energy through concentration can be detected and followed, no matter how rapid the process.' Now you are thinking with some astonishment, 'Why did Ahriman lead me to think he needed to develop this power? I will block his probing—'"

"But as you now see, Shepsut, you cannot do so. You are thinking—"

The Priest of Thoth stood up, a scowl on his face. "Enough! You are quite adept at following surface thoughts, which after all was what I would have taught you." Alan could see he was thoroughly annoyed. "I see no reason for continuing this session,'' he concluded stiffly.

"I quite agree," MacDougall said, rising and grasping Taliesin's arm, the Bard also on his feet. "I am sure, in accord with Ahriman's planning, we shall meet again."

In a breath the chamber of Thoth was gone, and they were standing under the palms, their horses grazing placidly a few feet away.

CHAPTER 7

Enter: Wave Sweeper

The City of Atu fell rapidly away behind MacDougall and Taliesin as they sent the white horses racing across the grassy plain.

"Lord Enki and Lady Inanna, what was that all about?" Alan spoke aloud. "And why all this haste?" Half-seriously he added, "Now I'll never know how to read minds."

"*Nonsense,*" Enki replied, making his thought clear for the Bard as well as Alan. "*You can do so now if you but try. The same power that enables you to sense happenings beyond sight and through solid barriers, with appropriate adjustments, will enable you to sense another's thoughts. It merely requires application and practice.*" The serpent-god seemed to brush the idea aside.

"*But that is unimportant. Things are beginning to happen, Amaruduk's doings. The next city, Axume, will be involved, which is why I thought you should be on your way as quickly as possible. Beside that, nothing of importance was going to happen in Atu.*"

MacDougall reverted to mental exchange, including the

Bard in his thought: "*Amaruduk. Not surprising. What is he up to?*"

"*He found* Wave Sweeper, *probably using as focal point one of the three gods of Tartarus who had pursued you into Marduk and whom some of the Anunnaki possessed. Leaving his body behind, he joined Manannan in the sea-god's body, Kindazi doing the same with Nuada. The other one of his attendants, Ashak, remains with the two comatose bodies.*"

The Lord Enki continued with his report, telling of Amaruduk's countering Ahriman's spell; with the *Wave Sweeper* again responding to Manannan's orders, they were even then anchored at a fishing wharf on the seaward side of Axume. Why there? Because this was the area where the Sumerian god's body lay. Even as Enki reported, Manannan sent his coracle well out to sea where, rendered invisible, it floated safe from curious fishermen. They had scarcely any difficulty with the fishermen; and without much question they were given horses to make their way to Axume.

Enki concluded, "*Unless you want to meet the crew of* Wave Sweeper *I suggest you get to the city, complete your visit, and leave, all before they arrive.*"

"Why go there at all?" MacDougall demanded. "Certainly no earthshaking ability remains for me to learn. I can't think of a single useful power that I don't have. Taliesin and I can ride past Axume and continue around the circle to Cuchulainn."

"*I should think,*" the Lady Inanna interjected, "*you would want Ahriman to learn of this new development on his own—if he doesn't know it already. If you bypass Axume he would expect an explanation. And I for one believe there is more reason than appears on the surface for these visits of yours.*"

Suddenly Alan burst into audible laughter. "Taliesin," he said aloud, "I can never become accustomed to these three-way conversations in my own mind. You are here and you haven't contributed a word, yet you're aware of all that was said, while an observer would swear we rode in complete silence. Crazy world."

The Bard chuckled. "There is much that is strange in this land, but I no longer marvel at the strangeness. One learns to accept anything during fourteen centuries in a world where magic works. Referring to this matter of mind reading—I can do it to a degree, and believe me, it is not an unmixed blessing. For this reason I have never tried to impart the secret to you."

Slowing somewhat for the sake of their mounts, they continued on their way. Mentally Alan pictured the crew of the copper coracle riding across the plain, approaching from his left. They still had a substantial distance to go, according to his visualization of the island. He had a sudden idea. Why imagine them? He should be able to see them.

He closed his eyes, concentrating on his recollections of Manannan, seeing him clearly in his mind's eye—and instantly he sensed a sharp image of the sea-god astride a black horse. Bunched behind him came: Nuada, King of the *Tuatha de Danann*; beside him to the left the red-bearded giant Beli; and to his right, Pryderi, jailer of Ochren, sullen and dark-browed as ever. Behind them rode Balor, god of the Fomorians, and four Druids. They were moving at a leisurely pace, in no apparent hurry to reach the city, if that indeed was their destination. Behind them Alan saw the gray of the fishing village and, stretched out to infinity, the calm waters of the sea, alive with the reflected aurora.

Suddenly he realized there was something wrong with the picture. Puzzled, he studied the scene. Then it struck him—there should be ten in the group! Mathonwy the Druid Master was not there.

He opened his eyes, frowning, then mentally shrugged. No reason for him puzzling himself about the matter. If it was significant, the answer would appear in due course.

He thought about the accumulating extraordinary abilities he was acquiring. In his own world he'd never been aware of what were called psychic powers. Oh, hunches that usually were best followed, and awareness of his being watched; but that was not unusual. He thought of mind reading, and he was intrigued. Enki had suggested it was merely an extension of the same perception that penetrated barriers and to which distance meant nothing. Why not try it?

Again he closed his eyes; again saw Manannan on his black mount. He strove by concentration to learn what the sea-god was thinking, in a way listening mentally as he did during telepathic conversations with Taliesin. He caught fleeting wisps of ideas, not his own—a sudden feeling of abhorrence, of a chilling fear. There followed a burst of defiance, of resentment, of protest; then the clear thought, *"This is not to be borne! I am the god of the sea, a being of power."*

Shockingly there came an answering thought, coldly calm. *"Manannan, will you not learn? Resistance is useless, and cooperation will benefit you greatly. You will not be harmed, and in a short time you will be released with your mind greatly expanded."*

There was more from Amaruduk; but Alan tried to probe more deeply, below surface thoughts, testing this new ability. He became dimly aware of an even greater wrath, of something carefully concealed, a gloating satisfaction, a repressed excitement. Then the sudden erection of a barrier, almost as if Manannan sensed his intrusion.

MacDougall cut off the thought. He stared across the plain with little awareness of the pale grass, his mind reverting to the sea-god's surface thoughts. The fear and the repressed terror were too real, stirring up memories of his own experiences when he was the intended subject of possession. He tried to blot the incident from his mind.

He didn't like it—any part of it, this mind reading. He imagined a peeping Tom must feel like this, a sense of secret gloating over forbidden knowledge, plus self-repugnance for his prying. Manannan's secret terror should remain his own. He understood why the Bard had called the ability "not an unmixed blessing." If he used the power at all, it would be reluctantly and out of dire need.

The rest of their ride to Axume was without incident except for an unexpected thought from Taliesin. *"It oc-*

curs to me, friend Alan, that there is one ability you have not mastered. You have used it several times but always assisted by the dwellers in your armlet. I refer to the creation of illusions.''

"True enough," Alan agreed, "and highly important when they were needed. Once during our escape from Lochlann, and twice when getting away from Scathach's Tower. I wonder if that's what I'll learn in Axume?''

Lord Enki interjected, "I fear not, Alan MacDougall. The creation of those illusions required the efforts of both Inanna and me, and would have been beyond the powers of you or any other single entity. You recall the phantom army defending Beli's castle. That was the creation of ten score Druids uniting their powers. And the illusions in Manannan's castle, again the combined efforts of teams of Druids.

"Perhaps you and Taliesin together—but why should you need to know? The results would be uncertain; and if illusions are needed, you always have the Lady Inanna and me at your right hand—or should I say—arm?''

MacDougall grimaced. If only that were not so, he could be out of all this.

When their destination appeared as a dot on the horizon, horses and riders became invisible, and the closer they came, the more cautiously they proceeded. At length when the gray walls with their skyward-pointing spears like an enormous, ancient stadium loomed about fifty yards ahead, Alan sent Taliesin a thought.

"With the passengers of Wave Sweeper on their way, we'll ride around to the other side of the city, well away from the wall, and let the horses graze. We won't have to walk back, obviously, and if we want to leave in a hurry our mounts will be waiting.''

Still invisible, they skirted the rounded walls on the seaward side, passing a great iron double gate, decorated in relief with heroic stylized human figures, turbaned and clad in link-chain armor. Like all the visible iron, it was rust-red and ancient. Well beyond the city they dismounted. Removing the bits from the horses' mouths,

Alan, feeling rather skeptical, tried to fix in their minds the idea of their staying where they were.

"Since time may well be important," he suggested, *"I'm inclined to bypass all but the essential individual, whoever that may be. I'll do a bit of visual exploring, starting at the gate facing Ahriman's Tower. Observe."*

Together, through MacDougall's new sense of perception, they watched the assembling of thirty or forty black soldiers on an expanse of gray flagstones just inside the gate. They were of mingled racial groups, all very dark, but some with broad noses and woolly hair, others with features more Arabic with straight black hair. All wore caplike white turbans and chain-link armor from neck to knees. Each bore an oval shield and a long iron-headed spear. Mail and spearheads, unlike the rusty structural iron, shone brightly, the obvious result of careful polishing. The soldiers were forming in ordered ranks to bar the gate.

The Commander, a most impressive figure towering above the others, differed in dress only in that the others were turbaned, and he wore a domed, gold-embossed iron helmet somewhat suggesting a crown. He was calling out his orders.

"There are nine of them, so Diviner Ela Armida has seen, and they are men of power. They are headed for Axume and they do not come in peace. They are not to be slain but are to be taken alive. Use whatever force may be needed, but do not slay! Another guard has been set at the other gate.

"Two others are on their separate way, but they have been sent by the One-Who-Speaks-for-the-Master. They are to be welcomed and are to be brought to me at once."

While the Commander was speaking Alan was probing his mind with his newly gained power. Clearly came the surprising fact: This was King Ezana, ruler of the old Axume, who had once been supreme over the Axumites, the Himyas, the Raidan, the Sabaens, the Tiamo, the Begu, and the Kasu. Now in this strange world—and the thought was bitter and ever-present—he was reduced to control over one small city.

MacDougall addressed the Bard. *"Have you followed?"* At Taliesin's affirmation he continued, *"It appears the one we should see is this Diviner Ela Armida, bypassing King Ezana, interesting though he might be. I don't want to be around when these spearmen tackle the magic of Amaruduk and the others."*

"Agreed," the Bard responded. *"They're expecting us, as were the other cities; but our suddenly appearing before the Diviner might well impress him with our—or your—powers."*

"I'll have to find him so I'll have a target for our transfer."

With eyes closed MacDougall sent his perception wandering through Axume. Here, as in the other cities, men—and apparently only men—wandered idly about, or stood in small groups, or sat on the low stone steps of dwellings in eternal boredom. A rapid tour of nearby grass-grown alleyways winding between the round stone dwellings with their conical iron roofs quickly convinced him that there was only one place to search—the great stone tower.

When Alan had seen the model of the structure he had thought of the Highland *broch* with its inward curving, tapering walls; on observation of the actual tower his impression was strengthened, except that this was more than twice its width and height, indicating a probable second storey. Its roof, like the dwellings, was a shallow brown sheet-iron cone.

The inside walls, revealed by the glowing ceiling, were manifestations of artistry, massive carvings in gray stone, figures stylized but skillfully rendered. Some were battle scenes obviously created from memories of life in Africa, armored elephants mingled with chariots drawn by armored horses; warriors clad in link-mail armor like that of the guards even then massed inside the gates. Other scenes depicted gyrating dancers; wrestlers locked in combat; hunters stalking prey.

Alan found the Diviner alone in a dimly lighted chamber on the ground level, a small round room in the center of the tower. The walls were covered with purple hangings; the floor appeared to be black pelts of animals. At one side, on a low, tall-backed chair of ornately carved dark wood, sat a tall, thin black man, in a purple robe, the fabric glistening with a velvety sheen. Before him stood a stone table holding three cupped metal vessels, from them rising twisting tendrils of white, gray, and black smoke, to mingle and vanish through a wide vent in the ceiling. On either side of the table stood a black pillar, carved to represent a giant serpent coiled about a tree trunk, twinned heads poised above the man.

As Alan and Taliesin watched, a curtain was swept aside and a white-robed man entered and bowed deeply.

"You summoned me, Master?"

"Yes. The two have suddenly appeared inside the Seaward Gate. Messengers are even now racing to inform Commander Ezana. Have the water veil prepared."

MacDougall cut off the vision and stared at the ghostlike image of the Bard. *"Did you hear that?"*

"I did indeed."

Alan pictured the gate they had recently passed; visualized the soldiers inside the wall. And fantastically he saw perfect doubles of himself and Taliesin at the center of an excited throng of soldiers. The shape-changing was perfect, and thus seeing himself was an uncanny experience. He sensed the pseudo-MacDougall saying in an imperious manner, "We have been sent by the One-Who-Speaks-for-the-Master. We command you to take us to Diviner Ela Armida."

Mentally Alan probed; and beneath the façade, as he expected, he saw the twisted form of Amaruduk. Examination of the Taliesin duplicate revealed Kindazi, the Annunaki. Again MacDougall cut off the vision; visualized Manannan.

The god of the sea still rode at the head of the group from *Wave Sweeper*; and as Alan touched his mind he sensed that his thoughts were all his own, that the awareness of freedom from Amaruduk gave him a feeling of great relief. But beneath the surface lurked apprehension and uneasiness. Would Amaruduk return?

MacDougall spoke aloud. "You were with me?"

"All the way," the Bard responded. "What will it be—a confrontation with Amaruduk or on to Cuchulainn?"

"On to Cuchulainn, of course. That was my original inclination. While we ride I'll follow what happens in Axume, and if there is anything worth my learning, any new ability, perhaps I can absorb it."

Moments later they were on their way across the grassy plain, keeping the Golden Tower on their right. Mac-Dougall observed the meeting between his double and the ruler, an interesting clash of strong personalities. It was obvious that King Ezana yielded only because of Ahriman's instructions. Finally messengers escorted the imposters into the presence of Ela Armida.

Sharp eyes examined the two who waited in silence. Finally the Diviner spoke.

"So you of the yellow hair are the Chosen One, selected by the Lord of Light centuries before you were born. He-Who-Speaks-for-the-Master tells me I am to teach you the art of the Diviner."

He turned his attention to the spurious Bard. "You, I was told, are merely observing; but you may as well gain the gift at the same time as MacDougall. At the front of the table you will find two small stools, placed there in anticipation of your coming. Seat yourselves on them facing me, and the lesson will begin."

Finally Amaruduk spoke, amusement in the Mac-Dougall voice. "Not so fast," he protested. "Perhaps I do not wish to learn what you plan to teach. Just what do you mean by the art of the Diviner?"

"Divination," Ela Armida said, a testy note in his grating voice, "means many things. What I refer to is its primary power, the ability to foresee the future, a gift sought by many in the Olden Time."

Not by me, MacDougall thought. A power he wouldn't accept under any circumstances. Unless the future could be changed, the knowledge would be a curse. And if the future *could* be changed, it would not be foretelling. He was glad he had bypassed this visit, thanks to Amaruduk.

"Interesting," his double observed noncommittally.

"I use incense and its smoke images with the veil of water, though other helps produce the same results. Turn about and face the wall." As they did so Alan saw something that had not been there when he first viewed the room.

Covering most of the wall stood what appeared to be a great, square, shimmering screen of crystal. On closer inspection MacDougall realized it was a sort of self-contained waterfall, a sheet of water falling like a veil over a mirror into a metal trough, evidently to be circulated in a continuous flow. Now from behind the Diviner came a beam of light, sending its rays through the tendrils of swirling smoke, projecting their shadows on the unusual screen.

Slowly Ela Armida drew his hands from beneath the folds of his purple robe, long, thin fingers stiffly outstretched. They entered the writhing white and gray and black smoke, weaving gently back and forth like sentient, disembodied things. The lighter skin of the palms and the inner surface of the fingers shone intermittently through the smoky mist. The Diviner spoke, little more than a whisper.

"Reveal now, god of the veil, what lies in this one's future."

An image began forming on the sheet of water, dim at first, misty and wavering, then growing clear. Startled, incredulous, MacDougall recognized the scene.

It was a view of a great, square gray building with a polished golden dome, a kind of Temple, the companion of the tipsy ziggurat that he had visited in Marduk, the home of Amaruduk. The scene changed to an interior view of the Temple, the long corridor encircling the outer walls, holding tier upon tier of transparent oblong boxes like crystal coffins, each holding the rigid form of a gray-clad Annunaki.

There was sudden motion, a procession of the Igiggi, the servants of Marduk, bearing another crystal box holding a still form. It was instantly recognizable to MacDougall, as it must have been to the two watchers, as Amaruduk.

There came a furious exclamation from Alan's double; and at the same instant the scene vanished to be replaced by a glowing image of Ahriman, glaring out of the water veil. The gem-blue eyes held hypnotically for silent moments, then the too-red lips moved, and the harsh voice of Lucifer's lieutenant intoned, "That, my ambitious Amaruduk, will be your future until the Master releases you. And your mischief-making ends *now*!"

With the words the water veil became a glimmering imageless sheet; and the Diviner Ela Armida was alone.

Alan MacDougall cut off the mental view, at the same instant returning himself and his horse to visibility. A second later Taliesin followed.

"No reason for concealment," he said grimly. "It appears that Ahriman is fully aware of what's happening." Shaken by the sudden climax, he added bitterly, "The devil—and I mean Ahriman—is calling all the shots."

The Bard looked at MacDougall doubtfully. "You don't mean you think he *is* Lucifer?"

"No—I know better—but he's as close to the real thing as I ever want to get."

They rode in silence for mile upon mile, each occupied with his own thoughts. Alan spoke only once.

"That last vision on Ela Armida's water veil must have been quite a shock to the Diviner as well as to Amaruduk. As it was to me. A very logical punishment for what he did." After a long silence: "Takes a lot of courage to defy Ahriman—as I am going to. I've done it before and I'll do it again."

"Never forget it," Taliesin said solemnly.

With one stop en route to rest the horses and to drink from—and empty—their canteens, they finally saw white-walled Cuchulainn ahead. Having ridden in a hundred-mile circle and approaching from the opposite side of the city, they passed along the edge of the clump of trees MacDougall had noticed in the model. It was far larger than he had visualized it, dark and forbidding, almost as closely grown as the strange woodland surrounding the portal into Scath. After passing it they rode along the edge of the carefully tailored park that held the entrance into Avilion.

And, Alan thought longingly, the way out.

Their approach was observed by white-robed guards who opened the city gates. They waited while a horseman was summoned to lead them through the streets. Finally they dismounted at the castle exit from which they had left. Here, too, they were met by guards who told them King Cuchulainn had left instructions that they be taken to their rooms to await dinner.

When the door of his Spartan chamber closed behind him, Alan hung up his cape and sword, then stretched out on his back on the bed. Suddenly he realized he was tired, physically and mentally played out. Nervous energy had kept him going. It was not merely the weariness brought on by the hours on horseback; indeed, that was a minor part of it. Rather, it was the drain on his strength by the succession of unnatural experiences he had been forced to undergo.

He stretched and tried to relax, his eyes on the glowing ceiling. Darkness might help; and with the thought the light was gone. Now if he could stop thinking—but despite himself his mind continued working. In memory he again sat with Ahriman in the Golden Tower. The Persian had mentioned instant transfer, adding quite casually "which in due course you will master." As he had. Ahriman had said, "You will know what people are thinking before they speak . . . whether they are lying or telling the truth." And now he had that ability.

He thought of the other powers he had gained, particularly that uncanny flight of his spirit from his own body. And as he summarized the abilities that were definitely supernatural, a chill coursed through him. He had sought none of this; it had been forced upon him against his will. Not quite true, Alan, he thought. He certainly hadn't fought against this educational tour. So why should he think he could successfully resist Lucifer's larger plans for him in his own world?

As he lay staring into the darkness, images began to form in his mind's eyes, a hodge-podge of grotesquerie, its ingredients fragments of memories out of all that had happened since his initial entry into Tartarus. He saw and heard again the pack of changeling wolves pursuing him through blinding fog; he sensed the swirling, intertwining clouds of whispering specters in the dark abyss of Annwn; the gyrating Daughters of Lilith in the Grove of Spirits in Scath; and the almost-seen shapes gibbering around him as his spirit floated free, lost in limbo. Then a face appeared, distorted, gloating Semias the Druid who had just thrust a dagger into his back.

In near panic MacDougall sought light, staring at the ceiling. Obediently the glow reappeared, and Alan sat up, mentally berating himself. Snap out of it, Mac, you idiot. Afraid of the dark!

Another thought formed, not his own. A word came from Taliesin in the next room.

"Alan, do not blame yourself for being disturbed by memories of all you've experienced. Anything else would be abnormal." Evidently sensing MacDougall's surprise at this awareness of his imaginings, he added, *"You are so accustomed to sharing your thinking, you do it subconsciously. Sorry for my intrusion."*

"No intrusion, my friend. And thanks."

Closing his eyes, MacDougall thought of the most fascinating part of his visits to the four cities, the time spent in the hexagonal chamber of Wu Chuangtse. He thought of the fanciful statement the Chinese Sage had made concerning the six carved jade panels that made up the walls: "If you were to spend time with me, we might venture into the depths of one or more of the Six Worlds, each a marvel in itself. Most of its wonders are concealed behind the surface."

Alan tried to picture the black jade bas-relief on which he had fixed his attention, the tiny cottage by the lacy waterfall, clinging to a steep cliffside; then suddenly he remembered he need not be content with visualization. He should be able to *see* the panel itself. And so it proved.

The chamber was empty, but the usual glow came from the ceiling. He saw the tiny cottage, half hidden in mist, and though the idea seemed absurd he tried to look beyond the cloud. He thought he caught a glimpse of movement on a path beside the cottage; it blurred, became a thing of uncertain shape, trailing into nothingness . . . MacDougall dozed.

A rap on his door brought him instantly awake. A voice, one of the guards, announced, "You are summoned by King Cuchulainn to dine."

"In a moment," he responded, sitting up and stretching. He had no idea how long he had slept, but he felt alert and rested. He headed for the necessary room. A short time later, minus cape and canteen, but with his sword at his side, he went into the hallway.

The Bard was waiting with the usual two guards. After exchanging greetings they were led through the marble corridors, up a stairway to the hall in which Alan had dined before his session with Ahriman. This time the table was set for thirteen, six on each side and the King at the head. All the others were there, already seated, the same group as before, Taliesin making the thirteenth. As the visitors entered, all stood up, including Cuchulainn. Alan was ushered to a seat at the King's right hand and the Bard across from him on the left. At a signal all sat.

"Welcome, travelers," Cuchulainn said heartily. "You, Alan MacDougall, have met all of us, and you, Taliesin, as we converse, will become acquainted with those you have not met. We are anxious to hear of your visits to the other cities, all of which have been barred to us, as I suppose you are aware. But first we eat."

At his signal servers entered with platters of steaming and aromatic food, the menu similar to the earlier dinner, and equally tasty. After all had eaten to repletion and the evidence had been removed, the questioning began. Cuchulainn started it, but the others soon joined in, all most curious about areas closed to them for fourteen centuries. Both MacDougall and Taliesin were besieged with questions; and it quickly became evident that none had ever seen anything within the outer walls of any of the other cities.

Alan answered freely except when questions touched on the purpose of his visits. Most of the queries grew out of the specific activities of the inquirer. The Druids, Cathbad and Broichan, were interested in religion and magic; Laegaire and Conall, comrades-in-arms of Cuchulainn in the Olden Times, were interested in weaponry and military organization, as was Artur, Captain of the Guard. Hagith the Tormentor asked few questions and these few Alan ignored.

The reaction of the two women, Eimher the Queen and Scathach, finally registered on Alan's awareness. For obvious reasons neither had mentioned their visits, and neither had asked many questions. But during the entire session they had their eyes riveted on MacDougall, and there was poorly concealed admiration, even adulation, on their faces. It was actually embarrassing. The King, it seemed, was too occupied with his own inquiry to notice.

After a time all ground seemed to have been covered; then Cuchulainn, who had not forgotten the Bard's statement about his passing through the Other World, asked the Bard for details. Scathach, of course, had long since told of what she had seen inside the tower. When Taliesin described his venture out of the tower into the Highland air, describing what he saw, he had the eager, breathless attention of everyone. But his emphasis on the shortness of the time he dared stay, and the penalty that would follow violation of the limit, put gloom on every face. On this note the session ended.

Back in his room, MacDougall crossed to the window and stared over the city. He saw little, his mind centered on one individual, Ahriman. The questions he had answered, the details brought to mind, emphasized again and again the presence of Lucifer's lieutenant. At this very moment there was near certainty that he was being observed, if not by the Persian himself, by one of his demonic helpers.

There was only one bright spot—his thoughts were still his own. Or were they? What of the armlet, the constant presence of Enki and Inanna? Could he in truth keep his thoughts from them even with conscious effort? He could not be sure. They had always expressed scorn for Ahriman; but they, too, were fallen angels.

A mental word from Taliesin interrupted his gloomy soliloquy. *"A very interesting group, Alan. I found Myrddn and Artur especially fascinating in light of what I have read in your copy of that book,* Mythology of the British Islands. *A great mass of mythology seems to have been built up around two figures, Merlin the Magician and a King Arthur. Yet the two at the dinner are the only ones from the Olden Times with the proper names; and Artur certainly was never a king. As for the Round Table and the Holy Grail—"* The thought broke off.

"I sense that you are deep in thought, and I interrupt. My apologies. It is sleep-time, and I shall do so."

MacDougall responded earnestly, *"Thanks for the interruption. My thoughts were of Ahriman and his constant presence. Depressing and pointless thinking. I appreciate your bringing me out of it. I believe I'll prepare for bed myself. Sleep well."*

Rapidly Alan stripped, tossing his clothes on the bed. A cold shower might bring him out of his blue funk. Before stepping into the bath he held out his right arm and gazed savagely at the golden armlet. As always he had to admire the fantastic workmanship, the twin heads of the coiled serpent with their gem eyes and ruby tongues, but it was nonetheless infuriating. This was at the heart of all his troubles. Damn you, he thought.

Came a silent reply from the serpent-god. "Not our fault, Alan. We merely obey the commands of the Master."

With a grimace MacDougall stepped under the primitive faucet. The chill stream diverted his attention, and a thorough lathering with a bar of motel soap drawn from one of his numerous pockets, followed by a brisk rubdown with a towel from the same source, brought him under full self-control. As he dressed he realized that sleep was far away.

No more moping, he thought as he sank to a seat on the single chair. What was the next development? That, he realized with annoyance, was up to Ahriman. Or was it?

He remembered a fleeting thought he had entertained at the start of his visits to the four cities—go around the circle, then find the portal and return to his own world! If only he had remembered to mark the spot; but even without marking it could be found.

MacDougall hesitated. What good would it do? He'd still be stuck with the armlet. But at least it would scramble Ahriman's plans for a while. And the means was at hand with his mastery of instant transfer. One detail first, the door. A thought to Enki, and it was locked. He stood up, strapped on his sword and canteen, then flung his cape over his shoulders. Should he tell Taliesin? Maybe just before he left Avilion.

He visualized the lawn outside the gazebo where he and the Bard had stood when they first saw the skeletal, starved victim of Hagith the Tormentor, spread-eagled on the floor. Better invisible, he thought at the last moment, vanishing. He concentrated on the combination of levitation and mental flight; felt breathless movement; and the aurora shimmered overhead. He had landed a few feet away from the marble structure. All signs of the monstrous torturing had disappeared, the floor bare.

He turned away facing down the gradual slope, his heartbeat quickening. The Gate should be somewhere to his left and farther down hill. Not a great distance, else they could not have heard the weak cry of the dying man. Slowly he moved in what he thought must be the right direction, intently scanning the slope, trying to remember each tree and flowering bush. No luck on his first try.

He tried again, seeking the wraithlike outline of the circular, yard-wide opening between the worlds. There should also be the ghostly suggestion of the ancient stone tower as he had observed it on his first entry into Tartarus.

Finally, after crossing and recrossing all of the area that could possibly be involved, he stood stock-still and closed his eyes, trying to picture the precise setting when the Bard had become visible and had greeted him. The white path leading up to the castle of Cuchulainn, the scattering of gazebos, the nearest tree under which Taliesin had been sitting. The scene formed clearly in his memory, a picture he was certain was accurate.

Everything fell into place. He should be standing on the very spot! He opened his eyes but could see no sign of the Gate. He grasped the armlet.

"Lord Enki and Lady Inanna, I am at my wits' end. I am seeking the portal and cannot find it."

"Nor will you," they replied. "We, too, have been searching; and there can be only one answer. The Gate has been closed!"

CHAPTER 8

Revelations

Alan MacDougall stared through narrowed eyelids at the castle of Cuchulainn, beautiful against the aurora. Unchanged from the moment he had first seen it through the fourth Gate, with its carefully landscaped lawn, bushes, and trees, it was the embodiment of tranquillity. There was no sound.

In contrast his thoughts were in utter turmoil, a confusion of anger, frustration, and helplessness. Why, why had he closed the other Gates? There was no way out. He was trapped! Who could have closed the portal? Certainly not Cinel Loarn or any of the Sidhe; and no one else could have. Except Ahriman. Either from the inside, though that seemed unlikely; or more probably through a fellow demon in the Other World. Logical. Through one such had come the attack on him in the Cameron home; and another had served as his guide during the mental tour of the world.

Alan inhaled deeply a half-dozen times, calming himself, then transferred back to his room. He flung aside his cape, sword, and boots and stretched out on the bed.

He dimmed the ceiling glow and tried to think rationally. No reason for panic. For the Persian to do what he planned, the Gate would have to be opened. And there was another possibility. His spirit out of his body could pass through the barrier into the Highland *broch*; and there was a chance that he could communicate with his brother Malcolm, now Cinel Loarn of the *Shee*. Anyway, what would his departure from Avilion have accomplished? Nothing beyond annoying Ahriman.

He began to feel better. He grimaced. He was glad he had said nothing to Taliesin about his intentions. And he wouldn't even mention it to Ahriman.

Abruptly he became aware of a faint glow on the bare wall above the head of the bed, and even as he swung to his feet he knew what he would see. The glow intensified, became brilliant, and a greatly enlarged image of the Persian looked down from the wall. There was an amused smile on his statuesque face as his deep, resonant voice spoke from the projection.

"I trust you enjoyed your stroll through the park. I have been told that a quiet walk helps to relax one and induce sleep, but you appear to be wide awake. I suggest that, though it is normally the time for rest, we sit down in the comfort of my quarters and talk. Taliesin is deep in slumber, so I think it would be rude to awaken him. We will be considering your visits to the four cities, and he would add little to the conversation." He waited for a response, but when none came he continued.

"You may wish to put your boots back on, even though the covering on my floors is thick and soft. Being well shod bolsters a man's morale."

Alan stared into the blue eyes of the image, then forced a sarcastic smile. "I'm inclined to tell you to go to Hell, but since we're already there, the directive would be rather pointless." He sat on the edge of the bed and drew on his boots. "And to say I don't want to go with you would be quite as pointless, since you'd simply take me by the scruff of my neck and place me where you wish." He bowed deeply. "Ready when you are."

In an instant MacDougall was again standing in a cylindrical room flooded with golden light, on a gold-colored rug. Unchanged were the furnishings and the blackness of starless space beyond the clear golden walls. He resisted an impulse to cross to the wall and look down again at the fantastic spectacle of the aurora seen from above.

At a gesture from the Persian he sank into one of the chairs.

"Wine?" Ahriman asked. At Alan's curt refusal he continued, "Then to business. We'll begin with the City of Cuchulainn."

MacDougall's brows rose in surprise. "Cuchulainn?"

"Yes. There was a twofold reason for the visits you made. One was for you to learn certain abilities from qualified teachers. This in part was accomplished. But perhaps equally important was your appraisal of some of the people you met. Hence my inclusion of the City of Cuchulainn."

"Why wasn't I told this?"

"Because I wanted your natural, uninfluenced opinion. Some of these, plus others, will be members of your staff when you assume your exalted position, when you become the Transcendental King."

Slowly MacDougall shook his head in mock sadness. "Here we go again," he lamented. "No amount of my protesting seems to do any good. You persist in your delusion no matter what I say. So let's take it from there. What do you want to know?"

"Simply your opinion of the people you met. You are observant, and people impress you favorably or unfavorably. You react strongly to some and weakly to others. If you were an employer and had a variety of positions to fill, would you hire certain individuals? Let us begin with Hagith."

"Hagith the Tormentor!" MacDougall almost shouted in his indignation. "He deserves to be squashed like any poisonous insect, and I would delight in the squashing."

Ahriman smiled faintly. "Yet he does his work well. Of course I knew how you felt about him. Seriously, let us begin with Cuchulainn himself."

MacDougall shrugged. Though it seemed meaningless, why not go along with the game?

"Actually, I know little about any of these people. From what I've seen I should say that Cuchulainn would qualify. I am influenced to a degree, of course, by what I know of his history in the Other World. The same can be said of his two chief aides, Laegaire and Conall. As for the two Druids, there are so many about on the other islands that to make a selection from among them would be most difficult. I know nothing about Myrddn, Artur, and Abred, and would not express an opinion."

"What about Eimher?"

Surprised, MacDougall asked, "You would consider women?"

"Why not? In many parts of the world women exert great power. To put men in women's bodies would create complicated psychological problems."

"In that case, Eimher is very lovely and, I suppose, is capable of doing what she wishes to do, but I can hardly see her in any responsible role. Perhaps I misjudge her since I don't really know her." After a pause he added, "What about Scathach?"

Ahriman frowned. "There is no question about her abilities, but as you know, she played a part in that stupid war with Amaruduk's awakened Sleepers. True, it was Ereshkigal who suggested an army of the dead, but Scathach cooperated. Punishment is inevitable. We will exclude Eimher and, obviously, Scathach. So for the present we have three from Cuchulainn.

"What about Magadha?"

Alan closed his eyes and pictured the leaders he had met in the Hindu city, four in all. "Under no circumstances could Despot Mihiragula be a possibility. I have mental reservations about Kalidasa the Poet, a schemer and a man to be watched. He might serve in a pinch. The King, Kumaragupta, impressed me very favorably. Varuna the Seer was quite impressive but obviously would not qualify because he is not a mortal."

"Let us include Kalidasa. Two more. What of Shenzhu?"

"I met only two of any stature. The Emperor Khau Ch'in Khih and the Sage Wu Chuangtse. I should say both are men of unusual ability."

Ahriman nodded. "And what of Atu, the city of the Egyptians?"

Vividly MacDougall recalled his visit to Atu where his lesson was to be possession, his spirit's ability to occupy another's body. "There are three there who might qualify if we include the Oracle, Hypatia. A brilliant woman, but I think primarily a scholar limited to her own field, philosophy. Horsaneb the Ruler is another story. A strong man, most impressive. And Shepsut the Priest should be useful."

"Two more," Ahriman commented. "I have other plans for Hypatia. Finally Axume, the city you did not enter. Too bad that Amaruduk decided to take your place. The gift of prophecy would have been most fitting in your arsenal of powers. And had you been permitted to have your own future foretold, you would have seen yourself in all your future glory."

Indeed, Alan thought, a vision of another link in the chain of his enslavement to the prophecy. He said aloud, "Though I did not enter Axume, I observed much. Both King Ezana and Ela Armida the Diviner appear to be quite capable men."

"Two more," Ahriman said. "Eleven in all, plus those you shall select from the other islands. Still others will be chosen from the five cities. I shall select these through my own observations over centuries. They, of course, will serve in lesser positions on your staff."

Frowning heavily, Alan MacDougall suddenly stood up and stared down at the lieutenant of Lucifer. "Will you tell me how all this makes any kind of sense? Five cities on this island, each containing a people of a different race. From these we have arbitrarily selected eleven to become members of my staff, so you say. To these will be added others you will select, plus still others from Scath, Ochren, and Tartarus. A total, shall we say, of thirty, or even fifty. This is assuming they are interested in becoming members of this mythical staff. Let's double the number—a hundred.

"To what end? Before these visits you arranged for my being shown a lot of the trouble spots of my world. And you informed me that I am to right the wrongs of ages. I have been called the Chosen One. Moments ago you referred to my future as the Transcendental King. And the hundred, presumably, are to be my royal retinue. Surely you have not forgotten that they cannot live in the Other World!''

Ahriman smiled blandly. "Nothing has been forgotten. Those chosen to assist you will be trained in the power you refused. They will be taught out-of-body flight, and they will master the art of possession. Can you imagine any of them refusing the opportunity to leave this monotonous existence for physical life, in positions of power, in the world from whence they came? There may be some but not many. There are capable teachers available as well as numerous subjects for practice; and no action will be taken until all is ready. Then suitable world leaders will be selected and one by one will be, shall we say, 'joined' by a member of your staff.''

While the Persian was speaking, Alan sank back into his chair, a hollow feeling in the pit of his stomach. What a horrible idea! And they planned to make him part of it. Worse! Its leader.

Ahriman's voice went on inexorably. "Now you can see why it was necessary for the Master to involve several of the races. A Caucasian does not think quite like a Chinese thinks, nor a native of India, nor an African, nor even like one of the peoples of the Near or Middle East. So representative races were chosen and kept in isolation so that no matter how long a period of time passed before the culmination of the plan, true representatives of the different peoples would be available.''

"But a hundred from this world, thirty of them leaders,'' MacDougall protested weakly, "even conceding that thirty key world leaders could be possessed and controlled—thirty would hardly control the world. There must be two hundred different countries.''

"No?" Ahriman's smile broadened, became genuinely amused. "The United States, the Soviet Union and its satellites, China, Japan, England, India, Canada, Germany, the rest of Europe, Korea—but why go on? Far less than thirty. In addition there are countries that are already under the Master's control through their present leadership. The one called Iran for example, formerly Persia. There are others.

"Or the leaders of world religions who could be possessed. The one at Rome; the famous television preachers with their legions of followers. All these under your guidance.

"I have not spoken of the thousands, the tens of thousands, waiting to enter the conflict at the proper moment." His eyes held MacDougall's with hypnotic intensity as he concluded triumphantly, "I refer to the Host, the multitude of dark angels, if you will, who follow the Master, the Lord of Light, and who are still on the Other Side!"

Alan felt a tightness in his throat, a mounting consternation. This was getting out of hand. Getting? Whom was he kidding? He swallowed hard, trying to conceal his trepidation. "With all that demonic power, why bother with me? Or with the others you speak of training? After all, I am a most unwilling participant. I'll be fighting your plan all the way."

Ahriman shook his head decisively. "It will not work with the Host alone. It has not in the past. Attempts have been made through the centuries with Lucifer's angels in full control and all have failed. The most recent occurred in your lifetime—a man named Hitler. It would be different if it were not for the Host who remain on the side of the Power, but there are such in great numbers, and they constantly oppose the army of the Master.

"No—this plan has been underway for fourteen centuries, and nothing can stop it now. And this time we will win."

"So *that* is the secret of the Scroll," MacDougall commented softly.

"Not in its entirety," Ahriman responded, smiling faintly. "In part—but there is more."

Again Alan MacDougall stood up, feeling drained, exhausted. By sheer willpower he remained calm, closing his mind against the fear that sought to overwhelm him. "Is there anything else you wish to discuss? I *am* tired."

"Nothing else at the moment. After you have slept and broken fast, we will consider and choose the rest of your assistants. I have issued instructions that you be returned to your room. Now!"

With the last word MacDougall sensed sudden indescribable flight; and he was standing beside his bed. He closed his eyes and stood there for dragging moments, trying to find a bright spot in the oppressive gloom, trying to see a way out of his dilemma. Never in his life had he been so shaken. Massive walls of blackness seemed to be closing in on him. Always before he had clung to a confidence in his ability to cope somehow with any circumstance, and when that wavered his Scot's stubbornness had exerted itself. Not this time.

The Persian had made wild statements before this, and he had been able to shrug them off. They had seemed so absurd, so farfetched, that he had been able to relegate them to an impossible future. But this seemed imminent, almost at hand. And there were no more Gates.

He flung himself across the bed, landing with an audible impact, rolled over on his back, and stared at the ceiling.

"*Alan—Alan MacDougall.*" The thought of Taliesin touched his mind. "*I heard sounds. You are back.*"

"Yes," Alan answered dully, "*I am back. But that's all that can be said.*"

There was deep concern in the Bard's words. "*I tried to reach you earlier and sensed that you were with Ahriman, so I waited. You seem troubled. Is there anything you wish to tell me?*"

Suddenly it seemed to MacDougall he was bursting with the burden of what he had learned. He *had* to unload. Starting with his attempt to leave Avilion, thwarted by the closed Gate, he told all that had happened. Etched in his mind as it was, he missed nothing. At the conclusion of his recital the Bard spoke.

"From my reading of the Scroll I had a general idea that something of this sort would happen. I can recall the very words, and I quote them:

" 'The One Who Shall Come, the Chosen One, shall be of the line of a king whose reign will end, through the seed of a serf. He will bear the jewel of the golden serpent. His day will be a day when the wonders of man's creation will far outshine the wonders of the gods, my faithful Host. In that day this One-Who-Shall-Come will lead a band of his choosing from among my servants who were dead yet live, from a world of my creation through a hidden portal, into the land claimed by the Enemy. They will possess the rulers of nations.'

"There is more, but this is all that applies at the moment. Yet despite all this, Alan, don't give up. I repeat it—don't give up!"

"Oh, I won't quit," MacDougall answered doggedly. *"I'm too stubborn for that. But I must say I don't see any great cause for optimism. The deck seems stacked against me, with Ahriman holding all the winning cards."*

"I quote another prophecy." Taliesin seemed somewhat hesitant. *"You recall during our ride to Manannan's castle on Ochren you gave me two books from the Other World, one the Bible. I have learned to read these, as you know. In the Bible in a section called The Revelation, I came upon a passage that I found very interesting. An unusual section about future things, hard to understand; but this statement was very clear. Again I quote as it is written."* He reverted to English with a strange, archaic accent.

" 'And I saw an angel come down from heaven, having the key of the bottomless pit and a great chain in his hand. And he laid hold on the dragon, that old serpent, which is the Devil, and Satan, and bound him a thousand years, and cast him into the bottomless pit, and shut him up, and set a seal upon him, that he should deceive the nations no more.'

"When this will happen I do not know, but that it will

happen I am convinced. Much of the rest of the book I know to be true from my own observation during the ages. So take heart, Alan. The Dark One is vulnerable, hence so must Ahriman be vulnerable.''

Strangely relieved, though he could not have told why, MacDougall said fervently, *"Thank you, my friend. Perhaps now I can sleep.''*

As before, Alan was awakened by a rap on his door and a summons to breakfast. He was surprised at how soundly he had slept, though he was not fully rested. In the moments before arising he decided on his course of action for the day—if day it could be called. To resist openly would be futile, accomplishing nothing. Ahriman would go ahead with his plan regardless of what Alan did. So he would appear to acquiesce—up to a point. He would have nothing to do with possession.

A hasty toilet was followed by a hearty meal with Taliesin, the two Druids, and Scathach, the others occupied elsewhere. While they ate a messenger came with an invitation from Cuchulainn for the Bard to join him after breakfast to talk about old times. A ploy of the Persian's, Alan was certain, to get Taliesin out of the way. During this interruption the Sorceress had asked Alan to join her for a stroll; he had graciously declined, citing a scheduled meeting with Ahriman. At the conclusion of the meal one of the guards led the Bard away while the other conducted Alan to his room.

Almost immediately upon his return, a full-length image of Ahriman appeared on the wall, extending casual greetings. He was dressed most impressively in full-cut pantaloons of silvery silk, gathered at the ankles, a vesture of crimson, and a black, gold-embroidered cape. His jewels for the occasion were black pearls. Moments later MacDougall was standing in the Persian's presence.

They were not in the room at the top of the tower. Instead, they were in a moderate-size auditorium complete with platform and a semicircle of seats, strangely like a conventional concert hall. It was on a level below

Ahriman's quarters, the familiar aurora visible through the walls.

They were on the platform where two chairs had been set, side by side. Not ordinary chairs, of course. Chairs of gold that might have come from an Egyptian tomb. Seating himself, Ahriman motioned for Alan to join him. They were facing the rows of empty seats.

"We will have company very soon," the Persian said. "Visitors familiar to you."

Waiting, MacDougall wondered at the anomaly of an auditorium in a Tower that for more than a millennium had been unseen by any of the human dwellers on the island. An auditorium without a doorway or visible means of entrance. He thought of the serpent-gods. Odd. Less and less he was involving them in his affairs. He asked Enki about the reason for an auditorium where no people assembled.

"No *people*" came the response. "But many conclaves have been held here, gathering of the Host from this and other spaces in Lucifer's vast domain."

Inanna added reprovingly, "Always in your thinking, Alan MacDougall, you limit the scope and power of the Lord of Light. Know that his activities are many and his Host without number."

Alan felt a momentary chill. Exaggerated, of course, but how could he resist a being like that? He checked the thought as the promised "company" started arriving.

Manannan, god of the sea, was the first to appear. He materialized out of thin air, standing at the center of the first row. Moments later Nuada followed, placed at his right side. Beli came next at his left, then alternately came the rest of the nine Alan had seen riding across the plain toward Axume. Their expressions without exception were a mixture of defiance, concern, and surprise at the sight of MacDougall. None spoke.

Ahriman inspected the lineup, his gaze moving from one end to the other, then finally he spoke.

"Gentlemen, be seated." As they obeyed, he continued, "Thank you. As you may have surmised, I was responsible for the temporary delay in your reaching your destination. Amaruduk, with whom some of you have had earlier dealings, saw fit to interfere with my schedule; he has been dealt with. I strongly recommend that you avoid similar errors in judgment.

"You have noticed, I am sure, that you have not been disarmed. Does this mean I trust you? Hardly. Even now some of you are considering the possibilities of a surprise attack, especially on Alan MacDougall, the object of your long-standing hatred. He is seated, his weapon is in its scabbard, and I am not armed, but something restrains you. Do I hold your powers so lightly that I fear nothing you can do? Precisely. And lest you think I speak empty words, look!"

At his exclamation there suddenly appeared a solid line of archers with drawn bows, steel-tipped arrows in place, completely encircling the chamber. At a wave of Ahriman's hand they vanished.

"And that," the Persian said quietly, "was not an illusion. My archers are very real. At my word any or all of you will relinquish the life in your present body; and you, Balor, have gone to great lengths to acquire the form you now possess."

Even this he knew, MacDougall thought glumly; the god of the Fomorians dispossessing the spirit of a newly animated Norseman to acquire his body. Ahriman had continued speaking.

"I appreciate your coming directly to the Tower. Your decision to avoid the walled cities and come to what you decided was the center of authority was wise, avoiding the useless expenditure of time and effort, not to mention conflict. I admit you were aided in reaching your decision by my minions.

"Why have you been brought here?" Ahriman paused, then continued with great deliberation, "To be offered the opportunity to return to the Other World in positions of power. If you meet the qualifications."

There had been little change of expression on the faces of the nine since their arrival, only a grim and stolid defiance greeting all that had gone before. But with his last statement, sudden intense interest and awakening hope, mingled with doubt and skepticism, appeared on every face.

Beli's deep voice rumbled, "And how do we qualify?"

"Initially, Alan MacDougall does the selecting," the Persian began, to be interrupted by a roar of derision from Pryderi, the jailer of Ochren.

"MacDougall! I will have nothing to do with anything in which he has a part."

Ahriman glanced toward Alan. "Your view?"

"My position exactly, reversed of course."

The Persian raised a hand—and the jailer's chair was vacant. "I have returned him to his skeletal prison in underground Ochren." He spoke to Alan. "Are there others completely unsuitable?"

"Without question Balor. Unworthy of any trust, his hatred for me is as great as that of Pryderi."

Again Ahriman raised his hand, and Balor vanished. "He is now back in his quarters in Murias." To MacDougall: "Are there still others who should be eliminated?"

Alan looked hard at Beli who glared back defiantly; then he turned his attention to Manannan. The god of the sea kept his face expressionless.

"I know nothing about the four Druids." Alan hesitated. Should he mention the absent Mathonwy? But Ahriman must know already. "The other three might well fit into your plans."

Ahriman looked at Alan quizzically. "I seem to recall some violent attacks on you by Beli in Amaruduk's realm, and before that in his own castle. Nuada also was involved in the Marduk adventure. Despite this you would trust them?"

MacDougall shrugged. "Beli, unlike Pryderi and Balor, is a man of reason. I think, when he is presented with all the facts, he will decide it is in his own best interests to cooperate. And he has great abilities. As for Nuada, he should be an asset to the enterprise, and I would not question his loyalties. Manannan, on the other hand, may well reject the whole idea. I doubt that he will leave his horse, Silver Mane, or his coracle, *Wave Sweeper*. If he were to do so he could serve well.''

Ahriman smiled cryptically. ''Time will tell. At the moment his mind is busy with—other things.'' To the Druids he said, ''You will move to my left and to the rear.'' And to Beli, Nuada, and Manannan: ''You will move to the rear on the far right. This is to make room for others.'' While they followed instructions, Beli obeying with evident reluctance, the Persian spoke to MacDougall.

''Now I ask you to consider those you remember from your visits to Tartarus and Ochren who might fit into the plan.''

Alan frowned in thought. ''As for Tartarus,'' he said finally, ''I see no reason why the others of the *Tuatha de Danann* could not be included—Danu the Mother, Dagda, Gobniu the Smith, Credne, master bronze worker, and the Physician Diancecht. I know little about Diancecht, but he should warrant consideration. Ochren is another matter. Perhaps Amaethon who, I believe, is Nuada's son, and the Roman, Titus Flavius Sabinus Vespasianus, to give him his full name. A third possibility might be the Seer Simon Magus.'' He added, ''I know little about any of them. As I know little about the many Druids on both islands, gifted men of magic, some of whom might be worthwhile additions.''

Ahriman nodded approvingly. ''Your choices coincide with mine. Simon Magus? He could be useful in Israel. As for the Druids, their selection will be the task of Taliesin. Though he is intimately acquainted only with those of Tartarus, he knows their kind very well. What of Scath?''

MacDougall was surprised. ''I had not thought of anyone except Scathach from the third island, and she has been eliminated. The Sorceress did not permit others to attain prominence. Unless you refer to the three Daughters of Calatin. ''But they . . .'' He hesitated.

''Are very strange,'' Ahriman concluded. ''However, they are gifted and quite intelligent. They could be very useful. And have you considered Brendah?''

"Brendah!" He pictured the Amazon now occupying Scathach's apartment. He could not see her as a world leader. Nor would she be interested. He shook his head. "I do not think she would be suitable." Another thought followed. Careful, Alan—you're taking this thing seriously.

"And of course," Ahriman added, "the Druidesses will be examined for capable ones among them." He stood up. "Even as we spoke, all those we named have been addressed by my image, preparing them for their transfer here. Even now they begin to appear."

One by one, starting with Danu the Mother, the five members of the family, the *Tuatha de Danann*, materialized before the front seats. Placed, Alan thought, with precision by the manipulators of Ahriman's forceps. The expression of each was a study. It was evident that none had been given time to prepare for the visit, both Gobniu and Credne in their blackened leather aprons and with toil-begrimed hands. The smith, in no way awed by the circumstances, grinned broadly and waved to Alan.

Following those from Tartarus came the three from Ochren, Simon Magus, Amaethon, and Caesar Vespasianus, the latter failing miserably in his effort to look the part of a Roman Emperor.

As soon as these were seated, the first of the Daughters appeared, to be followed immediately by the other two. For the first time Alan saw uncertainty on their ugly, witchlike faces, evidence of a situation beyond their experience. At a motion from Ahriman they seated themselves.

"Welcome." The Persian stood up, greeting the new arrivals. "Please find seats farther back. One more group will appear. When all have assembled, everything will be explained completely, and you will realize the importance of this occasion."

With the newcomers seated about halfway back in separate groups, the Persian also resumed his seat, then said, "All those who will now appear are from this island, Avilion. Because they are strangers to many of you, or in some cases all of you, at least in this life, I will introduce them as they join us.''

He raised a hand, and Cuchulainn materialized before them, facing the watchers. ''This is Cuchulainn, god of the sun in his own land in the Olden Time. Now he is ruler of the city that bears his name.'' Laegaire the Battle Winner and Conall the Victorious followed, presented as Cuchulainn's chief aides. ''Others will be chosen from the marble city.''

Ahriman continued, ''There are two from the City of Magadha, at one time dwellers in a land unknown to any of you, now called India. The first is King Kumaragupta, a ruler in the other life and now ruler of Magadha. The second is Kalidasa, a poet, but a man with other skills, especially in the field of diplomacy.'' They appeared in turn.

''Two also come from the city of Shenzhu; its dwellers a people like the Ch'in from Gorias on Tartarus. One is the ruler, Khau Ch'in Khih, who was an emperor of great power in the Olden Days; and the other, the sage Wu Chuangtse.'' At mention of his name, each appeared, a look of intense curiosity on the latter's face.

''The fourth city to be represented is Atu, named for a city in the ancient religion of the people of Egypt. For them Atu was the chief city of the land of the dead. The first from Egypt is Horsaneb, its ruler, and the second is Shepsut, Priest of Thoth.'' With their appearing, Ahriman concluded, summoning the final arrivals.

''Finally the fifth city, Axume, where dwell the dark people of a great land now called Africa. Here also are two, King Ezana and the Diviner, Ela Armida.'' As they materialized, MacDougall heard the first audible reaction from those of the other islands. Most had never seen a black man, and these two were very dark.

As the last group seated themselves, Ahriman stood up, moved to the front of the dais, and stood surveying the gathering. All eyes were fixed on him, an impressive figure in his red and gold garments, and an expectant hush fell over the gathering. A strange assemblage, Alan thought, with the varied and colorful dress of the several groups, especially those from the five cities of Avilion. The moments dragged by; and suddenly MacDougall blinked. Ahriman, it seemed, was emitting a faint glow like that of his projections. This bit of showmanship did not pass unnoticed, as the rapt expressions on the watchers' faces revealed. At last he spoke.

"There are twenty-five of you, and at the moment the four Druids. You Druids will withdraw, although some or perhaps all of you may rejoin us later." As if his words were a signal, one by one the four vanished. "You who remain," he continued, "have been chosen to play important roles in what may well be the greatest drama in the history of your race; indeed, your world." He reached into a recess under his cape and produced the vellum Scroll that Alan recognized instantly, the key, probably, to all that had happened on the four islands.

"MacDougall found this Scroll in an ancient stone tower in the Highlands of Alba or Scotia, now Scotland, in the Other World. It had been there in the keeping of a Celtic Druid for fourteen centuries, waiting for his arrival. It contains a prophecy written by the hand of Lucifer, the Master, the Lord of Light, may he be glorified. It tells in part of the creation of these islands in a realm parallel with the one from which all of you came. It speaks in detail of the early dwellers on the island MacDougall calls Tartarus, the Daughters of Lilith for whom the four cities were created. Though not on the Scroll, for your information I add that their spirits later were transferred to the island known as Scath or Marduk, depending upon which half of the island you visit. Here, too, at the beginning were placed Amaruduk and his followers; and in the top of a tower, later to house Scathach, one not mortal, bound in a stone image. All of these, not including the Daughters of Lilith, had displeased the Master.

"Later to the island called Ochren, into an undersea city named Lochlann, the Master sent the Fomorians who, in your time, for reasons that pleased the Lord of Light, were moved to Murias, one of the four cities of Tartarus.

"On two of the islands, Tartarus and this one, Avilion, were erected the Golden Towers, for my purposes and my dwellings. These were invisible and forbidden until I chose to reveal them. It should be obvious that you are in a chamber of one of those Towers.

"Later, much later, and all from the same time period, spanning a few centuries and according to the plan of Lucifer, came the Celts and Norsemen, the Ch'in and the Trolls, to Tartarus; more of the Britons and some from Rome to Ochren; the women under Scathach from Britain and Scotia to Scath; and to Avilion those you have seen, the five peoples of this island."

Ahriman halted and let his gaze wander over his audience. "Why have I told you all this? So you may fully appreciate the predictive powers of our Master. For it was in the time of the Daughters of Lilith that the prophecy of the Scroll was written. The Master, foreseeing events far in the future, set into motion happenings that would culminate in the experience in which you will participate. Mind you, at that time Man had not yet been placed upon the Earth!"

Alan MacDougall, listening, remembering the passage Taliesin had quoted from the Scroll, felt his heart sink. He tried to tell himself it was all coincidence—had to be—or it was a pack of lies. The Scroll older than the human race! Absurd. It showed no sign of such great age, the parchment flexible, with no sign of cracking. Yet even at fourteen centuries, how could it say what it had? But Ahriman had *not* said all this was on the Scroll. Clever deception by his emissary of Satan, the Father of lies. And how could what had been written be called prediction when the supposed prophet could control events to bring about what he had foreseen? Somehow this thought did not ease his mind in any way. When the Persian continued, Alan tried to set his face into an expressionless mask. His beard helped.

"When the peoples, according to the Great Plan, were placed on each island in new bodies fashioned by the Master, in the minds of the leaders was implanted knowledge of a portal, a Gate that led into the Other World.

Also in every mind was an awareness, a fear, of certain forbidden areas that dared not be entered. At the same time, in the stone tower in the Highlands the Gates were created, visible in this realm only to the wearer of the armlet and to me, the Master's mouthpiece. In the Other World, beside the Chosen One, the sight was given to certain others because of help they would afford him.

"The Scroll tells of One to Come, to enter this world through a portal, one wearing an armlet of gold fashioned in the form of a two-headed serpent, one who could enter and leave at will. Foreseen in a time long before the tower in the Highlands had been thought of; indeed, before the ancestors of its builders were born. This One would be the Chosen One of Lucifer who would lead in the deliverance of Man from himself. And this One is Alan MacDougall.

"He will come from a royal line, so declares the Scroll; and you from Tartarus know that MacDougall sat on the Stone of Fal and it cried out, thus proving his kingly descent. He will have the power to take with him into the Other World those whom he selects, though your present bodies can survive there for only a short time. This has been called the jest of Lucifer; but its purpose was *not* to trick the unwary into dissolution. The select few will be able to survive long enough to fulfill their mission—the possession of world leaders from peoples and nations compatible with your own origin.

"MacDougall has passed through the four portals and has faced the tests of the four islands. This, too, was predicted. He was left largely to his own devices, with some help from the gods imprisoned in his armlet. He received help only when he requested it, learning by his mistakes, gaining powers and abilities that now in total surpass those of any of you. During these visits he met you and sometimes fought you, but this was all according to plan. You are here because he chose you."

Ahriman unrolled a section of the parchment, letting it curl at the open end, scanning the writings as they passed before him.

"There is more that is foretold on the Scroll, details

you would find quite interesting. I could tell you of Volmar the Saxon serf who was the bastard son of a king, and MacDougall's ancestor. I could tell you of the ancient gods, Inanna and Enki and Ereshkigal, all of whom played a major part in your leader's preparation, but this knowledge is unnecessary for the performance of your assigned tasks." He rerolled the Scroll and thrust it inside his cape. Sharply a thought struck MacDougall. As before, Ahriman did *not* say the references to Vollmar and the others came from the Scroll; only that he could tell them, suggesting by his actions that they were recorded in the prophecy!

"Why should you follow MacDougall and do his bidding in the Other World? First, because the Master has decreed it. Second, because it will permit your escape from the endless monotony of this existence. And third"—Ahriman looked squarely into the face of Beli—"because you will be facing the greatest challenge of your lives in either world.

"Properly trained, fully prepared, you will be required to enter and control the body and mind of strong, capable people, men and women who are leaders of nations or religions or societies. It will be necessary for you to share with yet control those personalities so that they may continue to perform their normal functions while you adjust to a different day and different conditions, guided, of course, by Alan MacDougall. In time, when you have mastered your tasks, possession may become complete with you discarding, driving out, the spirit of your host—but this may not be done in haste.

"Are there any questions? Now is the time to ask—or withdraw, if that is your wish."

Alan had sat through Ahriman's speech with what he hoped was a poker face; but his mind was an arena of tumultuous thoughts and emotions. Helplessness mingled with growing wonder at the revelations he had heard; but above all rose a mounting wrath at the presumptions of Ahriman, taking his acquiescence as a matter of course. He was about to spring to his feet and flatly refuse to participate any further when Manannan stood up. There was a fanatical glare in the sea god's eyes. His deep voice rang out strongly.

"I will have nothing to do with this wild scheme. I will not leave my horse, Silver Mane, nor my coracle, *Wave Sweeper*, nor will I serve MacDougall. He dared to make off with my ship and has crossed me too often. I will oppose him in anything he attempts." A note of triumph entered his voice. "And because you, too, Ahriman, thought so little of my powers as god of the sea, daring to strand *Wave Sweeper* in the midst of the waters, even as I speak a fleet of thirty ships created by my magic, working through Mathonwy my Druid Master and his thirty Druids, is landing on the shores of Avilion. And they bring the army of Murias, the savage Fomorians, to attack your walled cities—and, victorious, the Golden Tower itself!"

CHAPTER 9

Invasion

Ahriman drew himself up to his full height; and Alan saw
his fists clench at his sides. He could see little of the
Persian's face, but he could picture its distortion as it
seemed to radiate diabolic fury.

"You dare to defy me!" Ahriman inhaled deeply, as
if striving for self-control. "You with your meager magic
and your futile attempts to deceive me. Think you I was
unaware of Mathonwy's disappearance from your coracle? It amused me to wait and learn what you and Amaruduk had devised. I am no longer entertained. Now you
shall feel the weight of my judgment. I have already dealt
with Amaruduk—" The Persian broke off in incredulous
surprise.

Manannan had vanished. MacDougall stared intently
at the vacant space, as did all in the room. Not invisible;
the sea-god was not there. He had evidently transferred
himself elsewhere—but, Alan remembered, he had lost
that power. Someone else must have whisked him
away. Alan glanced at Nuada, Beli, and the other Celtic
gods, but all appeared equally surprised at the vanish-

ment. Probably the work of Amaruduk, even if Ahriman, apparently, had removed him from action during his impersonation of Alan in Axume.

"The fool!" the Persian rasped. "He cannot hope to elude me. In moments—" He halted, apparently listening. "Impossible!" The word seemed torn from him. "How *could* he escape? Bunglers! I will join you."

After a momentary struggle for control, Ahriman again his imperturbable self, scanned his audience. "This minor problem will be cleared up quickly, after which preparation will continue. You from the other islands will be placed in comfortable rooms here in my Tower. You will have ample time to consider my offer, and if you wish to discuss it among yourselves you may do so in a central chamber where you will be served food. After sleep-time you will receive further instructions. You from the five cities will be returned to your own quarters to await my summons. You will not discuss this matter with those not involved."

He turned to MacDougall with an inscrutable smile. "You will be returned to Cuchulainn's castle to a room suitable for the Chosen One, to be entertained as a royal guest. You will be free to do as you wish until your chosen assistants have begun their training and have progressed sufficiently to warrant your inspection." He made a slight gesture; and Alan, after an instant's breathless flight, was alone in a luxuriously furnished bedroom.

He dropped into a chair and stared without seeing at a colorful tapestry, his thoughts chaotic. Those last disconnected words of Ahriman had to be uncharacteristically audible responses to one of his demonic staff. The subject matter almost certainly was the escape of Amaruduk. That would fit in with Manannan's sudden disappearance.

He thought of the sea-god's fantastic claim of thirty shiploads of Fomorian invaders landing on the shores of Avilion. Ships created by magic and captained by the thirty Druids under Mathonwy. He had read of such fleets in the book he had given Taliesin, *Mythology of the British Islands*. Logical that they could recruit the malformed Fomorians who had once dwelt in Lochlann, then under the rule of Manannan. How many of the invaders? Perhaps a thousand or more, fierce fighters all, and always ready for combat.

But how had they passed the dropping-off place? In his mind's eye MacDougall saw vividly the vast wall of darkness and the great chasm into which the sea seemed to be pouring. When he and Taliesin had fled from Ochren in *Wave Sweeper*, this had been in their way, a barrier between Ochren and Tartarus. An illusion; but to one who believed it was there, as deadly as fact. How convince a thousand Fomorians, or even thirty Druids, that what they saw did not exist? Unless—wild thought—Lucifer had removed the illusion since travel between the islands was now permitted. Whatever the answer, apparently they were here.

MacDougall thought of the rest of the proceedings in the Golden Tower and his own silence. Why hadn't he protested? Time after time he should have interrupted, disclaiming the whole idea. Instead, seemingly, he had acquiesced to everything. His courage gone? Damn!

He looked around the room. Tapestries covered the walls, and there were two comfortable chairs, a chest and a table, in addition to a large bed. Whom had he displaced? he wondered fleetingly, though he didn't really care. He checked the bathroom and found a mirror, a polished sheet of silver above the washbowl. A luxury previously missing.

He thought of Taliesin. He might have known the Bard would be drawn into the affair sooner or later. His job to select Druids to join—Alan grimaced—to join the class in possession. What, he wondered, would guide him in determining suitability? Would he still be in his bedroom? He pictured the Bard; sent the thought: *"Taliesin, my friend, I'm back in Cuchulainn's castle in luxurious quarters. Where are you?"*

The reply came instantly with the clarity that had become characteristic of their mental communication. *"Good to hear from you, Alan. I am in Tartarus, sent by Ahriman to choose Druids for his project. I must say I am not overly enthusiastic about the assignment. And what have you to report?''*

In a blend of words and images MacDougall related what had happened in the Golden Tower, concluding with Manannan's defiance of the Persian, the report of the invading Fomorians, and the sea god's disappearance.

"I am thoroughly annoyed with myself because I raised no objections to any of this. No matter what Ahriman thinks, I won't go along with this insane venture."

"Be sure you remember that," the Bard said solemnly, then added with a note of regret, *"I see a group of Druids approaching. Here, because I am the Bard of Bards, they come to my home at my call. How I will fare with Enki's Druids on Ochren, especially after the episode of the wasps and the dragon, will be a different story, I fear. Farewell.''* The conversation ended.

MacDougall stood up and began pacing the floor. That last solemn warning of Taliesin lingered in his mind. "Be sure you remember." How could he forget? Pressures were increasing, closing in on him—but there was no way he would go through with this madness. He shut the thought from his mind.

The Fomorians—had they actually landed? He had the means to find out. He checked the pacing, closed his eyes, and visualized the seashore to the far left of the castle. Instantly the picture appeared in his mind, the smooth sand of a narrow beach, the placid, barely rippling waters reflecting the brilliance of the aurora. He seemed to be hovering about twenty feet above the surface.

At will he moved, seeming to float, an exhilarating aerial survey, following the gently curving shoreline. Then ahead he saw what must be one of Manannan's ships. Mentally he floated above it, a craft of glistening copper, a much larger but less ornate version of *Wave Sweeper*, substantially wider and equipped with eight sturdy oars on each side and a rudder at the stern. Including the oarsmen, it could easily carry forty or more passengers. It was moored to what appeared to be a fisherman's wharf.

But this is ridiculous, MacDougall thought. This was a craft created by magic. It couldn't really be here. Obediently with the thought it vanished. For him it didn't exist. Would it still be there for the Fomorians? Probably.

Alan opened his eyes to the tapestried walls of his room. Like the army created by Beli's Druids, the copper craft was there only if you believed it; or the Roman village of Caesar Vespasianus in the abyss of Annwn; or the walls and chasms separating the islands. Somewhere he had heard the expression "If you believe it, it's so." A mad, mad world.

He closed his eyes and pictured the wharf. He'd follow the invaders' trail. Then he saw the first of the bodies, evidently a fisherman, brutally slashed, lying in a pool of blood. A short distance away lay another, then a third, the last decapitated. MacDougall's blood boiled. Killing inoffensive, unarmed fishermen, typical Fomorian conduct. As Alan's perception began moving across the plain, following an obvious trail on the trampled turf, a woman crawled from beneath an overturned boat; and he sensed her wail of grief fading into silence as his perception sped across the plain.

He caught up with the briskly walking monstrosities in moments, all afoot except the white-robed Druid who rode at the head of the group on a horse obviously taken from the fishermen. Despite the heavy silver chain with its massive *ankh* about his neck, he was not an overly impressive figure with his robe drawn above his knees, exposing thin, hairy legs.

The Fomorians, about forty, Alan estimated, were the distorted caricatures of men that he remembered, with every possible kind of malformation, including extra limbs, three-sectional arms, fangs, tusks, animal features; some almost chinless, others with enormous prognathous jaws, eyes protruding or deeply buried in their skulls. Utterly revolting, all were heavily armed, and every face expressed savage hatred.

Again Alan opened his eyes. The invaders still had a substantial distance to go before they reached Cuchulainn, probably to be joined by others on the way. If they were equally divided and attacked the five cities simultaneously, there would be about two hundred forty in each band. Certainly not an overwhelming force. And even if they concentrated their total army on each city in turn, Alan was certain that Ahriman would not permit this invasion to alter his plans. He had stopped the bloody war on Scath; he would cope with this one as easily.

In the meantime MacDougall decided he needed fresh air. Confinement had become oppressive. He thought of transferring to one of the gazebos; decided instead to walk through the castle unannounced to see what would happen.

As he stepped into the hallway he saw Scathach standing at the end of the corridor, apparently searching for something, a troubled look on her face. With a sudden smile of relief she hastened toward him.

"Oh, Alan, I'm so glad to see you. I was told you were in one of the rooms in this section, but I could not tell which it was. May we talk?"

"Of course," he answered, though without great enthusiasm. She seemed not to notice, bursting into speech the instant they were seated in his room.

"I confess I am troubled, and I don't know where to turn. Strange things are happening, people vanishing, and I am being ignored." She hesitated, then burst out plaintively, so unlike the Sorceress he knew, "Oh, Alan, I want so badly to return to Scath! And only you can help me."

"How can I help?" he temporized.

"By carrying me to my place. I have learned that you visited the other cities to gain new powers, and surely one of these must be the ability that so few have—instant transfer." She rose impulsively and dropped to her knees before him, her clasped hands on his lap. "Please, Alan."

"Well . . ." He hesitated. He had never tried the trick, but he could probably send her there, though with Brendah on the throne he didn't think he wanted to. Most certainly he would not go with her.

"Please," she repeated with almost childlike pleading, training the full power of her dark eyes and lovely face upon him. "And you can help me in another way. You have great influence with that awful Ahriman. I fear he plans to punish me for that stupid war with Amaruduk. You can tell him it was all Lamashtu's doing—the goddess in the statue—and the three Daughters of Calatin. In panic I suppose I agreed, but it wasn't my doing."

Lamashtu, the name that concealed the identity of the onetime Queen of the Underworld, Ereshkigal.

"I fear—" MacDougall began, then halted, his gaze fixed on the facing wall. A glowing area suddenly framed the face of Lucifer's lieutenant. At Alan's movement Scathach hastily turned, then caught her breath.

Ahriman spoke, smiling faintly. "Well, Scathach, I hear you wish to return to Scath. That awful Ahriman is here to help. You shall return, but as a member of the Castle Guard. Brendah is now Queen and she will remain in that position. You will serve her well. To insure your faithfulness, one of my servants, invisible, of course, will be your constant companion. This will be your punishment for your offense."

He shook his head sadly. "And you could have been of all women the most honored."

Suddenly the Sorceress was gone. And with no further word the image of Ahriman likewise vanished.

Shaken by the sudden turn of events, Alan stood up. He couldn't help feeling sympathy for proud Scathach, though she hardly deserved it. Disobedience of Lucifer's laws brought severe punishment. He scowled. Now he really wanted fresh air.

He started briskly through the corridors. The first guard he met stepped hastily aside and bowed deeply. He met another as he approached the exit; he, too, showed the same deference. One of the two at the door was the only one who spoke, saying as they swung wide the silver barrier "If we can help in any way, it will be an honor to serve you."

Oddly, the guards seemed unaware of the approaching Fomorians, going calmly about their usual activities.

Certainly Ahriman knew; but evidently his plans did not include defense by the local guards.

Outside, ignoring the zombielike strollers, Mac-Dougall walked slowly across the pale-green lawn, a grimace on his face. His fame had gone before him. The Chosen One. Just another indication of the Persian's power. Scowling, Alan headed for a gazebo containing marble benches. Seating himself on one of these, he gazed over the peaceful scene.

Peaceful! What a laugh. Deceit in all of it. A lovely park, beautiful trees and bushes, these skillfully wrought follies, the marble castle framed by the colorful aurora—all of it a sham. Why was it here? Seriously he asked himself the question: Why *was* the park here? There was nothing like it on the rest of the island. At no time had he seen any of the Cuchulainn dwellers use the park, though admittedly he had spent little time here himself. And of course, Hagith the Tormentor had been here, probably with helpers, attending to his revolting duties.

That suggested a grotesque idea. Were the follies erected to provide places of torture? Suffering surrounded by beauty to make the pain more unbearable? Two of the structures had been so used. The armlet. Perhaps the serpent-gods knew the answer.

"Lord Enki and Lady Inanna, have you any idea why this park is here?"

"What a strange question," Inanna commented. "I fear we have no definite knowledge. One possibility suggests itself. It provides a lovely and inviting setting for the fourth Gate. Which, by the way, is still closed."

Startled, MacDougall exclaimed aloud, "You can't be serious! This must have been created when the five cities were erected, fourteen centuries ago."

"Indeed. And at that time the four portals were built into the Highland *broch*. All to provide passage for the Chosen One foretold in the prophecy of the Scroll."

"Absurd," MacDougall exclaimed aloud but without conviction. He ended the mental contact. Was it absurd? It fit all too well into a pattern that became more consistent with every happening. And the fourth Gate was still closed? Of course. It was not yet time for him to pass through.

How big was the park anyway? Mentally he sent his perception around its edge. Not very large, roughly oval, narrowest where it met the castle in what he thought of as north; running along the woodland to the east and extending an equal distance to the west. The spot he pictured as the location of the Gate was at its center. Surrounding park and woods and city were level green grasslands.

In frustration MacDougall stood up and headed back to the castle. All this seemed to bear out Inanna's idea. A lovely frame for the Gate. And Hagith the Tormentor using the gazebos for torturing was merely an added value.

As MacDougall reached the flagging at the entrance, he found the great silver gates standing wide apart and, in the opening, a guard whom he recognized as one who had spoken to him on his way out. The man bowed deeply and said, "I have been instructed to tell you, Alan MacDougall, that dinner will be served whenever you wish. It is yours to command."

MacDougall checked a grimace and gave a slight nod. He wanted none of this kowtowing. He knew its source. "I'm ready now," he said curtly.

He was led to a room on the second level, small, luxuriously furnished, its walls heavily draped with rich velvety fabrics in blue and gold, the thick rug of navy blue setting off a massive gold-covered loveseat and divan. At its center stood a teakwood table set for three with vessels of crystal and gold. The chairs also were of teak, ornately carved. A chamber somehow intimate, probably usually used by Cuchulainn and his wife.

MacDougall was directed to a seat at the table's end, and as the guard withdrew, the curtains parted in the opposite wall and two smiling women entered. Eimher with her spectacular red-gold hair and Hypatia, the lovely Oracle of Atu. Instinctively Alan stood up, startled at Hypatia's presence, thinking with surprise, What an incredible transformation in the erstwhile lecturer.

The Queen, on the several occasions when he had seen her, had been dressed like a queen; and her violet eyes, fantastic hair, and skin of tinted alabaster had received just enough help to appear at their very best. But now in addition she wore a platinum tiara set with blue-green emeralds and diamonds; and her gown of palest green, leaving shoulders bare, seemed woven of spiderwebs, designed to reveal rather than to conceal. Incredibly she seemed shod in green glass slippers.

But the transformation Hypatia had undergone was almost unbelievable. He remembered her in a black academic robe, her long chestnut hair drawn back tightly and gathered in an oversized ponytail at the base of her neck. Now her hair was a crown of radiant curls becomingly arranged, her hazel eyes, unnoticed before, glowing in a frame of incredibly long lashes, her cheeks a delicate rose, her lips, full and sensuous, yet smiling modestly. A masterpiece of the beautician's art, but without a trace of artificiality. She, too, wore a tiara, hers of pale gold set with rubies and diamonds, and not quite as large or as ornately wrought as Eimher's. And her gown, of delicate rose, not quite as daring as the Queen's, revealed a figure quite as perfect.

A shape-change? For a moment Alan entertained the thought, then dismissed it as his gaze penetrated. Truly Hypatia, and she *was* that beautiful. Suddenly her cheeks flushed; and MacDougall realized he had been staring quite openly.

"I'm sorry," he said. "I fear I've been rude. But you appear so greatly changed, and so lovely."

Hypatia smiled with obvious pleasure. "It has been a long time since I concerned myself with such things."

Eimher looked surprised as they reached the table. "I did not think you two had met."

"We met briefly when I visited her city," Alan answered, "and without her knowledge I observed Hypatia during one of her lectures. It was most impressive, though I admit I found it quite unintelligible. Something about the mind and the soul and first principles and living the life of theory. Most confusing."

Again the philosopher smiled. "Intentionally so." She sobered instantly. "I am honored to meet the Chosen One a second time. I am grateful to the One-Who-Speaks-for-the-Master for making it possible."

"Let us forget that as we forget the one I know as Ahriman." Quickly Alan moved to seat them, the Queen first in deference to her position. As he seated himself, through another doorway behind the draperies came servants bearing platters of food. For an interval there was little conversation while they ate.

MacDougall, studying his lovely companions, thought, How obvious of Ahriman! With Scathach no longer "fated" to be his consort and out of the running, Eimher and Hypatia had been provided as alternates. But what of Cuchulainn? He supposed his scheduled role in the Other World changed the situation, making Eimher available.

"I am honored," Alan said politely, "to have two so very lovely dinner companions. But where are the others? King Cuchulainn, Laegaire, Conall, Myrddin and Artur, and the Druids?"

"I know nothing of Cuchulainn's actions since . . . Ahriman—" Eimher hesitated over the use of the name. "—appeared to the King and some of those you mentioned, summoning them to appear for a great honor. It was then they vanished one by one. Immediately afterward Hypatia appeared, and I was commanded to treat her as an honored guest." She forced a smile. "As I would naturally have done without orders.

"Later the image reappeared, and we were instructed to entertain you at dinner and during your stay in the castle, however long that might be." She hesitated, seeming somewhat embarrassed. "There was more, but nothing you would find interesting."

"And you." Alan turned to Hypatia. "I suppose the image appeared to you with instructions to join Eimher, and suddenly you had made the journey."

"More than that," she responded in awed tones. "A sleep before I was brought here, two strangely beautiful women appeared in my chambers. They said they were sent by the One-Who-Speaks-for-the-Master, and they told me I was to be prepared for a great honor. They brought with them lovely garments, and unguents and strange devices with which they wrought wondrously until I became as you see me now." She shook her head in unbelief. "Not for centuries have I felt as I do at this moment. A—a woman."

MacDougall thought, Demonic beauticians, of all things. He smiled and glanced from Hypatia to Eimher. "I am certain that you two are the loveliest women in Avilion. Fortunate that I do not have to decide which of you is the more beautiful." Again he gazed from one to the other. "An impossible task. Each perfect in her own way."

As one the women exchanged quick sharp glances, then looked hastily back at MacDougall. The Queen made a halfhearted attempt to conceal her displeasure at the comparison, but the Oracle beamed. Apologetically Alan added, his eyes meeting Eimher's, "You see how prudent I am. I am sure King Cuchulainn would not appreciate my expressing open admiration for and interest in his Queen." Better seek a safer subject, he thought.

"Are you two aware of the invasion that threatens the five cities?"

The women looked startled. "Invasion!" Hypatia exclaimed; and in the same breath Eimher said, "We know nothing about it."

At that moment the servers entered to clear the table, and while they did so MacDougall considered how much he should reveal. What would he do if the Fomorians actually reached Cuchulainn? Could he transfer himself and the two women out of danger? Worth a try, but nothing he'd mention. It probably wouldn't happen.

"I was about to say," he resumed, "Avilion has been invaded by the Fomorians from the island called Tartarus. A fleet of thirty magically created ships brought them here, and even now they are marching toward the five cities. The Fomorians are probably the most savage fighters on all the islands. They hate even themselves, and with good reason, for all are monstrously malformed."

Eimher stared incredulously at MacDougall. "You are serious? Yet you sit here calmly; and the city has not been warned?"

Alan shrugged. "Ahriman knows all about it, as does Cuchulainn and the leaders of all the cities. It would appear that they are depending upon the One-Who-Speaks-for-the-Master to turn back the invaders. He has that power, you know."

The Queen's face brightened. "Then there is no cause for alarm." With sudden animation she rose and said, "Why do we sit here at the table when these more comfortable seats are available?" She looked doubtfully at Hypatia as the latter also stood up. "We need to learn more about each other." Noticing the glance, Alan thought with amusement, Two's company and three's a crowd.

"I am sorry," he said, also getting to his feet, "but I feel I should observe all that is happening with the invaders and—at other places. For this I need to be alone."

Eimher's eyes widened, and Hypatia exclaimed, "You mean you can see what is occurring at a distance from within your room?"

"Yes, as I heard and saw your lecture to the monks and the Bishop of Alexandria though I was elsewhere."

"Oh." Her voice was very small.

The Queen's self-assurance was obviously shaken. "When will we see you again?"

"At breakfast, I hope." Alan smiled warmly. "Lovely companions make the food more enjoyable. And now, if you will excuse me . . ."

Somewhat reassured, though with awe still evident in her eyes, Eimher clapped twice, and in moments MacDougall's guide appeared, holding wide the draperies. Before leaving, Alan bowed deeply to each of the women and said, "May you enjoy a peaceful sleep."

Back in his room, Alan dropped into a chair and stretched out his long legs. He chuckled, thinking of Eimher's repeating Ahriman's instructions to entertain him and her concluding, "There was more but nothing you would find interesting." Sure as he was born, each had been told to do her utmost to win his affections. The Queen obviously resented Hypatia's presence, but her long-standing fear of Ahriman assured the visitor fair treatment. Certainly in a contest of feminine wiles, Eimher felt sure she would win. Except that since he was both judge and prize, neither would win.

He closed his eyes, thinking about the Fomorians. He wondered, Would it be possible for him to see the island mentally as from a high elevation? There was a great deal he didn't know about this ability, but the serpent-gods would know.

"Lord Enki and Lady Inanna, the student is calling the masters for guidance. Can I get a bird's-eye view of Avilion to see what is really happening?"

"Well! We *are* remembered occasionally," the Lady Inanna answered. "Since you have received your special education you appear to have become self-sufficient; but as you have just realized, mastery of the new abilities is not gained in a single sleep. And yes, there should be no difficulty in your getting a bird's-eye view of the island, or at least large areas of it. And the figure you use, a bird's eye, is a logical means. Picture yourself soaring as a bird in the vicinity of the Golden Tower, seeing the land far below. It is merely a matter of mental visualization."

It sounded simple enough, Alan thought; and it was. In an instant he seemed to be floating in the midst of the aurora, a great expanse of Avilion spread out below him like an enlargement of a portion of the model in Ahriman's Tower. And on his right rose the gleaming, rounded wall of the structure itself.

A fantastic feeling, almost like his out-of-body experience. And he could soar at will, dropping closer to the ground, or sweeping swiftly upward or across the landscape as he wished. Flying without effort or sound or danger of falling. Truly birdlike. For a fleeting moment he thought of soaring upward through the aurora and above it to look into the top level where he and the Persian had met.

Movement far below caught his attention, ending his

exhilarating mental gymnastics. Two cities lay below him
with another blending into the horizon far to the north.
Cuchulainn, Magadha, and the third, Shenzhu. Clearly
visible were the straight white roads leading from the
nearer cities to the circle of trees around the mound of
the Tower. And walking single file along the roads toward the Tower were people, a long column on each thor-
oughfare.

He sent his perception down closer to the white way
from Cuchulainn; saw men and women, some in white
robes, faces depicting the rapt dreamlike state of the drug
slaves; others in the dress of guards; about fifty in all.

An instant later in vision he was hovering above the
column from Magadha, colorful in their open-front tunics and full, wraparound lower garments drawn up between their legs to form quasi-trousers. With bare feet
and shaven heads, they bore no resemblance to the
marchers from Cuchulainn. There were no women, and
only about twenty men in number.

Swiftly he sped visually to the next road, that from the
City of Jade. He could see the other two, Aku and Axume; and there were columns of marchers on their way
from the three. Like pilgrims, came the unlikely thought,
flowing into Mecca. *Most* unlikely! Not pilgrims, came
the chilling realization, but subjects for the students of
possession to use in gaining their skills! Then Mac-
Dougall saw something else that drove all other thoughts
from his mind. Incredulous, he dropped closer to the
surface.

Ghostlike, invisible to other eyes, ignored by those on
the roads, he saw a succession of mounted warriors pouring out through the golden wall of the Tower at ground
level. Armored in gleaming bronze like ancient knights,
armed with lances and longswords, they were warriors
riding into battle. Their mounts were unicorns.

Unicorns! At least, a single spiraling horn projected
from their foreheads, though their bodies seemed more
feline in their litheness and the grace of their movements.
This had to be illusion, he thought. Yet, probe as he
might, he saw only armored men on strange steeds. And

those steeds, too, were armored, chests and heads and forelimbs protected.

They dashed swiftly down the hillside on the turf between the converging roads, their passing almost soundless and their number seeming endless. Endless! Unbelieving, he glimpsed a second and third tide of warriors pouring from the Tower between the stairways at the ends of the roads. Absurd, impossible, all these scores of mounted riders coming out of the Tower. There was no way it could hold a fraction of these.

"Lord and Lady—" MacDougall clutched the armlet. "—please tell me what I'm seeing."

The serpent-god answered promptly, an amused note in his thought. "Remember when you wondered about the conference room in the Tower? We told you it was used for conclaves, gatherings of the Host from other worlds and other spaces in Lucifer's domain. Well, these riders have been summoned from a world in a parallel space, and they merely pass through the Tower as through a doorway. Thousands are available, far more than are needed to repel the Fomorians. None of the five cities will be involved in the battle—if battle it may be called.

"Manannan's folly is understandable to a degree, since he had no idea of the powers he was challenging, but Amaruduk's stupidity is inexcusable."

Inanna added scornfully, "Arrogance and pride have addled his brains."

Alan broke contact and mentally followed the nearer riders down the slope and across the plain, quickly leaving the cities behind. It was at that point that the warriors shed invisibility; and MacDougall gained a clearer view of the horned mounts. Definitely not horses or the conventional idea of unicorns, they were giant dun-colored cats with goatlike faces—plus the spiraling two-foot-long horns.

He sent his perception soaring high into the aurora to watch the fight that must follow. The Fomorians, moving at their steady pace, were still some distance away, but the mounted attackers were rapidly closing the gap. They were now riding seven abreast and fifteen deep, with their ranks apparently complete.

Out of the western sky suddenly rolled a mass of gray-green clouds, sweeping over the sea at hurricane speed, evidence that the sea-god was aware of the new development. The mounted Druid halted, holding one hand aloft, probably having received a mental directive from Manannan. He appeared to shout something to the Fomorians, then sent his horse galloping northward, his troops following at top speed. The clouds speedily overtook them, hiding them from sight, and hurricane winds swept ahead of them, flattening the turf, roaring on toward the demonic riders.

But all of this was futile. The great cats sped on undeterred, and when the gale reached them, the winds parted, as a bit later did the bank of clouds. Magic meeting greater magic. On contact, five of the armored demons swiftly encircled the Druid and cut him away from the Fomorians. The latter, overtaken, faced their assailants and sprang savagely at the riders, swords swinging.

They hadn't a chance. Unlike horses, the agile cats, seemingly without guidance, twisted and turned to confront the Fomorians; and with sickening frequency the lances of the riders skewered the invaders. The outcome was inevitable. MacDougall cut off the vision and opened his eyes. Without question, the mayhem was being repeated wherever the Fomorians had gathered.

Revolting, MacDougall thought, staring at the tapestried wall. Despite the purpose of the invaders' coming, and their repulsive nature and appearance, this slaughter was unjustified. They could have been captured and returned to Tartarus. After all, they were only tools of Manannan. The Druids—apparently they were being captured, perhaps for Taliesin's later consideration. And, he supposed, the armored demons and their cats would return to the world from whence they came.

He thought of what Enki had said about their origin, and as he considered its significance, he felt a pang of dread. From somewhere in the recesses of his memory came a statement he had read, probably in the Bible:

"We wrestle not against flesh and blood, but against principalities and powers, and the rulers of darkness in high places." Probably not an exact quotation, but how precisely it described his circumstances. And to think that he dared to pit his puny will against a power so great and far-reaching. He gritted his teeth and scowled. Silly or not, he would continue resisting to the bitter end.

Restlessly MacDougall began prowling around the room. This inactivity was driving him up a wall. There was nothing for him to do. He might explore the castle, but to what purpose? He could communicate with Taliesin, but the Bard no doubt was engaged in selecting Druids to become part of Alan's future staff. He snorted at the idea. To stir things up he could transfer to one of the other islands, maybe visit Tartarus; spend some time with Einhurr Gurulfin, King of the Trolls. Better than being cooped up with a couple of women, no matter how beautiful, intent on seducing him.

MacDougall suddenly laughed aloud. Imagine him being in a mental state where he would find this unappealing. He sobered quickly. He wanted no entanglements. With preparations underway for what could only be called world-shaking events, if they ever took place, he wanted to be aware of what was going on and free to do whatever needed to be done.

He stopped short in his pacing. Dared he spy on Ahriman? What could he lose? If the Persian detected his prying, he'd merely block him. Certainly worth a try. He dropped into a chair, closed his eyes, and pictured Lucifer's lieutenant.

He saw Ahriman seated in his golden room at the top of the Tower, a round teak table at his elbow, on it a crystal goblet of wine and a crystal decanter. Before him stood a man, stiffly erect, tall, swarthy, impressive, clad in a military-gray vesture and full-cut trousers.

"Phaleg, make your report," Ahriman said crisply.

The demon—for such he must be, Alan was certain—bowed and said, "The Fomorian invaders have been destroyed without exception. Our own losses were negligible. All of the Druids have been captured—as was

Mathonwy, the Druid Master—and all have been placed in the designated Tower room to await your pleasure. Zadok is even now returning with his forces to planet five of Azriel's system. He asked permission to take the carcasses with him as fodder for the ka-ats, and since I could see no reason for refusing, permission was granted. I have reported the body count to Replacement.''

Ahriman nodded his approval. "Well done. Return to your post." Instantly the being vanished; and moments later a second figure appeared, differing little from his predecessor. As before, the Persian commanded, "Ceratron, report."

After bowing deeply the demon replied, "The subjects for practice are arriving and are being placed in designated cells to be called as needed. They were chosen from the cities according to your instructions. The instructors, most skilled of the Host in teaching possession, have been brought from the nine world systems. All have been impressed with the importance of their mission and are ready for your call."

` "Excellent. Return to your post." And Ceratron disappeared.

A third gray-clad figure followed; and Ahriman stared at him with his gem-hard blue eyes for a seemingly endless period. Finally he said in an icy voice, "And what, Bethor, have you to report? No evasion."

The demon named Bethor drew a deep breath. "Failure thus far, Master. They continue to elude us."

MacDougall saw the repressed rage on Ahriman's face; he seemed on the verge of exploding, but he said in an expressionless voice, "Your explanation."

"Amaruduk's skill at shape-changing and instant transport are responsible. I have all available agents on their trail, circulating about the five cities. Time and again they have been sighted, once in Magadha among the fasting Tantrics; and at the instant of discovery they vanished, appearing perhaps as wandering dreamers in Cuchulainn or among the monks in Atu. Of course, Amaruduk carries Manannan. And until the capture of Mathonwy they were in constant communication, directing the Fomorians. Now all their efforts seemed aimed at annoying us.''

"While Amaruduk plans further mischief." Ahriman stood up and transfixed Bethor with his glare. "Find them! There must be a way. Go!''

Alone, the Persian sank back into his chair, raised the wine goblet, and drained it. As he returned it to the table, another of his agents appeared; and at the same instant MacDougall cut off the vision. He had seen enough. He opened his eyes.

Very interesting, he thought, and frightening—especially the scope of Ahriman's influence. Able to call on demonic help from what must be other star systems. And— involuntarily Alan shuddered at the memory of one detail in the first agent's report—the Fomorians slaughtered to a man and their bodies transported by the warriors to another world to be fed, evidently, to their feline mounts. No matter how revolting Balor's followers were, they didn't deserve this. Damn such a place. He grinned mirthlessly. It was already damned.

Amaruduk. The ancient Sumerian god was leading the other demons in a merry chase. But eventually, even if he left Avilion for the other islands, he and Manannan would be caught.

The more he saw and learned, the more hopeless became his own situation. The magic of the Celtic gods, the *Tuatha de Danann*, or the other mortals on Ochren or Scath, was as nothing compared with that of these demons. Though they had given MacDougall powers and abilities little short of their own, he found small comfort in the knowledge. They were many and adepts; he was a beginner and alone.

He rose and removed his jacket, hanging it in the necessary room beside his cape and sword. Might as well try to sleep, though slumber seemed far away. His shirt followed as did his undershirt; and stripped to the waist, he began preparing for bed. He had considered a shower but the frigid water would have made sleep impossible. With his toothbrush and the rest returned to their proper pockets, he moved to his bed, only to whirl about at a startled feminine cry behind him.

"Alan—Alan MacDougall!"

A few feet away stood a vision of blond beauty, her blue eyes wide, her lovely lips parted in unbelief.

"Darthula!" MacDougall exclaimed. "I never expected to see you here—though of course you're welcome." Darthula, Princess of Gorias, the City of the Five Peaks. It was sight of her Dresden-doll perfection of feature and haughty demeanor that had led him into this world and into a succession of adventures that was rapidly approaching its climax. Now she was here in a clinging silken robe designed for the intimacy of her bedroom.

"Oh, Alan," she said fervently, "I have missed you so greatly and I never expected to see you again, especially after I heard of you being stabbed. Later I learned you were alive, but you never returned to Tartarus. Then moments ago the vision of a man who called himself the One-Who-Speaks-for-the-Master—but whom I knew instantly was the being you called Ahriman—appeared on a wall in my home and told me I would be transported to an island where you were. And—and, well, he said some other things, and suddenly I was here!"

She raised her arms and took a step toward MacDougall. "I—I had no idea it would be like this—but I'm so glad!" Swiftly she covered the remaining space and flung her arms around him.

Alan, taken by surprise, tried to step backward, felt the bed press hard against his legs, and, with the girl draped over him, sprawled on the covers.

"Ah, Alan," she breathed, kissing him with sufficient warmth to drive any objections out of his mind; but even as he returned her embrace, being quite human, he was striving desperately to think of a way out of his predicament. Even under these circumstances he could not forget that he held a body created by Lucifer, housing a woman who had died fourteen centuries ago.

A deep, quiet laugh came to his rescue, a voice that MacDougall recognized instantly. Ahriman. Awkwardly the two scrambled to their feet to face a glowing image of the Persian, a broad smile on his lips.

"A dreadful mistake has been made," he said with great sincerity. "You, Darthula, were to have been placed in the room next to this one, which will be yours while you remain in the City of Cuchulainn. Your clothing has already been placed there; and it was while this was being done that the error was discovered. I am sorry. The one responsible will be reprimanded.

"After your sleep—and may it be peaceful—you will join Queen Eimher, the Oracle Hypatia, and MacDougall at breakfast. The Queen has already been told of your coming. And now we will correct our mistake."

Darthula vanished. So did the image of Ahriman, but not before he gave Alan a sly wink.

MacDougall crossed to a chair and sank into it to think about this unexpected development. Darthula reappearing after all that had happened, materializing in his bedroom, lifted evidently from her own. He glanced down at his bare chest. A fine way to welcome a lady.

He began to grin and a low chuckle escaped him. A mistake! What a liar. Not a chance in a million that her appearing as she did was other than intentional. And that wink—could Ahriman have a sense of humor? Or was he an unusually clever psychologist? Or both? And why had he interrupted at that particular moment? Only the Persian knew. As for Darthula's appearing, he should have anticipated it; Ahriman was giving him the choice of three beauties.

He got into his pajamas, dimmed the ceiling glow, and crawled under the covers. He felt more relaxed after the latest happening, the gloom that had been engulfing him somewhat dissipated. He thought now he could sleep.

He was vaguely aware of the confusion of mind that presaged the ascendancy of the subconscious, when he sensed a mental exchange as he had done time and time again on the verge of sleep. The *Tuatha de Danann* were in conference. Danu as usual was in charge.

"*I find this easier,*" she said, "*and less likely to be open to eavesdropping than a physical meeting.*"

"*True enough, except for MacDougall's listening.*"
That was Nuada.

"*This is new to me—*" Alan recognized the personality of Beli. "*—since you were not even aware of my existence in Ochren, but it seems to be a good idea.*"

"*It is new to me, also,*" came an unfamiliar thought, probably that of Amaethon, the son of Nuada and grandson of Beli, late of the outlaw city of Flavius Vespasianus.

Danu continued, "*We found these conferences useful on our island because members of the Family were always accessible to each other no matter where they were. But to the matter at hand. What shall we do in response to Ahriman's proposal? I for one will not accept his offer, since we have a choice. I do not question his ability to fulfill what he offers. And I could work with MacDougall. But I find nothing appealing in possessing another's body and eventually displacing her.*"

"*I agree. I stay among the Trolls.*" That was Gobniu the Smith.

"*And I,*" said Credne the Bronze Master quite firmly.

After a brief interval Diancecht the Physician spoke. "*Since this is a matter of individual choice, I plan to accept the offer. One fact was not mentioned that to me is of paramount importance. Ahriman is offering us virtual eternal life in the Other World. Consider. I possess an individual. If that body becomes ill or injured or old and about to die, I can move to another. And another. Until I become weary of the game. Which might be never. Oh, yes, I will accept.*"

"*And I,*" Nuada exclaimed. "*It is true that MacDougall and I have had differences of opinion, but I would have no difficulty following his leading. And this is an opportunity to escape from eternal monotony.*"

Beli spoke. "*I never thought I would see this day, but I, too, can follow MacDougall's leading. He has bested me more than once, and I find this hard to swallow. But he is a strong man, and I can serve under him. I will accept.*"

"*I will follow the example of my father and grandfa-

ther.'' That was Amaethon. *''One tires of the same illusion.''* He was referring to the illusion of a city that he had maintained for the Roman ruler for many centuries in the depths of Annwn.

Dagda was the last to speak. *''It is my turn, I suppose; and the decision is difficult. The challenge is most enticing. But I shall remain here with Danu. My answer will be no.''*

MacDougall opened his eyes and stared at the dimly glowing ceiling. The mental voices were gone and he was wide awake. From all he had heard, one statement lingered most strongly, the startling thought of Diancecht.

This whole plan *had* to fail. Far more was involved than his own leadership in an impossible enterprise. Ahriman would be letting loose in the world scores of men and women with extraordinary powers who to all intents and purposes would be immortal! Perpetuating their lives at the cost of other lives—forever! There *had* to be a way out of this mess.

Sleep was far away, yet most desirable to block the nightmares of his thoughts. He tried to make his mind a blank, an impossible effort. He tried various mental tricks without success, finally picturing a grassy slope in the park with himself lying on his back staring into the aurora overhead. Gradually, with the vivid yet soothing image in his mind's eye, following the ceaseless yet subtle changes, a kind of self-hypnosis brought calmness and relaxation; and at last MacDougall slept.

CHAPTER 10

The Haunted Grove

The subdued sound of voices outside his room awakened
Alan MacDougall: feminine voices in excited conversation. He stretched and yawned, then looked curiously
beyond the door. Darthula and Hypatia stood with blond
and chestnut-brown heads close together, evidently getting acquainted. Each appeared at her loveliest, and each
had her gaze fixed on his door.

He had looked into the hallway!

Abruptly it dawned upon MacDougall; without conscious effort that trick ability of his had seen through the
solid barrier. Disconcerting to say the least. Something
he had to live with, had to control.

"Greetings, lovely ladies," he called out, enjoying
their surprise. "I see you have already met—the Princess Darthula from Gorias on Tartarus, and the Oracle Hypatia from Atu on Avilion. I am still abed. I
suggest you make your way to the dining room where I
am sure Queen Eimher will join you. As will I in a short
time."

"We came out into the hallway at the same time,"

Hypatia explained, "from rooms on opposite sides of yours, so we met. I hope we did not disturb you."

At Alan's reassurance they hastened along the corridor. Out of bed, he headed for the shower, shedding his pajamas on the way. No dawdling in the icy stream; he was wide awake as he completed his preparations for the day.

A question occurred to him as he thought of the attentions paid him by the three beautiful women. Obviously they were under Ahriman's instructions. Why was the Persian so intent upon matching him with one of the women? With Scathach eliminated, which of the three he selected didn't seem to matter. It really made no sense, since they couldn't live in his own realm. Unless they, too, were trained in possession; and then the woman, whichever it might be, would become a physically different person. The whole idea was absurd, and Ahriman must know it.

Another possibility—maybe their physical beauty and powers of seduction were intended to break down his resistance and make him more willing to go along with Ahriman's—and Lucifer's—plans. That made a kind of sense. Ruefully he thought as he pictured the three, It was a good thing Elspeth was there in the background.

Dressed as always in his black garments, minus cape and sword, Alan made his way through the hallways to the room where he had dined with Eimher and Hypatia. The three women were already there, seated at the oblong table. There was a place set for him at one end, with the Queen on his right, the Oracle facing her, and Darthula at the far end. They greeted him warmly, though Alan could sense an air of restraint, each secretly resenting the presence of the other females.

"I see you have met the Princess Darthula." He addressed Eimher. "I trust you will become good friends, as were the Princess and I during my first visit to this world. *Very* good friends," he added with a faint smile.

Breakfast began in a chilly atmosphere and conversation was sporadic and forced. After they had eaten the excellent meal—during which Eimher and Darthula traded a few subtle insults, Hypatia apparently considered out of the running—the Queen suggested a walk through the park. Alan agreed, secretly amused at the awkward situation.

At first he was careful to pay attention to each; then gradually he concentrated on the Oracle, leading her into a philosophical discussion, thus cutting the other two out of the conversation. Eimher, accustomed to having her own way, found this intolerable; yet she dared not exert her royal authority. Alan, finally tiring of the game—and of a dialogue that had become boring—again allowed the Queen to dominate the conversation.

They had been moving about aimlessly, paying little attention to their surroundings; but when Darthula asked about the gazebos, MacDougall suggested casually that they visit some of them. As he expected, Eimher— knowing what at least two had held—showed little enthusiasm for the idea, but when he headed for the nearest one, she reluctantly followed.

After visiting six or eight and finding no indication of the Tormentor's handiwork, Alan decided that Ahriman, or possibly Cuchulainn, had ordered such use discontinued during MacDougall's stay. The lovely structures varied in their use, some containing marble benches, others devoted to flowering plants, some a combination of the two. Then, strangely, as they approached one, quite distant from the rest, the three women halted.

"That is forbidden," Eimher said in a hushed voice. "I have never been here."

"Forbidden?" Alan asked, anticipating the response. "Why?"

The Queen shook her head. "I do not know why, but I dare not go nearer."

"Nor may I," Darthula added; and Hypatia nodded agreement. "It is instinctive knowledge."

MacDougall shrugged. Another manifestation of implanted restraint. Even the two from distant places sensed the psychological barrier. "To me nothing is forbidden. Await my return."

Briskly he strode toward the gazebo. He had a hunch concerning what he would find; and when he saw the opening in the floor, and a marble stairway leading down to a subterranean chamber, he became certain. The stream of chill air rising from the opening was further proof. A Hall of the Dead from which came new bodies replacing any from Cuchulainn who had died; bodies animated by the spirits of the dead. And so it proved to be.

At the foot of the stairway a short corridor led to a closed door that did not open at his touch. With closed eyes he gazed beyond it to see a long line of coffinlike boxes with transparent covers, each containing a marble-still, naked form, ghastly in the dim blue light that emanated from the ceiling and walls. Here, as in that frigid building outside Falias on Tartarus, he saw a great metal dome like a huge reflector sending forth an intense blue beam—the animator.

He turned away and started up the stairs. He had seen enough. He found the three women waiting silently, relief on their faces at his reappearance.

"Don't tell us what you saw," Eimher said hastily as he approached. "Even discussing it would be disturbing."

"I understand," MacDougall replied. "This is not my first experience with forbidden areas. And what do we do now? I think we've visited enough gazebos."

"Why not look for the Gate into the Other World?" Hypatia suggested. "The One-Who-Speaks-for-the-Master told of your passing through it into this one. I would find it interesting to look into the world from whence we came. Can you lead us to it?"

Alan avoided a direct answer. "I'm afraid you would see nothing even if—" He checked himself. He almost said "Even if it were open." No point in revealing that it was closed. "—even if you came upon it. I alone can see it as a portal. But let us look if you wish." If by some remote chance it had been reopened, he'd simply step through it and vanish.

He led the women in the general direction of the Gate, and after describing the ghostly circle and even more tenuous image of the tower, he set them to searching. He centered his attention on the area he was sure held the portal, but there was no sign of it. As he had expected, it had not been opened.

At length, when his escorts tired of the hunt, Eimher said to Alan, "This search is hopeless. You probably know where it is and are letting us make fools of ourselves."

MacDougall smiled faintly; and she exclaimed, "I knew it! We'll return to the castle; and after we've had lunch I'll take you on a tour of the city."

Back in the marble halls, the Queen suggested that they return to their rooms to freshen up, after which they would get together in the dining area. As she started to call guards to guide them, MacDougall objected.

"That won't be necessary. I know the way. And thank you for putting us in neighboring rooms."

Eimher frowned. "That was not—" She halted.

"Your idea," Alan concluded. "I know. Ahriman's arrangement." He hooked arms with Hypatia and Darthula. "It *is* convenient." He glanced over his shoulder to see a look of frustration on Eimher's face.

After lunch the Queen led them through Cuchulainn, as she had suggested. She showed them the street devoted to shops where necessities were dispensed according to need. Alan was reminded of a similar setup in Murias, where Darthula had been his guide. Here, too, people took no more than they needed, because shopping gave them something to do. And hoarding, when discovered, was punished.

There was also a building where the narcotic blend was dispensed to keep the addicts in a euphoric state. There was strict control, the Queen told them, though she did not explain how it worked. Nor did anyone ask. To Alan, with his knowledge of the basement chamber with its rows of addicts taking the enforced cure, this was completely revolting.

During their walk Alan found himself beside the Queen, the others lingering in one of the shops. With a twinkle in his eye he asked, "Why did you call on me that first night I spent in the castle?"

Eimher looked surprised. "How did you know? You were not there."

"Ahriman removed me at the instant you entered."

She tossed her head defiantly. "Cuchulainn had forbidden my speaking to you, so of course I had to do so. No man commands the Queen."

Logical, Alan thought, but not very complimentary. "I was curious," he said.

"Also," the Queen added, "I had been informed that Scathach had visited you, so I decided to investigate to prevent your being disturbed. She told me she was waiting for you to return, so we waited for a time, then left." She looked searchingly at MacDougall. "The Sorceress has disappeared. Do you know what happened?"

He smiled faintly. "I understand she has returned to Scath."

"How—" Eimher began, then desisted, joining the others.

Alan was glad when the tour ended. Though it was interesting, he felt frustrated at the lack of purposeful action. This was getting him nowhere. He wanted things to come to a climax, to find a way *out*. There should be something he could be doing.' Even the company of the three beautiful women could not relieve his frustration.

After dinner he went directly to his room. He was tired, as were his companions. They had been on their feet for the greater part of the day; all seemed grateful that activity had ended. Stretched out on his bed in his pajamas after his usual preparations, Alan thought ruefully of the futile hours. He had learned one thing, the location of the Hall of the Dead, verifying an earlier guess, but the knowledge was of no value. He would not spend another day like this one.

There was one place he planned to explore—that strange block of woods, unique on the island. There must be a reason for it being there. But not with the three women. Either alone or with one, no more. He'd tell them so, and annoy two of them by making a choice.

He thought of Taliesin, wondering how he was faring in his selection of Druids. If he was working by the same timetable—not a certainty in this crazy place—he should be available. He sent out a thought.

"Taliesin, can we talk?"

The reply came instantly. *"Indeed. It is good to hear from you. I am having an interesting time. What about you?"*

"Disgusting. From breakfast on I have had to spend my time wandering around the park at Cuchulainn with three beautiful women: Eimher the Queen, Hypatia the Oracle of Atu—you remember her—and of all things, the lovely Darthula has been brought here to add her beauty to the scene. I am to select one of them to be my consort."

There was amusement in the Bard's response. *"If I were you I should choose Darthula. She really cares for you."* He added seriously, *"I jest, of course. I, too, am surrounded by women, the Druidesses of Scath. Something unusual seems to have happened. A subdued excitement exists among them. But they refuse to discuss it."*

"Scathach's return," Alan commented, then told the Bard what had happened. *"Her disgrace would certainly stir up conversation."*

"An unhappy ending but not surprising. She invited her downfall. I believe Brendah in her new power will keep her in line." He changed the subject. *"I had a surprisingly easy time on Ochren with Beli's Druids. Ahriman paved the way by having his projection speak to them, explaining the purpose of my visit; and some of his assistants were there, perhaps as my bodyguards, but more likely to check on my decisions. As each Druid was chosen he vanished, evidently wafted away to the Golden Tower on Avilion.*

"Now I am interviewing the Druidesses. Some have surprising powers and knowledge."

"And all to no purpose," Alan exclaimed bitterly, *"for I am not going through with this farce! There must be a way out, and I'll find it. And now I'm going to sleep."*

There was no response from Taliesin as they severed communication.

* * *

During breakfast—same place, same people—Queen Eimher made an announcement.

"Before I slept the One-Who-Speaks-for-the-Master appeared with a—a suggestion." She paused, then corrected herself, "With a command. We are to take turns in our entertaining the Chosen One, and he is to select his companion, the other two to remain in the castle to become better acquainted, since, in truth, we are strangers."

The three looked at Alan with their most enticing smiles. He surveyed each in turn, frowning thoughtfully as if weighing their respective merits.

"Surprisingly, I had arrived at the same idea. I could never get to know you as individuals if we remained in a group. You could not be free to be yourselves. It is now my plan to explore the forest. It seems strangely out of place in this setting and I am curious about it." He saw a look of distaste on Eimher's face.

"I wouldn't go there," she protested. "It is an unpleasant place. Although it is not forbidden, no one goes there unless it is required. None save Hagith the Tormentor."

"Fortunately for you," said MacDougall, "I have decided to ask Hypatia to be my companion." With a broad smile he faced the Oracle, lovely in a lacy gold robe over a black silken shift. "That is, providing you have more suitable clothing for a woodland hike."

Hypatia beamed. "Thank you. I am sure I have—at least I hope so. There are so many garments—"

"Fine. After breakfast you will check your wardrobe and I will get my sword. I might need it in this unpleasant forest."

Shortly thereafter they met in the hallway outside their rooms, Hypatia in a shorter and more serviceable gray gown, and MacDougall with his longsword at his side. They made their way to the park outside the castle, expecting to see Eimher and Darthula on the way, but they were not in sight. Except for a few casual remarks little was said until they were crossing the stretch of lawn between the castle and the forest, when the Oracle asked,

"Why did you choose me as your companion in this exploration? I have been made attractive, but not beautiful like the other two."

MacDougall grinned. "Such candor is surprising but may be part of the answer. I think I chose you because you are the most intelligent. In part my selection was instinctive. I feel there must be an important reason for the forest's being there, probably an unpleasant reason; and your mental stability will be a help in facing whatever we meet."

Hypatia smiled her satisfaction. "Thank you, Alan MacDougall."

As they approached the forest, looming high and dark and somehow ominous before them, Alan felt a sudden foreboding, an instinctive dread. He hesitated with a sidelong glance at Hypatia. Her gaze was fixed on the woodland, uneasiness evident on her face. Side by side they entered the shadows, the thick canopy of leaves screening out the light of the aurora.

Alan thought of his first entry into the castle of King Arawn on dark Ochren—the overwhelming impression of evil. Here, too, as if hidden behind the twisted tree trunks and under waist-high bushes, lurked dark and secret terrors. Neither he nor Hypatia spoke, the atmosphere of the place quelling speech, as did the struggle through the undergrowth, until the Oracle glimpsed the path.

"Is that a walkway?" She pointed toward a line of white on their left.

"It is—and welcome!" MacDougall pushed his way through the bushes with Hypatia at his heels. "I should have hunted a path before we entered this thicket. There had to be one."

They reached it, a white gravel way about five feet wide, winding and twisting through the trees. "This is a lot better—" Alan began, then stopped short as he thought he saw movement in the undergrowth. He stood still, holding up a hand for his companion to halt. He peered intently into the brush, saw a wraithlike figure float past, soundless, eddying as in a breeze.

"Did you see that?" he whispered.

The Oracle shook her head, looking puzzled. "I see nothing unusual, only the trees and shadows, though strangely I feel as if I were being watched."

He glimpsed another wraith, and beyond it another. They were everywhere! He remembered the Grove of Spirits on Scath, though these spectral figures were less clearly defined, more like the whispering, constantly flowing shadows in the Pit of Annwn under Ochren. Despite all he had experienced in this Other World he felt a momentary chill. He had thought himself immune to shock.

"You don't see anything—moving wraiths?"

Hypatia looked intently around, then shook her head. "Nothing." Her face cleared. "Of course—your powers of sight are far greater than mine. After all, you watched me through stone walls."

Alan nodded. "Quite true. At times I forget. Powers not always welcome." What was he seeing? He thought of the serpent-gods, mechanically grasped the armlet. Mentally he asked. "Lord Enki and Lady Inanna, what am I seeing? Disembodied spirits? Why?"

Inanna answered. "Spirits indeed. The life force of hundreds who have been shut out of the normal cycle of successive reanimation."

"By what means? Is not the replacement automatic?"

"Not quite. Bodies must enter the system or be reported. You will understand in due time. Better you see for yourself."

They continued along the walk through the gloomy forest, MacDougall aware of their ghostly escort on each side. They seemed to be edging closer, as if boldness came with familiarity. He saw them more clearly now, but they were no less amorphous, though identifiably human. A sudden revolting thought came to Alan: Could they attempt possession? He stopped short and shouted, "Begone!"

Like wisps of smoke swept away in a sudden wind, the wraiths vanished into the shadows.

He looked at startled Hypatia with a reassuring smile. "We were being escorted by clouds of disembodied spirits. They fled at my command."

Solemnly the Oracle said, "The forest has always been the realm of dark and fearsome things, of forbidden terrors. Imagination fills its depths with strange forms and whispering voices, but not always are they imaginary." She halted, frowning. "Have you noticed? Here there is no sound save those we make."

Both listened, holding their breaths. Utter silence prevailed, without even the rustle of a leaf. Abruptly Alan hooked his arm in Hypatia's. "Let us see what other secrets this grove conceals, then get out of here."

After a time Hypatia asked, "What is that unpleasant odor?"

MacDougall sniffed the air, becoming aware of a smell somewhat like that of a burned-out building, though a bit more unpleasant.

"I suppose we'll find out quickly enough."

They moved briskly along the path until, following a sharp turn around giant, closely growing trees, they came upon a straight approach to a great circular clearing seventy or eighty yards wide. The sudden varicolored light from the aurora emphasized every detail of the scene. The path led to a white marble platform or dais in the form of a thirty-foot-wide disk; on it, raised an inch or two above its surface, was a five-pointed star, its points touching the edge of the disk. At a closer look, circle and star appeared to have been formed of a single enormous mass of marble.

In the center of the star, facing away from MacDougall and Hypatia, rose a great golden throne. Near the end of each of the five points stood a lesser throne, also of gold, all facing the same way. With Alan leading they stepped up on the star, rising about six inches above the grassy surface of the clearing. They crossed to the throne and stood beside it, staring at the remainder of the treeless area, seeing what an occupant of the throne would see. Here the odor of stale smoke was more intense.

Alan's eyes were drawn immediately to a heroic statue at the far end of the clearing. Eight or ten times the height of a man, it was the work of a sculptor of consummate skill, a godlike robed figure wrought of white marble seated on a backless bench. The right arm, palm down, was held out as if in perpetual benediction. As Alan stared at it, his vision blurred, the lines of the image seemed to become hazy, and there was a strange impression of movement.

Blinking to clear his sight, he lowered his eyes, his attention immediately caught by a great gray stone altar, its top ending just below the knees of the statue. Stone steps at the right end led to the upper level. The four corners of the top rectangle held great inward-curving horns of gold. Irregular dark markings stained the altar's side, as if liquids had gushed from its top, flowing down to the floor of the clearing. The blood sacrifices!

His gaze followed its inevitable course to the third and nearest object in the clearing—what appeared to be a circular, fire-blackened grid roughly fifteen feet wide formed of heavy pipes about ten inches apart. There was the suggestion of black space below the pipes, apparently a pit. From this rose the persistent odor of old fires mingled with the unpleasant stench of decay.

MacDougall could picture the sequence: a sacrifice performed by Abred the Vate, probably with appropriate ritual, then the offering burned on the grid, the bones and remnants of partially consumed flesh falling into the pit below.

From his subconscious came Inanna's reference to "hundred shut out of the normal cycle of successive reanimation," and her saying that in due time he would understand. Was this the means of disposing of the bodies of those tortured to death? The pit would tell.

He glanced at Hypatia. She was staring with rapt attention at the great image.

"Is it not beautiful?" she asked in a hushed voice. "Those golden wings and that jeweled crown!"

Incredulous, Alan looked at the statue, saw that it had changed, that indeed there now were great golden wings outstretched from its back and an immense glittering crown on its regal head. The arms were outstretched as if inviting worship, or offering refuge.

Shape-changing—in a stone image!

MacDougall felt a stab of fear followed by mounting anger. Magic or hypnosis be damned. "Stay here," he commanded, darting over the marble, crossing the stretch of grass to stare through the grid of pipes. A convenient auroral flare of light revealed far below him the irregular accumulation of ash and charred bones, among them, unmistakably, human skulls. He saw something else, regularly spaced holes in the upper surface of the pipes— vents for the flow of natural gas to fire the altar flames. Gas had illuminated Ochren; underground wells were part of this world system.

Alan turned away to find Hypatia at his elbow, staring with horror into the pit. "How dreadful," she breathed. "Human sacrifices."

He grasped her arm and led her hastily across the dais to the path. He cast a final glance over his shoulder and he thought he saw the image now in polished black, the wings and crown gone, standing with arms crossed. Absurd, he told himself.

They did not slacken their pace nor speak until they had left the somber grove behind them. Then Hypatia said in subdued tones, "So much is dreadful in this realm. Often I have wondered what I did to deserve my being here. You spoke of my intelligence, and I was pleased. But this, it may well be, is my folly. Once in the Olden Time I heard a humble wanderer in beggar's rags—one who was in the crowd to which I lectured— and he said, loudly enough for me to hear, 'The wisdom of the world is foolishness with God.' The thought annoyed me then, but it has lingered with me. Perhaps pride in my wisdom and knowledge brought me here. I never thought I could be mistaken."

MacDougall made no immediate response. As they were about to enter their own rooms he said solemnly,

"Who am I to say? I lack the wisdom to venture an opinion."

Slumped in a chair, his legs stretched out before him, Alan thought about what he had seen in the thicket. He was infuriated by the evidence of the skulls. Was it merely cremation of those who had died at the hands of Hagith, or was Hypatia correct? Were there human sacrifices? But more disturbing than the blackened bones was the illusion of the changing image. It *had* to be illusion.

"Lord Enki," he addressed the serpent-god, "statues don't shape-change. What is the answer?"

There was hesitation; then came the single word: "Lucifer."

Lucifer! Did he indwell the image—or cause the illusion—or what? Alan did not pursue the question, consciously directing his thoughts into other channels. How much time had passed since breakfast? Certainly not enough to make lunch imminent. Should he seek out Eimher or Darthula? Definitely not. This idea of Ahriman's was ridiculous, his being the prize sought by three lovely women. What was happening elsewhere? With Taliesin, for instance.

With closed eyes he pictured the Bard, centering his mind on observation, not communication. Instantly he saw the familiar round face with its bald head and thick circle of white hair like a misplaced broken halo. He was seated at a broad table facing one of the Ch'in of Shenzhu. But this was no Druid; there could be no Druids in the City of Jade!

A clear thought came from the Bard. *"But there are some with magic powers among the priests; and Ahriman instructed me to seek logical candidates among such in each of the four cities. I have already completed my search in Cuchulainn, where of course there are Druids, and in Magadha."*

"But I intended no communication at this time," Alan mentally protested. *"I was merely curious about your progress."*

He saw a faint smile appear on Taliesin's face. *"Unless we consciously block our thoughts, we exchange them."*

"Sorry," MacDougall responded. *"I meant no intrusion."* He cut off the vision. So the pointless search for helpers went on. Ahriman certainly was confident about the outcome. What was he up to now? Why not join him and find out? Or at least observe?

He found Ahriman seated in a room unlike any Alan had previously seen. Obviously it was in his Tower, one rounded golden wall revealing the aurora; it was wedge-shaped, the two side walls tapering toward the center. Strangely, the light from the aurora seemed blocked, sending only a dim glow over the One-Who-Speaks-for-the-Master as he sat in a teakwood chair facing away from the light. The side walls were black, as was the floor. The heart of the wedge seemed to grow misty and somehow to open into the vastness of a black and starless space.

As Alan watched, a dim glow formed in the heart of the mist, and within it a suggestion of a face. There was something strange about it, overly long and thin, the great, dark eyes obliquely slanted, but the features were not clearly discernible. The Persian spoke.

"What have you to report from the artisans of Shekinar?"

An odd and wheezing voice, little more than a hoarse whisper, came out of the dimness. "We do well. Even now its powers are being tested. We are confident that the Master will be pleased. Only the finest and rarest gems and metals have been used, and the most skilled among us has wrought in its creation. Messengers will deliver it well before your scheduled need."

"It is well," Ahriman intoned; and the image faded into the blackness. The Persian stood up and vanished.

Opening his eyes, MacDougall waited. He had decided to appear in Ahriman's presence, but it would not be wise to seem to be following his movements. He thought of what he had seen and heard. It had no meaning for him. The object the "artisans of Shekinar" had created could be anything. Evidently something important made of metal and gems, fashioned and tooled on another world.

When he thought a prudent interval had passed, he

pictured the Persian and found him alone in his luxurious golden room at the top of the Tower. He was seated in a massive chair, apparently deep in thought. Alan centered his thoughts on being there, his mind set on the airiness, the floating of levitation, the breathless flight—and it happened in an instant. He was standing on the softly yielding rug in Ahriman's golden room, looking down into the widening eyes of Lucifer's lieutenant.

Momentarily Ahriman frowned; then his face cleared. "Trying out one of your new abilities, I see. An unexpected visit. To what do I owe your coming?"

"As you surmised, I decided to exercise the power you so generously included in my schooling. Then, too, I did it out of boredom."

"Boredom! With three lovely women to entertain you! Perhaps you are not aware that they are fully at your disposal. And though obviously their present bodies could not exist outside this realm, any or all of them will be taught possession, hence could provide you with the loveliest women in your world and time. If you desired, all three could be your—companions."

MacDougall gave a short, mirthless laugh. There was nothing ambiguous about the other's statement. He spoke slowly, emphasizing every word. "First, I do not plan to be your world ruler. I have made this clear repeatedly. And second, if through some impossible circumstance I were to occupy this exalted position, I should still choose Elspeth Cameron. And not Elspeth possessed by Darthula or Eimher or Hypatia. This is my final word on the matter."

Ahriman's face stiffened into an expressionless mask as he stared unwinkingly at Alan. When at last he spoke his voice, too, was expressionless. "Your last word? So be it."

Abruptly the Persian stood up and, to Alan's surprise, changed the subject. MacDougall had expected a more violent reaction to his defiance. Ahriman said quietly, "I had planned to summon you a bit later to have you observe our progress and a recent interesting development; but since you are here, you shall see it as it now is. The performance may not be as smooth as one might desire, but it should be fascinating to watch nonetheless."

MacDougall looked doubtfully at the Persian. "If it has anything to do with possession—" he began, only to be interrupted sharply.

"I will not take 'no' for an answer. It is highly important that you see what is being done." He grasped Alan's arm; and instantly their surroundings changed.

They were still inside the Tower as the curved golden wall attested, in a portion of a large circular room partitioned into small cubicles by heavy night-blue draperies. There were three people within the confined areas before them, seated in broad, massive chairs of bronze. That is, two were seated in normal fashion, one of them the Lord Beli of Ochren, the other a stranger. The third, Manannan, god of the sea, was manacled to the arms and legs of his chair. His face was fixed in a grim glare of defiance. The stranger, MacDougall decided after a penetrating look, was a demon, evidently the instructor. In addition to the chairs, there was a low cot along one side.

"Manannan, finally, has been caught, as inevitably he had to be," Ahriman said coldly, "and now he is adequately guarded. Not again will Amaruduk release him. He has arrived just in time to help in advanced training of the more apt among the students. Beli is one of these. And, for your guidance, nothing you can do or say can be sensed by the three. We only *seem* to be in this room."

The instructor was speaking to Beli, probably on a mental directive from Ahriman, telling the giant redbeard to lie down on the cot, release his spirit from his body, and to enter Manannan's, taking up joint possession. He must overcome resistance and take control.

As Beli stood up, Manannan ground through clenched teeth, "No man can do that to me, not even Beli!"

Face expressionless, the god of the underworld stretched out on the cot, arms at his sides, closed his eyes, and relaxed. Silence fell as tension mounted. Alan held his breath, aware of Beli's sensations, since he had undergone the same separation of body and spirit under the tutelage of Varuna the Sage in the Hindu city, Magadha. But not to the same end!

With a rasping gasp Manannan began to writhe, his features contorted, eyes squeezed shut. As he himself must have writhed, Alan thought, on his bed in the Cameron home when the black cloud had closed over him and an alien presence had sought to possess him. Here was no cloud, no visible sign of the battle being waged in Manannan except for the gyrations of the victim. His body twisted and squirmed, trying to wrench his limbs from the manacles, to tear himself free of the chair.

Abruptly he relaxed, all struggle ended, his features sickeningly flaccid, his head slumping against his chest. Beli had overcome. Slowly animation returned, facial muscles tightening, and Manannan spoke. The voice was his but the words were Beli's.

"A strong man, Manannan, but I have won. And this, though he knew what to expect, having had a similar experience with Amaruduk. What is the next step?"

The instructor replied, "You are to seek full access to Manannan's knowledge, to learn to use his brain. This is essential for your future task." After a pause he added, "And you, Manannan, are to resist, to strive with all your power to expel this intruder."

"And expel him I shall!" The sea-god's voice and words.

The scene changed; they seemed to be floating above a series of similar small cubicles where trios were enacting similar procedures, differing in that none of the victims were known to Alan. This, too, vanished, and they were back in Ahriman's quarters.

"Sit." The Persian motioned toward a chair. "As you have seen, preparation is quite thorough. It is not enough that possession alone is accomplished. For this major second step in the training, the ordinary subjects used thus far will not suffice. They lack the strength of mind and will to provide the necessary resistance. Hence some of those who chose to remain here, or whom you rejected, as well as Druids not selected by Taliesin, will be pressed into service. I should think Balor and Pryderi and his son Pwyll will provide excellent subjects. None of these, however, have incurred my wrath like Manannan, so they will render limited service. The sea-god will serve until he has reached total and permanent exhaustion.'' There was gloating savagery in his final statement.

"Is this really necessary?" MacDougall asked. "I mean, this intensive training."

"Without it what we plan would be impossible. There must be continuous mastery and the ability to utilize fully the knowledge and experience of each host."

Frowning thoughtfully, Alan said, "But all that will take a great deal of time. Somehow I gained the impression that you were planning to set events in motion in my world in the near future."

"As I am. But all that is involved will require time, including your own actions. Initially you will be virtually alone, humanly speaking. You will have the help of Powers, of course, as well as your newly mastered abilities. You will establish yourself as a world figure, control vast funds through an enterprising money power whom you will select and who will be taken over by one of your staff. Possibly an Arab Sheikh who will be possessed, perhaps, by Kalidasa the Hindu, who is a born schemer.

"But such planning is premature. Details will be worked out as conditions dictate. But time will be required, months, even years for the consummation of the Great Plan. And while events move forward in the Other World, training will continue here, so that skilled helpers will be ready when you need them."

MacDougall looked off to one side into the blackness beyond the Tower wall, trying to control his thoughts and his facial expression. He closed his mind to the growing revulsion this matter of possession aroused; he shut out thoughts of its diabolic ramifications for his own world, and concentrated on one idea. Somehow the concept of a gradual working out of plans outside of this bewitched world had never occurred to him. This meant he would be free of Ahriman's direct supervision and influence, back in Britain and the United States, and "virtually alone."

Of course there were demons in his own world, as well as human followers of Satan, but there were multitudes not under his control. Alan became aware of a sense of vast relief. He looked back at the Persian, hoping none of this had shown on his face.

"I should have realized," he said with a weak grin, "that world control could hardly be gained overnight. Though, as you know, long range or short, it is of no interest to me."

Ahriman smiled, as usual without mirth. "You may well change your mind." He stood up. "I'll return you to your room. Lunch has been prepared and is awaiting your arrival."

CHAPTER 11

The Transcendental King

Not in ages, it seemed to Alan MacDougall, had he felt the relief, the lightness that followed his session with Ahriman. Not, in fact, since his initial return from Tartarus; and that seemed in the remote past. He would be back in Scotland, back in America, free of the bonds that held him to Sheol, never to return. He'd see to that. Not quite free, he thought with a momentary frown. There would still be the armlet—but on his own turf he'd find a way to get rid of it.

A diffident rap on the door interrupted his train of thought, and a respectful voice said, "The Queen and her visitors invite you to join them for lunch, if you wish."

"Tell her I'll be right there. Don't wait."

As he headed through the corridors a short time later, some of MacDougall's exuberance began to fade. Easy, Alan, he told himself. You're overreacting. After all, this development merely meant that he'd have more time to find a way out of his troubles in his own world, something he should have realized all along. Nonetheless, the prospect of leaving Avilion, and soon, made him more cheerful than he'd been in a long time.

He joined the three women in the intimate dining nook, greeting them warmly. They were already seated. As he took his seat he noticed that they were dressed alike except for color. Each wore a full, wraparound robe of delicate silken fabric, Eimher's pale green, Darthula's pastel blue, and Hypatia's light yellow. To complete their dress, each had a broad red-gold band circling her head and long pendant earrings of a single great teardrop, the Queen's emerald, Darthula's sapphire, and Hypatia's a yellow gem, probably topaz.

Fantastic, Alan thought. Certainly this had been planned for his benefit. And as they ate, and sparingly, he noticed the conversation was strained, the three striving to conceal their excitement, as if they were bursting with a secret. Momentarily he was tempted to pry into the thoughts of one of them, but he checked the impulse. Let them spring their surprise.

It came after the servers had cleared the table. Queen Eimher rose and announced eagerly, "We have prepared some unusual entertainment for you. It awaits you in the next room. Will you follow?" She led the way through a doorway, Darthula and Hypatia at his heels.

The room they entered was thickly carpeted in black and, strangely, it held only a single heavily upholstered chair centered at one wall. At the far end stood five women dressed in flowing robes, each holding a musical instrument—three with panpipes, the fourth a lyre, and the fifth a hand drum. As Alan entered they began to play, a soft, wild, rhythmic melody.

The Queen ushered MacDougall to the chair, and the three women moved to the center of the room.

"We dance," Eimher said softly, and as the ceiling glow dimmed, with one movement the three kicked aside their sandals, swept off their robes, flung them away, and began to sway. They stood revealed in cobweb-thin shifts ending well above their knees—full-cut garments, pastel green, blue, and yellow.

Alan MacDougall caught his breath. They were three

beautiful women, faces and forms well-nigh flawless, voluptuous yet slender, designed to awaken a stone statue. As the moments passed the musicians increased the volume and the tempo, the sound more exotic, and the swaying became a spontaneous dance, uninhibited and erotic. Here was no choreographed form, no practiced repetition, each dancer expressing with graceful movements of limbs and torso the emotions and desires awakened and intensified by the wild melody and rhythm.

Gradually the gestures and motions became less graceful, more elemental, the whirling and posturing yielding to a wilder abandon. The voluminous webs of garments floated free, cloudlike, as they whirled, revealing fully the graceful forms. Each seemed to be vying with the others to gain his attention, to hold his gaze on her alone.

MacDougall watched in fascination, his pulse accelerating, his breath shortening. Incredible that these three—Queen, Princess, Philosopher—could free themselves of all restraint. As he himself felt restraint slipping away, desire growing. Remember, he tried to tell himself, these are bodies created by Lucifer, which accounts for their perfection, bodies fourteen hundred years old, and now under the command of Ahriman. He tried to close his eyes, to picture the warmly smiling face of Elspeth Cameron, but his eyes seemed to have a will of their own.

He was sitting on the edge of the seat, his mouth dry, when the music and the dancing ended, the three panting women flinging themselves at his feet with bare arms outstretched. Their breasts were rising and falling swiftly, their lips parted, their eyes fixed on his, seeking his approbation.

At that instant a deep and familiar voice jarred through the chamber. It was like a dash of cold water. Ahriman! With the voice a glowing face appeared high on the wall facing MacDougall.

"Beautifully done! I thoroughly enjoyed your dancing, my lovelies, and I regret that I must interrupt. But it is expedient, Alan MacDougall, that you return to your room. I will explain when you arrive there."

As the three women scrambled for their robes and sandals, Alan stood up, applauding even as he mentally berated the Persian. "That was—fantastic," he said huskily. "All of you are fascinating dancers, and so lovely. Each deserves—this." And with fervor he kissed them in turn, crushing each against his chest. "Perhaps the performance can be repeated. Later. In concert or each alone." Turning, he left the room.

As he moved through the corridors, MacDougall mentally damned Ahriman. A sadist! Gloating over another's frustration. Like someone dangling candy before an eager child and snatching it away at the last moment. Abruptly Alan grinned. Not a very apt comparison—likening those three beautiful sirens to candy, and his desire as that of a hungry child. Suddenly it made sense. This was Sheol—Hell. Desire aroused, then frustrated. By the time he reached his room he was almost inclined to thank the Persian. But not quite.

Outside his doorway he found two men waiting, one with a blue garment draped over his arm, the other with what appeared to be cloth-of-gold. They bowed deeply at his approach, and one said, "Your Majesty, we are tailors and we have come to fit the garments ordered for you."

MacDougall arched his brows in puzzlement. "Garments? I ordered no garments."

"He-Who-Speaks-for-the-Master ordered them; and we must complete them before the banquet. May we enter?"

"Banquet?" Alan stopped short. Ahriman had said he'd explain. "Very well," he said resignedly. After all, he had lamented the fact that he had to live in one suit for what must be weeks on end. A change would be welcome, though the cloth-of-gold looked strange.

Inside his room, at the tailors' request, he removed his black outfit and slipped on the medium blue, silken trousers, patterned after Ahriman's garments—full-cut, gathered snugly at the ankles—a white collarless shirt that had been folded under the cape, and the gaudy cape itself. Only the waist of the trousers and the sleeves of the shirt required adjusting.

When the tailors had gone and Alan was fully dressed, the glowing image of the Persian appeared on the wall.

"I told you I would explain—"

"Before we go into that," Alan interrupted, "why in the world did you order so gaudy an outfit for me? I appreciate a change of clothes, but that cape is ridiculous."

Ahriman forced a smile. "Trust me, my friend. It will be most appropriate for the occasion. As for my interruption—"

Again MacDougall broke in, saying with all the sincerity he could muster "I've been thinking about your intervention, and I want to thank you for appearing when you did. Had you delayed, I might have done something indiscreet, and that would have been most regrettable."

Ahriman stared doubtfully at Alan, then smiled. "Almost I believed you. However, I saw *you* as well as the dancers. The reason for my appearing, as you must have surmised, was the arrival of the tailors at your room and the need for the prompt completion of their work. You must have the garments in time for the banquet, which will be served here in Cuchulainn's castle at dinnertime. With this we start the ceremonies that precede your return to the Other World and the beginning of your ordained reign. Initially none there will know, but in due time they will learn."

MacDougall checked an impulse to laugh. The whole idea was so absurd. But the prospect of his leaving Avilion outweighed everything else. No matter what Ahriman proposed—up to a point—he'd cooperate. As for the Persian's appearing, the timing was too perfect. Dangling bait, then pulling it away. Somewhat sarcastically he asked, "And what am I supposed to do to occupy myself until the banquet time arrives?"

Ahriman smiled. "Since any of the three lovely dancers would welcome your company, you should find no difficulty in passing the time. Your garments will be placed in your room when they are ready; and no matter where you are I will find you in ample time for you to prepare for the festivities.'' The image faded and was gone.

Alan sank back into his chair. Hard to believe, but his time in this world seemed to be drawing to a close. He thought of the incredible events that had occurred since that far-off day when he had ventured into the Scottish Highlands to search for his missing brother, Malcolm. The chiming of the singing blades leading him to that ancient stone *broch* where he had found Malcolm's body, the armlet, his longsword, and the accursed Scroll. The tower with its four Gates. His entry into Tartarus and his meeting Taliesin, who had played so vital a role in all his adventures in this ensorcelled world. Not in his wildest imaginings could he have conceived all that had followed. And soon, if all went well, it would end! All in this world at least.

A tentative rap on his door broke in on his thoughts. He glanced into the hall beyond, saw Eimher standing there, a tense expression on her face. She still wore the same robe, evidently having come from the dining room.

Alan scowled. He didn't think he wanted company. He was certain she was there at Ahriman's command; her pride would not have allowed her pursuing him otherwise, despite his new status. He made no sound; and after rapping once more and waiting a few moments she left. Who would be next? he wondered. He had not long to wait for the answer.

At a more confident rap, he observed Hypatia standing before his door. She seemed quite self-possessed, almost businesslike, as if she had a duty to perform. It might be entertaining to admit her—but, no! He had no intention of yielding to the seductive powers of any of them. He remained silent, and in moments the Philosopher turned away, entering her own room.

Darthula would be next; and at the thought of her blond loveliness MacDougall stood up. He liked the Princess as a person, and he knew of her affection for him. He might be tempted to admit her in spite of Ahriman. He made a quick decision. When she came he would not be there. He wanted solitude and quiet, a place to think without interruption.

He pictured the white-pebbled beach and the tranquil waters of the tideless sea; and he was there, the rounded pebbles underfoot. No longer marveling at this magic manifestation, he crossed the narrow beach and sank to a seat on the turf at its edge. After pulling his knees up under his chin, he clasped his hands around them and stared out over the ever-thrilling spectacle of the aurora and its mirror image.

There was no denying it, there were sights of fantastic beauty and wonder in this Other World. The ice-blue city of Falias with its Temple of crystal; the valley of the waterfall with its lacy veil careening over the rocky wall to form the blue lake far below. The cliffs of massive outcroppings of gemlike greens and reds and purples, of raw gold. Indeed, each of the four cities of Tartarus was beautiful in its own way. But beauty merely formed the setting for ugliness, grotesquerie, brutality, and evil.

Ochren, the second island, was devoid of beauty. Its eternal dusk, with the aurora barely visible, tried vainly to conceal the closest approach to the conventional idea of Hell in all this world. He thought of the torture chambers in the castle of King Arawn, then shut the image from his mind.

Beauty in Scath? He could think of none except the aurora and the sea. The wide patch of giant fungi with their distorted shapes and sickly colors was fascinating but hardly beautiful. The stately trees in the Grove of Ghosts were handsome in themselves, but the impression of the copse as a whole was eerie and revolting. Even the castles and other structures of Scath and Marduk, the two halves of the third island, were erected without beauty in mind.

Avilion? Handsome architecture, genuine beauty in the City of Jade; the park surrounding Gate four manifesting formal beauty; but underlying all of it was gross evil. There was no escaping it—nothing could conceal the fact that this was Sheol. It would be good to leave, never to return. A chilling thought flashed through his mind, to be blocked out instantly. What assurance had he that after death he would not awaken in another part of Lucifer's domain?

MacDougall sank back on the turf, stretching his legs out before him, clasped his hands behind his head, and closed his eyes. He listened. There was no sound save his own steady breathing. He could sense the pulsing of his heart. Strange to be so completely alone.

He dozed.

A quiet but commanding voice filtered into his consciousness, a voice he recognized instantly. "It is time for you to prepare for the banquet." Ahriman.

Alan opened his eyes, fully awake, and sat up. The Persian stood a few feet away, observing him with a half smile. "Apparently you find nothing menacing in Avilion, sleeping thus in isolation. But then, Enki and Inanna are always alert." As MacDougall got to his feet he added, "When you are ready, you will be escorted to the banquet hall." And suddenly he was gone.

MacDougall frowned. Somehow Ahriman always annoyed him; something in his superior attitude. He shrugged. That, too, would come to an end with his return to the Highlands. He visualized himself in his room in the castle, and in a breath he was there. If only he could travel the same way into his own world!

He stared into vacancy as if transfixed. Why not? He had made the trip during his out-of-body experience; why not physically? Certainly worth trying. With closed eyes he pictured the interior of the *broch*; visualized himself standing before the fireplace; willed himself there.

Nothing happened.

He grasped the armlet. "Lord and Lady, why did I fail in my effort to transfer to the Other World?"

"The answer should be obvious," Inanna answered impatiently, "even to you. If that could be done, through the centuries those of this world with the ability—the *Tuatha de Danann*, for instance—would have discovered the secret and would have returned to their own destruction. No; only the Gates provide passage between the worlds. And only the plan of the Lord of Light as predicted in the Scroll makes possible the return of dwellers in this realm.'' Oh well, MacDougall thought, life could never be that simple.

A flash of color on the bed caught his attention. His costume, like something out of the *Arabian Nights*. Blue silk trousers, white collarless shirt, and cloth-of-gold cape. Quickly he stripped, took a hasty cold shower, combed his mass of blond hair before the mirror, and in freshly laundered underwear and socks put on his new garments. Only the black boots remained of his former outfit, and the pantaloons covered the tops. For a moment he surveyed his gaudy splendor, grinning broadly.

With perfect timing there came a rap on the door, and a deep voice announced, ''Your Majesty, we have been sent by the One-Who-Speaks-for-the-Master to escort you to the banquet.''

Outside MacDougall found four of the elite guards, splendid in their blue tunics and dark-green kilts. At his appearance, as one they drew their swords and held them against their chests, points upward, the same pose they had struck for King Cuchulainn. With two marching in step before him and two behind, they escorted him through the marble corridors to what he recognized immediately as Cuchulainn's great throne room, where he had been led upon his arrival at the castle. They entered through a doorway beside the dais.

As Alan halted just inside the doorway, seventy or more people, already seated at a great U-shap ed table, rose quickly and stood stiffly at attention. MacDougall repressed a grin as he surveyed the room with what he hoped was proper regal bearing. This was insane, but he'd go along with the conceit. He was especially amused to see Cuchulainn and Queen Eimher among those at the table at the far end of the room. With them were the others—Beli, Nuada, King Kumaragupta of Magadha, Emperor Khau Ch'in Khih of Shenzhu—all those chosen to assist him in world rule, plus Hypatia, Darthula, and Taliesin. At the side tables stood the Druids, Druidesses, and magicians in a mixture of white and gray and black robes. Quite a gathering.

Alan nodded to his guides, and they led him to a small table centered below the black dais with its empty golden throne. There were places for two; and as Alan paused behind one of the chairs, a golden light shimmered at his left, and Ahriman suddenly appeared. He bowed to MacDougall, then addressed the assemblage.

"We have gathered here with a twofold purpose. We have come to pay homage to the Master, the Lord of Light, the Bright and Morning Star, Lucifer the Lord of all Lords whose Great Plan is approaching consummation. And we are here to honor the Master's Chosen One whose coming was foretold millennia ago, who has passed every testing, who has overcome every obstacle, and who is now ready to accept his high honor, Alan MacDougall."

Ahriman bowed deeply toward the object of his eulogy, and Alan bowed in turn, even as he thought, Enough of this mumbo-jumbo. He drew back his chair and seated himself, and as if on signal, all the others followed suit, including the Persian. The latter raised his hand and announced, "Let the banquet begin."

The feast that followed must have strained the resources of all Avilion, but MacDougall gave little thought to the abundance of food. Indeed, he felt most uncomfortable. Ahriman's reference to him and Lucifer in almost the same breath had brought home his frightening position. And it *was* frightening. He was entangled in a web spun by beings with powers that must be called superhuman. Oh, he had learned many of their tricks, certainly more than any other man, even more than any one of these Celtic gods. He had mastered all their magic and much more. But though on occasion he had defied Ahriman and had tried to minimize his powers, in honesty he had to admit Lucifer's lieutenant was more than human, with powers beyond any that mortals could acquire. Even his calling him a Persian was phony; if he'd ever been a Persian—and that was most unlikely—he was one no longer. As for Lucifer—he refused to pursue the thought. Damn! How had he gotten himself into this mess?

At last the servers removed the remainder of the food and cleared the table. Then Ahriman stood up, raising a hand. Instantly all conversation ceased and complete silence fell.

"We have arrived at the moment I have long anticipated," he announced solemnly, "an honor for me that is the culmination of a great cooperative effort in which many of you have had a part. For some it was the shaping of the Chosen One through adversity. Others of you have been teachers. For others your role lies in the future. But, great or small in the Master's plan, you, too, have been chosen, hence you share this honor."

He turned to the waiting object of all this buildup, who was thinking impatiently, Get to the point, and whatever it is you plan to do, finish it in a hurry.

"Alan MacDougall, will you join me on the dais?"

Together they made their way around to the side of the platform, mounted a short, black stone stairway, and crossed to the throne. Ahriman gestured toward the golden seat, his gem-blue eyes meeting Alan's, his manner solemn, his voice commanding.

"Your throne, your Majesty."

Mentally protesting, MacDougall, almost as if under hypnosis, seated himself and, with head held high, fixed his gaze on the rear wall. Where would this end? In moments he learned.

"But one thing is lacking," Ahriman said. He raised his voice, calling to someone outside the chamber. "Nuriel!"

Responding instantly, a tall, gray-robed figure appeared in the doorway at the right of the dais. As every eye stared in his direction, MacDougall also turned his head. He gasped.

On outstretched arms the newcomer bore a padded square of black velvet, on it a jeweled crown of unbelievable splendor. Not gold, nor yet silver, it was wrought of a whiter metal, probably platinum, intricately chased, gleaming with mirrorlike brilliance. At the tip of each of many gracefully curved peaks glittered an enormous gem, alternating diamonds and emeralds. The central peak, taller than the rest, held a faceted stone like none Alan had ever seen, pulsing with internal fire, emitting every color of the spectrum.

As the man approached—not a man; almost certainly one of Ahriman's demonic servants—there flashed in MacDougall's memory the vision he had seen while spying in the Golden Tower. The glimpse as in a black tunnel of a strange being who had reported on the progress of their labors in a place called Shekinar. Their fashioning something of metal and gems that had to be delivered in time for some event. This must be that object.

The being called Nuriel halted before Ahriman, presenting the crown. Lucifer's lieutenant removed it from its padded bed and held it high before him, his eyes closed as if in prayer while the messenger backed away, then vanished. The scene held interminably, Alan's gaze fixed on the splendid jewel. Again he pictured the strange being with enormous, sloping eyes, again heard his report: "Even now its powers are being tested."

Powers! Unknown powers built into the crown. Sudden dread sent a chill coursing up his spine, awakened near panic. Ages ago he had slipped on the armlet and incredible experiences had followed. He did not want that alien creation placed on his head! He saw Ahriman open his eyes, move toward him, the crown poised; heard his deep voice intoning "In the authority bestowed upon me by the Master of Myriad Worlds, the Great God Lucifer, I declare you to be the monarch of all monarchs, the Transcendental King." Slowly he moved the crown toward Alan's head.

Escape! A single thought drove MacDougall. He pictured his bedroom, willed himself there, and instantly he was alone, seated in his great chair. Startled by his own impulsive action, for a fleeting moment he thought of hiding, then dismissed the thought. Not for him the role of fugitive with eventual capture inevitable, as Amaruduk would learn.

He tried to picture the consternation that must prevail in the banquet hall. Why imagine it when he could observe? He closed his eyes, saw Ahriman on his dais.

He stood in frozen rigidity, his face suddenly pale, incredulity giving way to cold fury. In seconds his features became expressionless, and as if all had been planned, he carefully placed the crown on the seat of the throne and faced his stunned and silent watchers.

"The actual coronation will take place in the Master's forest after the next sleep. All of you will be transferred to quarters in my Tower for rest." Again he called, "Nuriel," and the gray-robed being reappeared, the black velvet square in his hands.

"See to the crown," Ahriman directed, then vanished.

Alan opened his eyes to meet the unwinking stare of Lucifer's lieutenant, towering above him. "Explain your actions," he demanded.

MacDougall shrugged. "I decided on the spur of the moment that I did not want to be crowned, particularly with a diadem possessing unknown powers."

"What makes you think the crown has unknown powers, as you call them?"

"It is not merely an opinion. The being from Shekinar who made a progress report to you spoke of testing its powers."

Ahriman raised his brows. "So? Quite interesting. You have been observing matters not intended for your eyes."

"Why shouldn't I use the abilities I have acquired? As for my observing, you do it all the time."

Ahriman nodded approvingly. "The fault is mine. I should have been on guard. As for the powers that you seem to fear, they are physical abilities that the crown will impart. For example, you will be able to emit a golden glow as I regularly do. These abilities will become apparent to you as you need them. And if you fear that, like the armlet, you could not remove the crown, the idea is absurd. It is merely a symbol of your power, intended at this moment to impress those who will be serving as your helpers. Eventually it will fit into the scheme of things in the Other World; at present it would be completely out of place.

"Now I suggest you rest. You will need all your energy to play your part in the happenings in the Master's Woods.'' With the last word Ahriman vanished.

MacDougall sank back into his chair, trying to relax. As always, after a confrontation with Lucifer's lieutenant he felt tense. Mentally he reviewed what the demon had said and immediately decided it was nonsense. A symbol to impress the Chosen Ones, true enough; but as a means of supplying him with additional physical powers—this made no sense at all. Whatever the answer, he wanted nothing whatever to do with that crown.

The coming ceremony in the woods, what would it entail? A sacrifice, certainly. And was it to be followed by his immediate return to the Highlands? Ahriman's statement implied as much. In any event, sleep was in order. He stood up and stretched. He was tired. Quickly he shed his gaudy blue and gold garments and prepared for sleep.

By the time he stretched out on his bed his eyelids were heavy and he felt quite weary. As he dimmed the glow of the ceiling, there came into his mind the familiar thought of the Bard. *"Alan—can you sense my message? I have been trying—"*

"Yes, Taliesin, I receive you clearly."

There was great relief in the other's response. *"Wonderful. It is so important. I must warn you—"* As abruptly as it had come, the communication ended. Blocked again by Ahriman's agents, MacDougall thought angrily. This was not to be borne. He visualized the Bard; saw him seated in a small, sparely furnished room with golden walls, his bowed head held between his hands. Vainly Alan tried to reach him mentally. He thought of joining him, but decided that if he made the transfer the Bard would be snatched away; and he didn't feel up to another confrontation.

With the vision cut off Alan lay staring at the ceiling, sudden overwhelming weariness besetting him. In moments he was asleep.

How long he slept before he began to dream he had no way of knowing. But he began to dream, and strangely he knew he was dreaming. Not the half-waking, half-sleeping eavesdropping on the *Tuatha de Danann*; clearly the coherent and vivid creation of his subconscious mind; and quite unlike any dream he could remember. He was both participant and visual observer. Visual, because at no time was he aware of any sounds.

It began in the familiar, deeply shadowed interior of the Highland *broch*. He saw a full-color image of himself and Elspeth standing before the fourth Gate, his arm around her waist. He was dressed in his usual black attire, and she wore a simple frock of figured blue. As Alan watched, his double reached out and swung wide the Gate, a flood of auroral light dissipating the deeper shadows. They stood thus, gazing at the tailored perfection of the Avilion landscape, Elspeth's interest indicating that she, too, could see what lay before her.

To MacDougall, a slumbering watcher, the spectacle was uncanny. It became even more dreamlike as he saw the pair step through the portal, Elspeth leading the way, then grasping the arm of the Alan-figure and hastening across the lawn with elfin grace. After a few moments the girl halted, staring up into the aurora, then gazing in wonder all around her, apparently speaking to her companion. After the brief pause they continued on their way, their destination becoming evident—the woodland that Ahriman had called the Master's Woods. They reached it and, dreamlike, vanished in its depths.

Vainly MacDougall sought to follow, but with the perversity of the subconscious his imaging became confused, disordered, finally fading into nothingness.

Time passed; and again he became aware that he was dreaming. He found himself approaching the still-open portal into the stone tower. As he reached it, he beheld a ghostly procession emerging from the Other World. Amazingly, at the head of the column appeared the Highland lad, David Cameron, walking with sure steps across the pale turf. Behind him in single file came Cinel Loarn and his green-clad warriors, the Sidhe, marching with military precision, their bronze swords and shields in hand. There was no hesitation in their movement as they headed toward the woodland behind the marble city. The vision ended, as had that of Elspeth, when they reached the dark grove. Dreamless slumber followed.

Slowly Alan MacDougall awakened, coming out of a nearly trancelike state. Every detail of what he had envisioned was clear in his mind, as if through one of his unusual powers he had actually observed Elspeth's entry into Avilion, with himself her guide. But the idea was absurd, as was the sight of her brother David and the Sidhe following.

He opened his eyes and sat up. Should he try to check . . .

"Alan MacDougall!" Strongly the mental call registered in his consciousness, a familiar personality but not one instantly recognized. *"Have you forgotten me so quickly?"*

"Amaruduk!" Alan responded. *"What brings you here?"*

"My hatred for Ahriman." The thought was cold and venomous. *"I know you, too, can bear no kindly feelings for him after all he has subjected you to; and I have discovered a way to help you and to annoy him greatly. I have found and opened the Gate in Marduk—what you think of as Scath. It has been your desire to return to your own world, but the portal out of Avilion is closed."* Eagerness appeared in his thought. *"I dare not pass through; but in moments you can be back in the Highland tower."* The thought went on, *"I know you would not betray me to this self-styled Speaker-for-the-Master. As you may see, I am actually here with you."*

For a fleeting moment an image of the onetime Sumerian God of gods appeared seated across from MacDougall, first handsome, regal, in the form he had assumed; then twisted and misshapen as he actually was.

Alan was torn with indecision. Could he trust Amaruduk? He'd be out of Avilion, and he'd avoid wearing that crown . . .

Suddenly the room was crowded with entities, scores of beings centered around the chair where Alan had glimpsed Amaruduk; and in their grasp appeared the ruler of Marduk, invisibility gone.

An incredulous thought touched MacDougall's mind. *"You did betray me. Why?"*

"Not MacDougall." Coldly triumphant, another thought formed, evident to Alan and Amaruduk, the thought of the Lady Inanna. *"It has taken a very long time, but at last I am avenged. Perhaps as you lie rigid among the sleepers through the ages to come, you will recall the vengeance of the Queen Inanna whose form as Tiamat the Great Serpent you shamefully misused."*

Abruptly MacDougall was alone except for the perpetual presence of the serpent-gods. Gone were the demons and with them Amaruduk. An area of the wall began to glow, and the coldly smiling face of Ahriman appeared.

"At last that source of annoyance has been dealt with, and the Master's decree is being fulfilled. Immobility and silence coupled with full consciousness will be Amaruduk's lot for ages to come, as it is that of Ereshkigal, once goddess of the Nether World. The Master may not be disobeyed, even by those—no, *especially* by those whom he has greatly honored."

After a pause Ahriman added, "A new day, as you would think of it, has begun. The conclusion of your coronation and the beginning of your ordained task in your own world will follow your breaking fast. Do not delay. Appear wearing your royal garments. Your escort is already in the corridor." Ahriman's image vanished.

CHAPTER 12

The Wicker Giant

With gnawing irritation Alan MacDougall stared at the wall where the image of Lucifer's lieutenant had appeared. Why the urgency? What if breakfast were delayed a few additional minutes? After all, it was *his* coronation.

His coronation. Alan dropped to a seat on the bed. He was *not* going to wear that crown! He glanced with distaste at the blue pantaloons and gold cape hanging from pegs in the bathroom wall. Nor was he going to put on the so-called royal garments. If their only purpose was to impress the seventy Chosen Ones, they could be dispensed with. If there was some other reason for his wearing the crown—as he suspected—he wanted no part of it.

He knew his decision would annoy, even anger, Ahriman, but all the planning and preparation was centered upon one Scots-American who had not died, so they'd have to make the best of things. There was another factor—and the thought of it sent a chill through MacDougall: Ahriman's statement about Lucifer's displeasure with those who disobeyed him, especially those he had greatly honored. He wanted nothing to do with the king-ship.

As he got into his black garments he thought of the unbelievable sequence of events that had befallen him within so short a time, starting with the dancing of the three lovely women, ending with the capture of Amaru-duk. Especially strange was his dream of Elspeth, her brother David, and the Sidhe. For a fleeting second, he considered trying mentally to reach the girl or Cinel Loarn, then discarded the idea. It was only a dream. He was strapping on his sword belt when an impatient thought came from Ahriman.

"Please, MacDougall, can you not hasten? It is im-portant that there be no delay in our program. The Mas-ter himself is involved."

"I'll be there in moments," Alan responded. He was ready to go, but he lingered. There was a gnawing thought, an idea concerning something he should remem-ber. Something important—then it came to him. Ama-ruduk's statement that he had opened the portal on Scath! That *was* important. If worse came to worst, this was a way of retreat.

He glanced beyond the door at the four guards waiting in the corridor. Why walk to the breakfast room? He pictured Ahriman, saw him in the room where he had broken fast with the three women. The Persian was seated on the edge of a great chair just inside a doorway, evi-dently impatiently awaiting his arrival. There were five men at a nearby table, the rulers of the five cities. Cu-chulainn at one end, King Kumaragupta of Magadha and Emperor Khau Ch'in Khih at one side; and Commander Horsaneb, ruler of Atu, and King Ezana of Axume at the other. Instantly MacDougall transferred himself to the vacant space opposite Cuchulainn, a place apparently set for him.

Startled, the others at the table hastily stood up, whereupon MacDougall raised both hands, palms out-ward. "Relax, my friends. I am sorry about my tardi-ness." As all seated themselves he smiled toward the scowling figure of Ahriman.

"Perhaps you should dismiss the guards at my doorway. I did not require their services."

Rising to his feet, the other glared at MacDougall, his face pale with anger. "Why have you come dressed as you are?" he demanded. "I told you to wear the royal garments."

"The blue and gold didn't do a thing for me," Alan answered with a faint smile, "and I find this outfit more comfortable." His expression became sober. "Besides, I have decided not to wear that crown. If this means forfeiting the kingly status, so be it. I never wanted to be a king." He heard the sharp intake of breath of those at the table; saw Ahriman stiffen, his eyes growing wide in momentary unbelief, fury mounting. Then his iron control took over and his face became expressionless.

"You have gone too far to back out now," he said with deadly quietness. After a brief pause he went on, "The guards have been dismissed. Breakfast will now be served. I regret that I cannot join you, but there are matters that must be attended to." He looked squarely at MacDougall. "I shall return." Simultaneously curtains parted, servers entered with platters of food, and Ahriman vanished.

The meal began in awkward silence, with the city-kings under obvious restraint. Initially MacDougall found the situation somewhat amusing, but when he realized that their unwillingness to talk came from their fear of Ahriman and awe of one who would defy him, he felt a pang of uneasiness. What would follow? Whatever that might be, he told himself doggedly, he had no regrets.

As the servers were clearing the table, the city-kings vanished one by one. Not on their own, Alan was certain. The first disappearance was a bit of a shock; but after the five had gone, MacDougall waited for his turn. When time slowly passed with no action he recalled Ahriman's emphatic "I will return." Should he wait, Alan asked himself, getting to his feet, or should he transfer to the portal on Scath? The idea was tempting; but as he pictured the cleared area in the junglelike thicket, Ahriman materialized at his side, close enough to touch.

He stared at MacDougall thoughtfully through narrowed eyelids. "Have you reconsidered?" he demanded coldly.

Alan shook his head. "No! Call it an obsession if you wish, but I will not wear that crown."

Instant bedlam followed, with MacDougall engulfed by a score of demons, a repetition of the scene in his bedroom when Amaruduk had been captured, but now centered upon himself. He felt a suffocating weight of beings pressing against him, of tightly clutching hands. There was no time to react, no way for him to free himself.

Suddenly he felt a weight resting upon his head, was conscious of a surge of vast power flowing through him. At the same instant all restraint was gone, and he was seated out in the open, the aurora overhead. For an instant objects formed images in his brain—giant trees, faces with staring eyes, a great golden statue, a strange manlike object formed of interwoven white branches—then deliberately MacDougall closed his eyes to adjust to the flood of impressions crowding in upon him.

Strange, the exhilaration pulsing in waves in his mind, as if he had found sudden release from an intolerable, lifelong repression. Incredibly, he was *free*. And power, limitless power was his. Words echoed in his memory, Ahriman's words:

"I declare you to be the monarch of all monarchs, the Transcendental King." As he was, although the ceremony had not been completed because of his flight. As now it would be.

Why for so long a time had he fought the inevitable, with so many proofs that he indeed was the one foretold in the Scroll? His Scot's stubbornness might be to blame. That same will and determination would stand him in good stead as he ventured upon his great mission.

Where was he? He must be in the Master's Woods. With eyes still closed he scanned his surroundings as from above, recalling his earlier visit with Hypatia. He was seated on the golden throne at the center of the five-pointed star, a marble pentagram. The five lesser thrones were occupied by the city-kings of Avilion. On either side of the turf stretching before the pentagram, standing side by side and equally divided, stood the seventy who had been at the banquet.

In the far end of the clearing towered the heroic statue as he had seen it in its second form, an image of gold with extended wings. At its feet rose the gray, stone, bloodstained altar with its inward-curving golden horns; and between the altar and pentagram something new had been erected.

On the circular grid of blackened pipes where sacrifices must have been burned rose a manlike figure woven of white barkless branches and twigs that, somehow, seemed strangely familiar though he knew he had never before seen its like. He remembered. It had been described to him by the self-styled Saint Caradoc in Manannan's castle on Ochren. This was a Wicker Giant, an instrument of sacrifice where in Olden Times prisoners of war and others of the priests' selection had been burned. Oddly, there were dry branches heaped around the base of the figure. He wondered why, when there were gas vents in the pipes. Tradition, no doubt.

Through spaces between the branches he saw movement inside the structure and momentarily wondered why there were no outcries. Probably the subjects were gagged and tied. A coldly impersonal thought flashed into his mind, a question concerning whom Ahriman had chosen as victims. Probably Mohists from the City of Jade, violent troublemakers whom no one would miss. Or possibly the Tantrics of Magadha who were seeking death. He dismissed the thought.

All this he had absorbed in moments. Now he opened his eyes, his gaze sweeping the clearing and immediately focusing on the giant winged image. Again it had changed. Not in form or position, but now it emitted a brilliant glow, and the face seemed radiantly alive. The Lord of Light!

MacDougall's focus changed, his attention caught by a golden glow at the forward edge of the marble circle. The light solidified slowly, taking form, becoming Ahriman, clad from head to foot in cloth-of-gold. He faced the mighty figure of Lucifer. He raised his right arm high in salute as he cried out, "Hail, Master!"

Incredibly the statue seemed to nod in acknowledgment.

Ahriman addressed the spectators. "The coronation that you witnessed was incomplete when King Mac-Dougall, moved by momentary doubt of his adequacy for the monumental task he faced, left the throne room. These doubts have been resolved with his recognition of the important role all of you will play in curing the ills of a world gone awry through the weakness and ineptitude of its leadership. He now wears the crown and verifies the truth of the Great Prophecy—he is truly the monarch of all monarchs, the Transcendental King." Ahriman faced MacDougall.

"Before we continue with the conclusion of this unparalleled moment in history, perhaps our King wishes to speak."

Quickly Alan rose, with a nod barely acknowledging Ahriman's invitation. Of course he wanted to speak. King? He *felt* like a king. A ruler of limitless power who could accomplish whatever he chose. He raised his voice, projecting his words through the clearing, his thoughts seeming to flow from a source outside himself.

"My eyes have been opened and now I see. I have beheld a vision of the Other World with nations at peace, with the resources of all divided with equity among all peoples. With each of you playing your part in the Great Plan under my guidance, empowered by the Master, all that I thought impossible will be accomplished.

"A new age will dawn, an Age of Law and Reason, an age when lawlessness shall end with swift and final justice meted out to the rebellious, and appropriate rewards accorded the faithful.

"Continue with your training so that when you are needed, when I summon you, you will be ready to take your place in the rulership of the world. Remember—you are the Chosen."

As Alan resumed his seat, Ahriman turned to the silent

watchers. "It has long been the custom of the dwellers in the City of Cuchulainn to sacrifice a white bull to the Master when seeking his special favor; and on a few occasions during the long centuries other kinds of sacrifices have been made with the five city-kings present. For this unique event we have gone back to a very ancient custom, creating the Wicker Giant for a unique sacrifice." He raised his voice.

"I summon Abred the Vate!"

There was a stirring in the shadows under the trees to the left of the effigy, a sudden flare of light; and five men in black, hooded robes entered the clearing in single file. The leader, Abred the Vate, held aloft a flaming torch; and the others with right hands thrust above their heads gripped long, rapierlike swords. They ranged themselves in a row facing the central throne and as one bowed low.

Why the swords? Alan wondered; and somehow he knew the answer—to thrust back any who might seek to escape the flames.

"We await your command to begin the ceremony," Abred said solemnly as they straightened up.

"You may begin," Ahriman announced; then with a startling change, an inexplicable reversal, and in a totally different voice he cried out again.

"Hold!"

He turned slowly to face MacDougall; and as their eyes met Alan felt a sudden inexplicable chill. It was as if another personality, another being stared through the gem-hard eyes. With sudden knowledge—imparted, it must be, by the other—and with mounting awe and dread, he realized this had to be Lucifer himself. In the same voice of unparalleled power, not loud, yet audible to all in the clearing he continued.

"Alan MacDougall, I have chosen you among all men to accomplish my purpose. Put away all doubt, all uncertainty. I will guide you; I will be with you; and when need arises I will be *in* you. Your task will not be easy, for the opposing powers are strong, but we cannot fail!" He turned toward the Wicker Giant. "Let the ceremony begin."

Alan MacDougall's mind was a battleground of war-ring emotions: Excitement; incredulity; dread; exalta-tion; fear; and, weakly in the background, protest. And this, he suddenly realized, was the actual secret of the Scroll—not only his elevation to kingship, but his pos-session by the Lord of Light. No wonder Taliesin had withheld this from him. In his mental turmoil he was barely aware of the five Vates, led by Abred with his flaming torch, circling the crude manlike figure. They were chanting what seemed to be mere sounds without meaning. They were moving counterclockwise, had completed their second revolution, when a wild cry broke the stillness.

Charging with startling speed, Taliesin dashed across the turf toward the throne. The move was so sudden, so shocking, the distance so short, that he reached Mac-Dougall before anyone had time to react. With a single motion he swept the crown from Alan's head, sending it clattering across the marble.

"Elspeth," he shouted, "is in the Wicker Giant. Wake up, Alan! Hear me! Elspeth is here and in the Giant. She will be burned!"

MacDougall's shocked senses grasped the import of the Bard's cry, and in flashing thoughts, free of the crown's influence, he recalled the dream that was no dream. A shape-changing demon from the Other World deceiving Elspeth, giving her power to see, to enter Av-ilion. He thought of his defiance of Ahriman, his insis-tence that he'd have none but Elspeth. This was the diabolic solution. Even as he dashed across the marble and turf, his sword in hand, he looked within the Giant.

There she was, bound, gagged, lashed to a supporting branch.

He heard a shout from Lucifer-Ahriman: "Abred—the flame!"

As the Vate hesitated for a split second, Alan reached him, swung his blade viciously toward the torch—and severed the hand at the wrist. The torch arced through the air, still in the clutch of lifeless fingers, to fall to the grass where it lay smoldering.

MacDougall swung around to face the gold-clad figure glowering down at him. He was barely aware of the agonized howling of his victim; knew only that all hell must break loose at any moment. Already Taliesin lay on the marble, under the weight of gray-robed demons; and he could hear the first rumblings among the seventy watchers, could sense the movement of the four Vates with their rapiers a few feet away.

"This is not to be borne!" The Lord of Light cried out, "Approach, Alan MacDougall. Even you—" He halted, interrupted by a chorus of bell-notes ringing through the clearing. Alan could not believe his ears; then he remembered the second part of his dream. The Singing Blades! And never had he heard them ring so clearly, nor with such strength.

Out of the shadows under the trees on the right came Cinel Loarn and his thirty Sidhe, led by eight-year-old David Cameron. The green-clad *Shee*, swords in hand, shields on their left arms, marched in single file to form a curved line across the grass between MacDougall and Lucifer-Ahriman. They parted at the middle and David Cameron entered the breach. While this took place no one stirred, even the wounded Vate checking his moaning. All eyes were fixed on the Scottish lad, as if hypnotized.

Alan MacDougall gazed in wonder at the back of the slender figure, no taller than the Sidhe. Yet he sensed he was in the presence of a Power, a Majesty—a strange word to come to his mind—a Holiness. Somehow he felt unclean. There was a radiance surrounding the lad, a glory enveloping him. And somehow Alan knew that all in the clearing were aware of the same impressions. Some of the watchers, he saw, had bowed their heads and hid their faces in their hands.

Now the lad spoke, and MacDougall held his breath. Not David; it was a voice indescribable that could never have been formed by the vocal cords of the Highland lad.

"Lucifer, Son of the Morning, I have given you freedom to follow your own will within limitations and until the Time. Now you have gone too far. Elspeth Cameron is mine, under my protection, and when you tricked her into entering your domain you overstepped your bounds. Your reasoning is clear. MacDougall was to participate in the sacrifice of the woman he loves, thus binding him to you with the shed blood. To prevent her destruction I brought her brother and the Sidhe through the Gate, the lad in his innocence completely under my control.

"Alan MacDougall is not yet mine—nor is he yours. While he lives he has freedom to decide between us. Here again you used trickery with the Crown of Power, trickery and physical force. His intervention in the effort to release Elspeth with the aid of my servant Taliesin has freed him from your present control. Your Scroll and its prophecy, your careful planning through the centuries have all come to naught. Alan and Elspeth will leave, and you will not interfere." A solemn note entered the Voice. "And a little child shall lead them.

"As for Taliesin, the Bard of Bards, my servants have removed him to a realm beyond your reach." At the words MacDougall raised his eyes to the area of the throne where the demons had swarmed over Taliesin. They were still there, floundering, but the Bard was gone.

David Cameron faced MacDougall. The same stirring voice directed, "Free Elspeth—and all the others. There will be no fiery sacrifice."

Quickly Alan turned, found the entrance to the Wicker Giant, and slashed the cords that bound it shut. After returning his sword to the scabbard, he found his pocket knife, and one after another drew the intended victims from their prison, severing their bonds. Elspeth was the last, perched in the very top of the effigy. As he carried her out, their eyes met, the girl's tearful, filled with pride and much more. With the gag removed they embraced briefly, and she whispered, "I saw—I heard it all. But David . . ."

Without forethought Alan repeated softly, "And a little child shall lead them. All will be well."

Already the boy was on his way, moving across the marble platform past six motionless figures, his short strides setting the pace. Arms linked, Alan and Elspeth

followed immediately with the Sidhe at the rear. Last
came Cinel Loarn. Just before they reached the first bend
in the marble road, MacDougall glanced back. It appeared to him that no one had moved, all held in thrall
by the Power in David Cameron. The Power, Alan
thought with strange timidity, of God. There would be
no pursuit.

They left the woodland and continued through the park
with its tailored trees and graceful gazebos, moving un-
erringly toward the portal. Almost upon it, Alan again
glanced back for a last look at the scene of his incredible
adventure. He stopped short with a shocked exclamation.

"Look!"

He and Elspeth turned about, as did the *Shee*, to stare
in wonder at misty gray emptiness. There was no sky,
no castle, no woodland, no turf; only formless gray nothingness like an intangible wall extending into infinity. In
awe they turned in time to see David step through the
Gate into the Highland tower. Elspeth followed, with
MacDougall at her heels. Quickly they moved aside to
make way for the Sidhe who vanished as they stepped
into the *broch*. As Cinel Loarn came through, Mac-
Dougall said fervently, "Thank you, Malcolm."

The other vanished; but Alan felt a feather-light touch
of a small hand striking his and heard the quiet words,
"Farewell, brother. I feel we shall not meet again until,
perhaps, in another life."

The open portal lay before Alan MacDougall, the wall
of gray blotting out the last vestige of Avilion. Close the
gate, he thought; then felt a suggestion of movement on
his upper right arm. The armlet, so long immovable, had
slid down to his elbow. Quickly he rolled up his sleeve
and moved the jeweled serpent the rest of the way. He
held it in his hand, looking at its gemmed perfection,
and thought, "Lord Enki and Lady Inanna, we have come
to the parting of the ways."

There was no response, no glow in the gem eyes. Taking the armlet in his right hand, MacDougall hurled it
with all his strength into the gray mist. The instant it left
his grasp he saw no portal, only a rough rock wall; but

there was no sound, no clatter of metal striking stone. The armlet of the gods was gone.

He turned away, saw Elspeth in the light from the doorway, and caught her in his arms. Their lips met and clung; then he whispered, "I told you, darling, when I left, you would bring me back."

"Elspeth, where are you?" The treble voice of David Cameron came from the shadows; he sounded close to tears. "You must be here. I followed you."

"Here I am, David," his sister called reassuringly. "Alan, your flashlight."

Hastily MacDougall groped in his pockets, found his torch, and the powerful beam swept the interior of the tower, revealing Elspeth with her arms around her brother.

"Alan here, too!" the boy exclaimed in delight. "What luck. I'm so glad I found ye. Let's gae hame. I don't like this place." He moved toward the square of light that marked the exit, his hand in Elspeth's, tugging strongly.

"Yes, David," she answered quietly, "we'll go home. Come, Alan."

"In a moment," he responded, giving a final glance at the walls. There was no trace of the four portals, only the ancient, roughly hewn stones of the centuries-old tower, the blackened fireplace, the dust marks above it where once small swords and shields had been mounted, and a great oaken table. There were two narrow rooms on opposite sides of the fireplace; in one of them lay his hiking outfit and knapsack. There they would remain. There, too, was the case he had made to hold his sword. He hesitated briefly, then retrieved it. He would keep the sword as a memento of his adventure. Swiftly he removed the belt and, recalling its last use, he drew the weapon from the scabbard. Of blood there was no trace. Feeling strange, he replaced the sword and put it in its case.

Still he lingered. The abilities he had mastered in the Other World—were they still his? He had to know. He tried to reach out to Elspeth's mind. Nothing happened.

He closed his eyes; tried to see beyond the walls. Again nothing. One more test. He visualized the great rock outside the tower, willed himself beside it. He did not move. Indescribable relief swept through him. He was free! He felt as if a crushing weight had been lifted from his shoulders. With buoyant step he hastened out of the *broch* into the clean light of the Highlands.

The armlet, the Sumerian gods, they must have been the enabling power behind his abilities. Unless—the thought came timidly—unless that other, greater Power had removed them, that Power that had enabled Taliesin to start over. He knew so little about such matters.

He looked searchingly at David Cameron. He was the David he had known, unchanged and apparently without knowledge of what had happened. The boy peered up at him with a twinkle in his eyes. "I'm glad ye're comin' wi' us," he said cheerily, "an' maybe this time ye'll stay."

MacDougall smiled warmly, with a quizzical glance at Elspeth. "Maybe I will. If your father—and sister—invite me."

Anxiously David looked at his sister. "Say he may, 'Speth, say he may!"

"We'll talk to Father," she said reassuringly.

Halfway down the hillside, a vagrant breeze carried the faint chime of distant church bells.

"Listen," David exclaimed. " 'Tis the Sabbath."

"Perhaps if we hurry," Elspeth said, looking at Alan, "we can attend service."

"I was about to make the same suggestion," MacDougall agreed. "If we're in time, we can take Norah and your father with us."

They quickened their pace, and just as they reached the road leading to the Cameron farm, Alan thought he heard other bell-tones, faint and far away, the chiming of the singing blades. There was something sad about the sound, like a farewell. He listened intently, but it was not repeated. Then from across the valley, as if in answer, through the clear morning air came the cheerful ringing of the bells from the white kirk in Kilmona.

Side by side they hastened along the road toward the farmhouse with its gable roof reflecting the sunlight and a welcoming tendril of smoke rising from one of its two chimneys.

ABOUT THE AUTHOR

Lloyd Arthur Eshbach was born on a farm in southeastern Pennsylvania on June 20, 1910. He still lives in Pennsylvania and has spent most of his years in the same area. He began reading science fiction and fantasy in 1919 with the fanciful tales of Edgar Rice Burroughs, A. Merritt, and their contemporaries in the pages of the Munsey magazines. He wrote his first salable SF story in 1929 and in the 1930s became a "big-name" writer. He began publishing SF books as Fantasy Press in 1947. Although he was not the first specialist publisher in the field, he was the first to present a full line of science fiction titles. His own writing, always a spare-time effort, included, in addition to SF, tales of fantasy and the supernatural, mystery stories, adventures, romances, and juveniles, some published under pseudonyms. With his entry into publishing, his writing became quite sporadic, and his last story appeared in 1958.

After the failure of his publishing venture—a fate met by all of the SF specialist houses—he became an advertising copywriter, a religious publisher, advertising manager of a major religious publishing house, and a publisher's sales representative.

In 1978, in retirement, Eshbach began writing again, his first effort being *Over My Shoulder: Reflections on a Science Fiction Era*, a memoir of his life in SF, concentrating on the history of the fan hardback book publishers of the 1930s, '40s, and '50s. This was issued in a limited edition in 1983. He completed E. E. "Doc" Smith's last novel, *Subspace Encounter*, left unfinished at Doc's death in 1965, which was also published in 1983. *The Scroll of Lucifer* is the conclusion of a four-volume fantasy series, THE GATES OF LUCIFER, that began with *The Land Beyond the Gate*.